"I want you D'Andra," Night said huski[

"What? Right here, right now?"

"Yes."

"But what if people see us?"

"The gym is closed; nobody's here."

D'Andra looked around. How long had they been in the sauna?

"Nobody's here," Night repeated, just before his lips pressed against hers.

The kiss seared her body like a branding iron. She craned her neck to give him all of her, even as she opened her mouth to his probing tongue and let him inside. Their tongues swirled in the age-old dance, their hands moving, exploring, touching new territory. D'Andra gasped as she felt Night's hand slip below her athletic bra. She was surprised at his gentleness, even as he massaged each nipple into a hardened peak within seconds.

"Night," she moaned against his lips. "Night, Night, Night . . ."

"Aunt DeeDee!" Wake up, Aunt DeeDee!"

D'Andra fought sheets and little hands for air as she came out of what felt like a deep fog. She opened her eyes to three sets of wide-eyed brown ones with expressions that ranged from quizzical to comical.

"You were dreaming, Aunt DeeDee," Kayla said matter-of-factly.

"Yeah," Tonia said. "And talking, too!"

Also by Zuri Day

LIES LOVERS TELL

Published by Kensington Publishing Corp.

Body By Night

Zuri Day

Kensington Publishing Corp.

http://www.kensingtonbooks.com

DAFINA BOOKS are published by

Kensington Publishing Corp.
850 Third Avenue
New York, NY 10022

All Kensington Titles, Imprints, and Distributed Lines are available at special quantity discounts for bulk purchases for sales promotions, premiums, fund-raising, and educational or institutional use. Special book excerpts or customized printings can also be created to fit specific needs. For details, write or phone the office of the Kensington special sales manager: Kensington Publishing Corp., 850 Third Avenue, New York, NY 10022, attn: Special Sales Department, Phone: 1-800-221-2647.

Dafina and the Dafina logo Reg. U.S. Pat. & TM Off.

ISBN-13: 978-0-7582-2882-6
ISBN-10: 0-7582-2882-1

First mass market printing: March 2009

10 9 8 7 6 5 4 3 2 1

Printed in the United States of America

This book is dedicated to instructors Mike, Ryan and Steve, and all the Bally Fitness step-a-holics, especially those of us who get our groove on at six A.M.!

Acknowledgments

I have to thank Spirit . . . this is so much fun! And one question for Selena, "Do we know what *time* it is?" ::wink::

Hugs and kisses to my "More Perfect Union" family. Your energy during our production was the fire that fueled the completion of this work. Especially Valarie Kaur, who knew that when asked, I'd be crazy enough to say yes.

A huge thanks to the men and women all over the world who specialize in health care, fitness, nutrition and making us *feel* better so that we can then *be* better.

And last but not least, to the nurse who has provided outstanding service for over fifty years, my mama, affectionately called "Miss Flora or Mama Flora" by doctors, staff and patients alike, for your expert contribution to this work along with my niece, Tanishia, who is continuing this service tradition.

1

D'Andra Smalls gazed at the entrance to Bally Total Fitness as if the doors led to a gas chamber. Her dread at entering couldn't have been much worse than that of a woman doomed to die, since that's exactly what she thought she'd do the minute she positioned her hefty behind on a treadmill.

With a slight twinge of guilt, she eyed the empty spicy-hot pork rind bag that along with hospital memos, a Bally pamphlet, a workout towel and a bottle of water occupied the tan-colored passenger seat of her recently purchased maroon Suburban. Her favorite snack had tasted good going down, especially with the sixteen-ounce diet soda that accompanied it, but now she wasn't so sure about the wisdom of this hastily eaten pre-workout meal. Her stomach growled its disagreement and called for more, still angry from smelling but not tasting the bacon, eggs and fried potatoes D'Andra had fixed her mother for breakfast. In stark contrast, D'Andra had opted for a single can of Slimfast, just as her co-worker Elaine had suggested. Elaine had recently lost twenty of the fifty pounds she was trying to shed after having two babies in as many years. Seeing how much better her friend looked had been a

motivator for D'Andra to lose weight. Not to mention
the most literal wake-up call she'd experienced in her
twenty-nine years: recently waking up to find herself in
Martin Luther King Hospital's emergency room.

Thinking about that brush with death reenergized
D'Andra. Picking up the towel and bottled water, she
looked again toward what instead of her doom was
hopefully a pathway to good health and a noticeable
waistline, both of which were currently lacking. Just
then two size-fours walked into the gym, laughing,
talking and looking fit as fiddles. One, a curvy Latina
with thick, black hair, could have modeled in a com-
mercial on how to *gain* weight. Her friend, a rail-thin
blonde who D'Andra thought could blow away in a
two-mile-an-hour wind, looked picture perfect in her
tight-fitting top and boy shorts.

D'Andra sighed and dropped the towel back on the
seat. She rolled down the window, perched her elbow
on the doorframe, and rested her head on her fist.
This is never going to work, she thought with resigna-
tion. Her mother's earlier question, posed as D'Andra
prepared to leave the house, echoed in her mind.
*What do you look like taking yo fat butt to a gym? People who
go there are already in shape.* It looked like her mother
was right.

"Maybe I'll come back tomorrow," D'Andra said
out loud, pulling the seatbelt back over her sizable
belly. She should have known that Saturdays would be
busy. Especially now, the beginning of the year, when
millions of people had undoubtedly made resolutions
to lose weight. The Sunday crowd, especially if she
came in the morning around church time, should
be much lighter. At least this was the rationalization
she used for backing out of her workout. "That's it.
I'll come back tomorrow with Elaine."

"How can you leave before you even get started?"

a male voice asked. The sound was as deep as the ocean and its silkiness matched the flawless onyx skin stretched over the perfectly sculpted six-pack abdomen filling her seated, eye-level view. So far, the only thing D'Andra could find wrong with the man standing next to her car door was his timing; walking by at the exact moment she was blabbering to herself.

"Uh, excuse me?" D'Andra stuttered, shielding her hazel eyes from the sun as she looked up. Granted, she garnered a fair share of testosterone-laced attention but rarely from someone who looked like the man standing here. He was gorgeous.

"Didn't I hear you tell yourself you were leaving? Looks like you haven't been in yet."

"I haven't but—"

"No buts," Six-Pack stated firmly, his hand reaching for the car handle and opening the door. "Come on, doll, I'll walk you inside."

D'Andra was horrified. After seeing America's next top models walk inside the gym, not to mention the ebony Adonis holding her door, she felt inadequately prepared to exercise and inappropriately dressed in her hot pink oversized T-shirt and black leggings. How in the world had she imagined herself cute when she tried the outfit on in Ashley Stewart's dressing room? Now, she thought she looked like the proverbial pink elephant getting ready to walk into the room.

"I like Betty Boop," Six-Pack said, nodding toward the cartoon character gracing the front of D'Andra's T-shirt. "That color looks good on you."

D'Andra exited the car but made no move toward the gym. "Thanks," she answered, convinced he had said that just to be nice.

Still, she became self-conscious of how Betty rose and fell with her 42DDs every time she took a breath, which was more often than normal since the man in front of her was taking her very breath away. This fine specimen was definitely not good for her blood pressure. D'Andra guessed that if she wasn't careful she'd end up back in emergency before midnight. Yet she risked her health to take another look at the dark chocolate standing next to her. Yes, she quickly deduced, he was still as fine as he was the first time she saw him, a whole sixty seconds ago.

"My name's Night. What's yours?"

"D'Andra."

"D'Andra . . . that's a pretty name."

"Thanks." D'Andra knew her simple, monosyllabic answers were belying her intelligence but any form of smart, casual banter eluded her. A thousand thoughts of things that might impress him ran through her head but not one of them came out. Sometimes it took her a minute or two to warm up to people, but it wasn't like her to act shy. This man had her all discombobulated.

Then she remembered something. She hated men. Something else, or rather someone else, came to mind. Charles, the reason she hated them. What did her friend Elaine call them? *Walking dirt,* in reference to the biblical story of God forming man from the dust of the earth. D'Andra used this analogy to try and temper the flutters in her stomach. But she couldn't lie to herself. If this man beside her was *terra firma* then she'd like nothing better than to get her hands dirty.

But that's exactly what she'd done with Charles, literally, when she spent two grueling weekends—two weekends more than she should have—helping him with his so-called professional cleaning service. The dirt she'd cleaned from the office floors was nothing compared to the mental and emotional filth left behind by the dirty deed she witnessed the night of their breakup. D'Andra stopped the memories abruptly, before pictures from that nightmare night could crystallize. But that wisp of a memory had done the trick: stilled the flutters and renewed her resolve. She hated men. But the least she could do was be polite.

"You said your name is Night?"

"Yeah, that's what they call me."

Ignoring the obvious, she continued. "Why do they call you that?"

Night laughed. "You can't guess?"

"I might guess it's your skin color," she said honestly. "But that could be an offensive assumption."

"It could be," he admitted. "But in this case it would be at least partly accurate. Skin color, scrawny body, big eyes and a small head; my friends back in Texas said I looked like a type of worm, a night crawler, and stuck me with the label when I was around six years old."

D'Andra stifled a laugh. "That's mean," she said while trying to imagine scrawny or small ever describing the man before her.

"It is, but you know how kids are. Then my aunt started calling me Night. But she said it as a term of endearment, saying that the blacker the berry, the sweeter the juice. I started wearing my color like a badge of honor. The final approval came from Sabrina, the prettiest second-grader in all of Dallas. She declared to the playground in the middle of recess that Night was the 'coolest name ever.' That did it. I went from pitiful to popular before the back-to-class bell rang. You might say I grew into my moniker, which now has a whole different meaning."

His voice dropped to a near whisper. "I do some of my best work at night."

D'Andra smiled but remained silent. *Is this brown sugar brotha actually flirting with me?*

"I meant working out, of course, in my home gym." *No, he's not flirting.* "Of course."

"What else could I have meant, right?"

What else indeed! D'Andra felt Night's eyes on her but refused to meet his gaze. She could just about imagine what type of work he was referring to and since it had been a while since a man had gainfully employed any baby-making skills in her bedroom, felt it best not to speculate too long. Besides, the long lashes surrounding those dark brown orbs were bringing back her flutters and making her forget to hate.

"Do you work here?" she asked, nodding toward the gym as she consciously changed the subject.

"I teach a kickboxing class on Wednesday nights, but other than that, their environment is too restrictive for me. I don't like to follow rules." He licked a set of thick, perfectly proportioned lips. "I am a personal trainer though and pretty soon I'll have my own gym. I've got my eye on a prime spot in a strip mall over in Ladera Heights."

"The one with Magic Johnson's Starbucks and T.G.I. Fridays?"

Night nodded. "That's the one. The mall gets good traffic, customers who work out and care about their health. Plus, people who live in that area will more than likely be able to afford my rates. My prices will be slightly higher than some of the chains but I believe my customized workout programs, personal consultations and full-service approach to fitness will make it worth the higher fee."

D'Andra nodded but again remained silent.

"I'm sorry," Night said, realizing he was going on and on about his dream. "Get me started about my business and I can talk all day."

"I don't mind. I like your enthusiasm. I'm really into fitness too. I mean, I'm not fit yet but I'm determined to get there."

Night raised his eyebrows. "Oh, really?"

"What do you mean *oh really?*" she asked with as much attitude as she could muster while looking at an unexpected display of dazzling white teeth against his dark skin. She thought about Night's nickname and concluded that it suited him. Only someone as fine as he was could pull off a name like that though, and not have it sound funny or insulting. On him it was neither; it fit perfectly. But that didn't mean he could talk to her any kind of way!

"What I mean is, you could have fooled me," he said matching her attitude with his own. He'd seen that façade before, attitude that covered fear, and in her case, fear of working out or worse, of failing. He wasn't known as the motivator for nothing and decided to put his skills to work.

"If you were really serious about getting fit, we'd be in the gym by now. Let's go."

Before D'Andra could react, Night gently grabbed her elbow and steered her toward the doors. She didn't know whether to be pissed or impressed. On one hand, who did this stranger think he was to treat her like this? On the other hand, he was right. She'd been in no hurry to go into the gym and while she was genuinely interested in health and fitness, she'd been even more interested in delaying her own, happy to pass the time talking about nicknames. And truth be told, she liked the firm, authoritative way Night had taken control of the situation. She'd probably never let him know it but his actions were a welcomed change from those around her who were content to let her do everything: family, co-workers, her sorry ass ex-boyfriend and backstabbing former best friend.

D'Andra shifted her thoughts. She didn't want to think about any of them right now. While lying horizontal and staring into bright white hospital lights, D'Andra decided life was too short to pay attention to or worry about a-holes. She needed to focus on making herself happy, and that involved flipping the script on almost every thing in her life. Joining a gym was the first of many changes she'd vowed would happen this year, and getting in shape just part of the plan to turn her life around.

She listened as Night continued to make small talk, asking what she did for a living, about where she grew up. *Maybe this man can help it happen,* she thought. But could she be around him on a regular basis and not fall in lust? Lost in thought, D'Andra's foot caught in the door's rubber jamb and she stumbled into the hard body that was the source of her distraction.

"Careful now. You don't want to hurt yourself before you even get started."

D'Andra froze against Night's hard frame. Physical injury was a possibility she hadn't considered. With a strenuous full-time job at a nursing home and physical rehabilitation facility, and an equally demanding mother who mistook her daughter for a personal maid, she couldn't afford to get sidelined.

"I never considered hurting myself," she said, forcing herself away from Night's warm body and taking a step backward, out the door. "Maybe I'd better not . . ."

Night stopped D'Andra's retreat with a firm hand. "Come on now, you'll be fine. I'll take care of you doll, all right? So stop trippin' and yes, the pun is intended."

Once inside the gym, Night walked a couple steps ahead of her and approached the turnstile. In that instant she took in his close-cropped hair, wide shoulders, strong, muscular legs and a butt that looked as hard as it did round, even encased as it was in baggy pants that rode just below what she later saw was an inward navel. Then and there she determined it his best feature, the best bootylicious she'd ever seen. His tight red T-shirt had been ripped to show off the perfect set of abs that had caught her attention from the start. The arm that had guided her through the door was thick and strong; his Nike shoes long and wide. D'Andra gulped. Nobody had to tell her twice about the meaning of a man with big feet . . .

Night's physique had shifted D'Andra's attention from her body to his, but only for a moment. The sights and sounds inside the gym quickly brought back her purpose for being there, to get in shape, something that now seemed impossible as she looked at all the fit bodies around her. Not one person looked more than ten pounds overweight, twenty tops; there was definitely no one in there big as she was. Her heart sank. She wished Elaine were here. It seemed simple enough when, at her co-worker's urging, she'd signed up online. Then it had been easy, fun even. But where was Elaine now, when she needed her? Home nursing two kids with the flu. How she'd allowed her friend to talk her into coming by herself, she'd never know.

Night turned to see D'Andra still standing near the door. "Where's your card?"

"Card?"

"Your ID to get into the gym." Night held up the card he'd just scanned.

"I don't have one. I just joined online a couple days ago."

Night motioned to a young man working behind the counter, even as he walked over and once again placed a reassuring hand on D'Andra's elbow. She stiffened. *Why does he keep touching me?* she thought. Didn't the man know he was in danger? It had been almost six months since she'd had sex and her kitty had been meowing ever since her day turned to Night.

"She needs an ID," Night told the worker.

D'Andra once again forced her mind away from sensual thoughts. She needed to get ahold of herself

though truth be told, she'd rather that Night got
ahold of her. But she knew she wasn't ready for another relationship. She couldn't expect someone else
to love her until she learned to love herself. That's
what she'd read in a book on relationships Elaine had
given her. And while she was working on it and
making progress, she wasn't there yet. Until she was,
men were off limits.

"Hey Night; what's going on buddy?" A jovial, handsome man with a tanned face, thick, brown hair and
a hoop hanging from a pierced brow asked as he
joined the worker behind the counter. He and Night
did a soul brother's handshake.

"Nothing to it, Marc. Just here to help my friend
D'Andra, uh . . ." Night paused and looked question-
ingly at D'Andra.

"Smalls. D'Andra Smalls."

"Yes, here to help my friend D'Andra Smalls get her
workout on."

D'Andra warmed at Night's words. Her last name
had always been a hindrance, like a bad joke fate had
played. Her surname was the only thing about her
that was little, and ever since she could remember
she'd been teased about this fact. But Night breathed
her last name like a song; as if it was a promise instead
of a lie.

"You ready for your picture?"

D'Andra looked at Night as if he'd cursed. "Oh no,
I don't do pictures."

"You have to take one for your ID," Marc interjected. He pointed to a spot at the end of the counter.
"Just stand over there."

In that moment, D'Andra wished Night gone. How
could she stand there and pose with a man like him
staring at her? *This is stupid! Why did I listen to Elaine?
Coming here was a big mistake.* These thoughts whirled

in D'Andra's head as she walked to the end of the counter and turned around.

"Now, doll, don't stand there looking like you're about to get shot," Night coaxed. "Let me see that pretty smile."

D'Andra willed herself to not be self-conscious. Then, for some unknown reason, she imagined Night's hard, bare-naked ass, the one she'd admired as he stood at the counter, being the picture on the back of his ID card. His butt was surely as unique as a fingerprint; God couldn't have sculpted that masterpiece twice. She stopped short of laughing out loud, but showed almost all thirty-two pearly whites as the camera flashed.

2

Night's vast knowledge of exercise equipment was apparent to D'Andra as they walked around the gym and he explained each device and its function. Promises to herself aside, it was a continuous struggle for her to turn her mind from the curve of his luscious lips to the words coming out of them. But she would need to; he'd just asked her a question.

"D'Andra?"

"Yes?"

"The treadmill. I was asking if you're ready to give it a try."

D'Andra looked at the other exercisers—some walking comfortably, others running on the fast rotating rubber. An image of flying off the device and landing spread-eagled on the gym floor rose up unbidden in D'Andra's mind. It was not a pretty picture. She shook her head no, slowly at first and then more vigorously. Her bouncy black curls added to the objection.

"I can't take that chance; I'll fall off that thing and break my neck."

"No you won't," Night said softly. "I'll be here to catch you."

One look at Night's muscled biceps and D'Andra

went from praying she wouldn't fall to hoping it would happen. Having that man put his arms around her was worth a broken toe. She looked in his eyes, full of assurance and kindness, and back at the treadmill.

"I don't know," she whispered.

"Come on, doll," he said, taking her arm and coaxing her toward the daunting machine. "It's not as hard as it looks. Step up."

"But I can't run like that." She looked over at a woman sweating profusely as she moved her size-fives vigorously to keep up a fast pace on the machine.

"You don't have to run like that. D'Andra, look at me."

D'Andra looked down. In that instant she was back in grade-school gym class: not fast enough, skinny enough, or good enough.

Night placed a finger under her chin and raised her head to meet his eyes. "You're not here to compete with anyone in this gym. The only person you have to impress is yourself. Don't worry about what others are doing, their routine or how they look. We all have to start somewhere and your deciding to come here was the hardest step of all. Compared to that decision the rest is easy. Now step up, doll."

Night started D'Andra off on an easy walk, with very little incline. She thought it was too easy for the first two minutes. But two minutes later she was wondering if she could last the full ten. *Good thing I kept my mouth shut*, D'Andra thought as she worked to shift the focus from her labored breathing to the football game on the wall-mounted TV screens. On her drive to the gym, she'd planned to walk at least a half hour, and had almost shared this idea with Night.

While she was trying to figure out where all the air in the room went, a man who could have passed for The Rock's brother greeted Night.

"Hey, how you doing, man?"

"It's all good, bro. How are those plans for your gym coming along?"

Night stepped away from the treadmill and turned to fully engage his friend.

It was just as well. She was already sweating like a pig on a spit and to make matters worse, her spandex pants refused to expand and, like her, were not breathing well. Her thick thighs in the nonporous fabric resembled two pieces of wood being rubbed together: fire starters. With Night around she was already aflame, the last thing she needed was a match from her thatch. Thank goodness her hot pink T-shirt hid the incendiary action going on above her knees, and since she knew she was sweating enough for people to believe she'd peed on herself, thank goodness her leggings were black.

She felt like a hot mess, but decided to do her best. So dabbing at the sweat pouring down her forehead, she concentrated on moving her arms as well as her legs, as Night had instructed. *I'm walking my weight off with a huff and a puff. And in a few months I'm gonna strut my stuff.* She smiled at the diddy that popped into her head and began whispering it aloud. Her confidence began to build, and she imagined herself looking as good as anybody else in the gym. She pumped her arms more vigorously, determined to prove she had what it took to take on this treadmill. It would take more than ten minutes and a piece of moving rubber to beat D'Andra Smalls.

Her mind was in agreement but her body had other plans. Only thing is, D'Andra didn't get the memo; not at first. She frowned as Night came toward her in what seemed like slow motion. His hard, defined thigh muscles bulged with each step while his mouth formed words she couldn't hear. His stark white teeth glistened and his dark brown eyes sparkled . . . part mischief, part seduction. Was the treadmill still moving underneath her feet? D'Andra couldn't tell, mesmerized as she was by Night's arms reaching toward her in an unspoken invitation. *Come to me doll. Come inside my chocolate paradise and let's run some laps together . . .*

"D'Andra!" Night reached D'Andra just as she was about to tumble off the treadmill. He caught her, as he'd promised. She stayed on her feet, but just barely.

"D'Andra," Night said again, keeping his arm around her for support. "Are you all right?"

D'Andra shook her head, trying to make sense of what just happened. One minute she was cognizant of being on the treadmill, the next she was off it and in the arms of her dream man—albeit not as she had expected. She gave Night a confused look, even as she tried to clear the fuzziness from her head.

"Come on, sit down." Night lowered D'Andra to the now still treadmill and sat down beside her.

"Take deep breaths. That's it; stay calm. You're going to be fine." He checked her pulse, looked to see if her eyes were dilated. Then he reached for her water bottle. "Drink some water, D'Andra," he quietly commanded.

D'Andra kept her head down as she slowly drank from the water bottle. Embarrassment replaced the confidence she'd felt only moments before. Here she'd been worried about looking like a fool and that's exactly what had happened. She knew she shouldn't have done this, come to the gym thinking she could actually act like she wasn't an obese, out-of-shape woman about to die. Maybe her mother was right; maybe some women were destined to be fat. She'd been heavy her whole life.

The words of her doctor replaced those of her mom. *D'Andra, for your health's sake, you have to lose weight.* But was this the way? She thought of trying a different approach, perhaps starting with a food plan like Nutrisystem or the more drastic lemonade diet she'd heard about. Maybe it would be better to start exercising after she lost twenty, thirty pounds, when her thighs didn't resemble tree trunks and she could actually stay upright on the machines.

"What did you eat today?" Night's voice was calm and full of concern.

"Some pork rinds and a diet soda."

D'Andra's shame deepened. She knew that the word salad, vegetable or fruit should have been somewhere in her answer. But it wasn't. Night probably suspected that all the food she ate was either junk or fried, and here she was living up to the hype.

"Is that all?"

D'Andra nodded; then remembered breakfast. "Oh, and I had a Slimfast this morning."

She missed Night's look of compassion mixed with chagrin as he shook his head slowly. "Keep taking deep breaths, slow your heart rate. I'll be right back."

If she'd had the energy, D'Andra would have run out of the gym; away from Night and the illusion that she could change her life. But she was too out of breath. She glanced around the room, expecting to see eyes on her from every direction. But aside from a middle-aged Mexican man who smiled flirtatiously and nodded when their eyes met, no one was paying her any attention at all. Everyone seemed to be into their workout; watching TV, listening to their iPods, chatting with friends.

D'Andra turned the other way and saw a fifty-something, slightly heavyset woman sit down on a stationary bike. Looking like a cross between the food channel's Paula Deen and the actress Cathy Bates, she seemed not at all self-conscious of the varicose veins that ran down her exposed thighs to her ankles, or of the mounds of flesh hanging over her tight, sleeveless top. The woman adjusted the seat and the handle bars, settled herself onto the bicycle, plugged in a pair of earphones and began peddling to a rhythm D'Andra couldn't hear. D'Andra continued to look around and was struck at the focus with which people went about taking care of their bodies: the men lifting weights or doing bench presses, the women doing crunches on pilates balls and push-ups on floor mats, and the step class taking place at the back of the gym. She so wanted to feel a part of this world, to know what it was like to exert energy and feel good as a result, instead of how she'd felt just moments earlier, like she was borrowing breath from her next life.

"Okay doll, drink this." Night stopped in front of D'Andra and handed her a plastic bottle filled with a thick, brown liquid.

"What is it?"

"It's a protein drink, with all the vitamins and minerals of a full-course, well-balanced meal." Night sat down next to her and continued. "What are you trying to do, starve yourself skinny or something?"

"Or something," D'Andra responded. "To make a long story short, I have to lose weight. My doctor said I need to change my diet, exercise . . ."

"But did he say you had to do it by Monday?"

D'Andra smiled even as she shook her head no.

"Did your doctor recommend a specific exercise program for you?"

D'Andra nodded at the treadmill. "He specifically mentioned treadmills or walking to start. Once I lose a few more pounds, he suggested I buy a bike. Basically, he said as long as I didn't try and do too much too soon I'd be okay, that my body would tell me when I'd overdone it. Like now."

"No, what your body just told you is 'I'm hungry!'

It's like trying to drive a car without gas, or in the case of your rinds and soda mini-meal, with fake fuel.

"Look, working out takes a lot of energy; especially when your body isn't used to it. The last thing you want to do is come in here for the very first time on an empty stomach and more than that, you don't want to stop eating to try and lose weight. That's just going to throw off your metabolism and encourage your body to hang on to the very fat you're trying to get rid of."

"But you don't understand, Night, this is about life and death for me!"

"It's about life and death for everybody. But just like you didn't gain the weight overnight, you're not going to lose it overnight either. The more methodical you are about taking the weight off, going for a change in lifestyle instead of a change in diet, the better you'll be at keeping it off."

D'Andra turned and looked at Night. Who was this man? And why was he paying attention to her? She decided to find out. "Why are you doing this?"

"Doing what?"

"Taking all this time with me, helping me?"

Night shrugged. "I don't know; I guess it's because I saw you in your car, struggling with whether to come in here or not . . . and then you decided to do it, even though you were scared. That took courage. I like that."

Except for her exceptional work ethic and make-you-slap-somebody home-cooked meals, it had been a long time since D'Andra had heard anything about her being likeable. She couldn't remember the last time such words had come from a man; compliments from Charles had been as rare as a homeless man with a house key. But it didn't make sense; this gorgeous specimen named Night was paying all this attention to her and she couldn't figure out his true motive.

"My favorite aunt was a big woman," Night continued as D'Andra sipped her protein drink. "I spent the last five years trying to get her inside a gym. She never made it though . . ."

"Why, what happened?"

"They say it was cardiac arrest. She threw a birthday party for my uncle; we partied all night long. She did the electric slide until the power went out, danced until the sun came up. It looked like she was having the time of her life. That was the last time I saw her alive."

So that's it, D'Andra thought. *I remind him of a dead relative he couldn't save and now is his moment of redemption.* It was just as well she knew the truth; that his attention was driven by sympathy, not male-female desire. She knew all along there had to be a reason for his kindness, but the fact still made her sad. She didn't want his pity.

"I'm sorry for your aunt, Night," she said. "But you don't have to feel sorry for me. I'm not trying to leave this earth any time soon. That's why I'm here. I appreciate what you're doing and all but really, you don't have to feel obligated to help me. I may have taken on a little too much anyway; maybe it's best I lose a few pounds before trying to move all this weight around."

D'Andra struggled to her feet; Night immediately jumped up to help her. She started toward the door.

"Do you feel better?"

"Yes; that drink really helped."

"Then where are you going?"

"Didn't you say I shouldn't—"

"Exercise on an empty stomach? Yes, I did. But now that you've had a meal," Night pointed to the empty bottle, "I think you should finish your workout. We'll skip the bike, but you can handle a few weights. I have a feeling if you walk out that door I won't see you again. I'm not going to let that happen, and not out of some kind of *obligation* as you put it."

"Then why? You don't even know me."

"Personal training is more than what I do, it's who I am. I like helping people feel better, look better. And I'd love helping you work on that body and further enhance those light eyes and sexy dimples."

A slow blush crept across D'Andra's butter-colored skin. Her heart raced as if she were exercising even though she was standing still. And while she knew she should say something coherent, thought once again fled from her head. What was it about this man that left her speechless?

"Let's go over to the weights; keep your body moving."

Well, she determined, it definitely wasn't his bossy attitude. "Night, I'm not sure I should do weights today."

"Yes, you should. I won't start you off with anything too heavy. We have to add weights to your cardio workout. I said I've got you, right? I'm not going to let you hurt yourself, doll."

"What's with this 'doll' stuff; is that the new *in* word I haven't heard yet?"

"Naw, it's an old school term and the goal I'm setting for you. Speaking of old school, remember the Commodores song, 'Brick House'? Well, I'm going to turn you into another type of house, a *dollhouse.* When I get through with this body you'll be 'D'Andra the living doll.'"

D'Andra laughed. "That's so corny."

Thankfully Night had gotten over the pain that being laughed at used to cause him. "Yeah," he drawled. "But you liked it."

D'Andra tried but couldn't stop the smile that lit up her face. For the first time since they met, she felt comfortable. To be that fine yet talk that dorky . . . maybe they could be friends after all. And even though she hated men, the least she could do was be polite.

3

"Who was that fat chick?" Marc, the Bally employee who'd checked D'Andra in and taken her picture, grabbed a dumbbell and began doing curls next to Night.

Night copped an attitude. "What do you mean, fat chick?"

"Well, she was; no disrespect or nothin—"

"It sounded disrespectful . . ."

"My bad, man; but she is a big girl. What, you tappin' that ass or something?"

Night held himself rigid as he executed perfect chin-ups. "What are you trying to do, Marc, piss me off?"

"I'm not trying to jock you man." Marc laughed. "You came in with her, helped her work out and everything. Just wondering who she is, that's all. You're acting all protective and stuff, like she's either your girl, or your little sister. What's up with that?"

It was a good question. Night didn't know why he felt protective of D'Andra, but there was something about her that brought out his chivalrous side. He also thought she'd be perfect for one of the workouts he intended to offer at his gym, and had shared these thoughts with her. Still, Night couldn't fully explain why his friend's comments had riled him. Maybe it was because unlike Marc who'd been a pretty boy all his life, Night knew what it was like to be teased.

"I don't know what's up," he answered finally. "I just met the girl out in the parking lot. It took a lot for her to come in here, trying to lose weight and what not. I thought I'd help her out a little, that's all."

Sweat gleamed from Marc's toned body as he moved from the dumbbells to the bench press. He added forty pounds to the load and grabbed the bar with his hands. His arm muscles rippled like coordinated ocean waves as he repeatedly pushed the bar toward the ceiling.

"What's this, the new and improved Night? I've never seen you help a girl without an MO. Jazz got you seeing the error of your ways?"

"Man, the only error Jazz showed me was the judgment I used in messing with her as long as I did."

At one time Jazz Anderson was the love of Night's life and would-be business partner. But that was before jealousy and insecurity overshadowed beauty and intelligence. Night had conducted private workouts in his home gym for years. Jazz didn't have a problem with it, at first. Not until she started hearing wedding bells. Night heard them too, was helping to make them ring. Then she had to go and mess up the melody by demanding he not work with female clients in his home gym unless she was there. He refused. "Them or me" was her ultimatum. "Them *and* me" was his counter offer. After months of arguments and false accusations, he chose them.

"When's the last time you seen her?" Marc asked.

"Jazz? About a month ago; ran into her at a concert."

"Is she still fine?"

"Is the sky still blue?"

Marc let the weights fall with a clang. "My money's on y'all getting back together. She's a walking ad for sexy, dude. No man walks away from something like that."

"This man did."

And unlike when Jazz walked away, as she had several times over the course of their relationship, Night had no intention of returning. He couldn't argue Jazz's classic beauty: jet black hair, her own, which cascaded over smooth café au lait skin, feline eyes, high cheekbones, satiny lips. Her breasts were lush and full, booty nice and tight. She could easily fill the pages of any beauty or fitness magazine.

But for all her beauty, Jazz had an ugly side. She could be witty and charming, but she could also be verbally vicious and unnecessarily rude. It was enough that Night witnessed this treatment by Jazz to strangers. But when she used these antics with the one and only Val Johnson, it was the last straw. Nobody disrespected his mother and remained his friend. Not even someone as beautiful as Jazz.

He finished his workout and headed for the exit. Passing the treadmills on his way out, he thought of D'Andra. His mother would love her, he decided. Not that there was any reason for him to think such a thought. D'Andra would never meet his mother. She wasn't his type. He liked women who were confident, comfortable in their own skin. He'd sensed the opposite in D'Andra. Unfortunately, he was a builder of muscle, not self-esteem. It was a moot point at any rate. For now his focus was on one thing only: opening his business by the Fourth of July weekend. But even as he envisioned his luxury facility of rubber, steel, music and flat-screen TVs, somehow the scene was not complete without a dollhouse.

4

D'Andra turned up the radio as she navigated traffic on her way home. She was still trying to process all that had happened to her at the gym. It was enough that she'd successfully gotten through almost thirty minutes of exercise, but with the aid of a fine personal trainer? That she hadn't expected. She thought the afternoon could contain no more surprises but as she discovered in a conversation as she left the gym, she'd been wrong.

"You did well today," Night had said when her workout was over.

"For somebody who almost passed out I guess I did all right."

"You were fine, and it will only get better."

Night continued to walk with her from the gym to the parking lot. She didn't have long to wonder why.

"I have a project in mind that you'd be perfect for," he said.

"Me?" D'Andra couldn't imagine any type of project she'd be good at where he was concerned.

"It's for my gym. See, I want to reach out to big women," he imagined how that might have sounded to D'Andra and hurried to explain. "All women, of course, but I especially want big women to feel comfortable in my gym."

D'Andra immediately knew the reason, and said so. "For your aunt?"

Night nodded. "I plan to structure a program in her memory specifically for large women. Her name was Jewel, and that's what I'll call this special group, my jewels. I'm getting a banner designed to go across the wall of the main group exercise room: *Join Exercise With Enthusiasm & Look Sensational . . . J.E.W.E.L.S.*

"That's a sweet tribute to your aunt and a great idea," D'Andra admitted. "The first thing I noticed when I walked into the gym was that hardly anyone in there looked like me. Most everyone else was already fit; it was a bit disconcerting."

"I usually charge a steep hourly rate," Night continued. "But I'd like to offer you my services for free in exchange for your becoming the poster girl, so to speak, for this project."

"But what if I don't lose the weight?" D'Andra was moved by his thoughtfulness. Being fine *and* nice was quickly wearing down her man-hater wall.

"If you don't lose, then I don't win. I figure you want to lose, say, forty-fifty pounds, right?"

D'Andra nodded.

"I can help you do that over the next six to seven months, right around the time my gym opens. I'll put together a program that's aggressive without being over the top. You can run the regimen past your doctor and once he gives the okay, we'll be ready to roll. I'd like to get before and after shots of you, and use you as a motivator to get other women to first join then continue the program."

"I, I don't know what to say."

"Well if you're not going to say yes don't say anything. Just come by my house this Tuesday so we can

get started. You'll be in shape in no time and healthy
as ever."

He'd given her his card then, and with a wink turned
and jogged back to the gym. Now, thirty minutes later,
the shock had worn off and D'Andra was warming to
the idea for a variety of reasons. First, she'd get serious help in losing weight. Second, his desire to help
women get healthy mirrored her own desire.

After being diagnosed with high blood pressure and
Type II diabetes, the reasons for her unexpected
emergency room visit, D'Andra had gone online to
find out more about what her doctor had casually mentioned as "a problem common to women of
color." She'd been offended until she'd gone online
and read the facts: that two of the leading causes of ill-
ness and death in the Black community were diabetes
and heart disease. D'Andra had clicked on the various
links offered on the site for further information and
was shocked but not surprised at what she read: as of
2007 one report showed that one out of seven African-
Americans suffered from diabetes and that they were
twice as likely as Whites to develop the disease. There
was also an alarming increase of Type II diabetes, the
diabetes most closely linked with diet and exercise,
among children. Some experts suggested diabetes was
reaching epidemic proportions in Black America.

As D'Andra neared her home, she recalled how she
felt after watching a panel on cable television about
the state of Black health:

"We're seeing a shortening of life spans," the moderator said.
"People are dying earlier from heart disease and strokes,"
added Dr. Duane Smoot, chair of the medical department at
the Howard University Hospital.
"There are just so many problems associated with diabetes. It
causes people to have more problems with aging. For example,

it causes aging of your blood vessels, so hardening of the arteries occurs more frequently. We talk about aging gracefully, but with this disease, it makes it more difficult to have a good quality of life. We have very firm data that tells us that diabetes itself has reached epidemic proportions in this nation as a whole, but more specifically in the African-American community."

Recalling the program and focusing on her conversation with Night, D'Andra realized how she could accomplish the second major life change she wanted to make as a result of her "emergency gurney journey" brought on by a blood pressure spike that had reached 210/120—to study nutrition and somehow help teach her community the value of proper diet and exercise.

She hadn't told anyone of the life changes she was working on but meeting Night today felt like some kind of sign that she was headed in the right direction. Maybe by helping him, he could help her reach the community through his gym. *Fate must be smiling down on me,* she thought as she turned the corner on to her block. And for the first time in a long time, D'Andra was smiling back.

But not for long. Her smile turned upside down as soon as she noticed the blue, four-door Toyota parked in front of a row of small, yet well-kept townhouses. Cassandra was home, which meant the peaceful Saturday afternoon she'd imagined wasn't going to happen. Ever since her sister had moved in with her three children two months before, the house had been pure chaos. Cassandra had sworn at the time that the situation was temporary. But temporary was turning into permanent, which brought D'Andra's thoughts to the third thing she wanted to change in her life . . . her address. Even as she walked toward the house, her mind whirled with thoughts of where she could go to escape. *Maybe I'll go to the mall, or see a movie.*

"It's about time you got home," her mother yelled before D'Andra got completely in the door. "I told you I wanted those greens for dinner."

"Ooh, Aunt DeeDee, you fixing greens?"

"What you fixing with them Aunt DeeDee?"

"Can we have some Kool-Aid, Aunt DeeDee?"

Cassandra's three children, seven-year-old Kayla and five-year-old twins, Tonia and Antoine, bum-rushed D'Andra in the foyer. She loved her nieces and nephew but it still didn't stop her from wishing they'd click their heels three times and go home. That was the problem: they were home. She'd thought the two-bedroom townhouse just big enough when her mother had asked her to move in after the breakup with Charles. Now that the two-person household had become a six-person one, five of them female, the living space was downright suffocating. D'Andra took a deep breath, and tried to keep a rein on her blood pressure.

"Where's y'all's mama?" she asked, pushing her way through tiny hands and feet.

"She gone," Kayla responded.

Oh no she didn't leave these kids here again for me to watch, D'Andra thought, her blood pressure rising despite her resolve to keep it down. When the doctor had asked if there had been any recent events that would have precipitated the spike in her blood pressure, D'Andra knew Cassandra's returning home was part of the reason. That she was selfish enough and felt entitled enough to think she could dump her children on D'Andra without asking was too much. She marched into the living room where her mother was lying on the couch flipping channels with the remote.

"Mama, I told Cassandra I can't be watching these kids every weekend. I've already got a job. I'm tired after working all week and need to be able to relax on the weekends."

"Those kids ain't bothering nobody," Mary said as she grabbed a pillow and placed it under her head so she could see the TV better. "Your sister's been through a lot, it's good for her to go out and have a good time. I told her I'd watch the kids."

Bringing up Cassandra's messy divorce didn't change D'Andra's position. She knew how her mother watched kids. What she watched was D'Andra, making sure her orders to feed, clothe and entertain them were carried out.

"She's been through a lot and I haven't?" she argued. "Two weeks ago I was in the hospital, in emergency. And I was there because of all this added stress from Cassandra and her drama. I can't work, cook, clean *and* take care of her kids."

"Cassandra had nothing to do with you being in that hospital," Mary said with a big yawn. "Yo' big fat ass is what got you there. Cassandra's out with that pro baseball player she just met, trying to make a better life for herself, and for her mama in the process. He's got money, owns his own house and everything. She's my only hope of getting out of this rundown neighborhood. It ain't like you're ever gonna find a man. Charles was probably the best you were gonna do, and you couldn't even keep him."

D'Andra felt a slow throb begin at the back of her head and fought down a series of snide comments. She hadn't told her mother what happened between her and Charles. And for all of Mary Smalls' issues, she was still her mother and deserved respect. But Cassandra was another story. She was tired of putting up with her sister's crap and today was the day she was going to tell her so. It was also the day she was going to get on the computer and find another place to live. Enough was enough.

D'Andra decided to keep this impending change to herself, as she had all the others. Her mother and sister derided everything she tried to do. Plus she knew her mother would try and convince her to stay, for the portion of rent she paid if nothing else. But she was through being pushed around. Let Cassandra's baseball boy foot the bill. That decision made, D'Andra ignored her mother's comment and headed upstairs to take a shower.

"Aunt DeeDee, we're hungry," Kayla said quietly, her big, brown eyes looking up expectantly as D'Andra came down the stairs.

"What have you eaten?" D'Andra asked.

"Just some cereal," Antoine piped in. "We want some real food."

"And I don't want no more of that baked chicken," Mary said as D'Andra headed toward the kitchen. "We like our meat fried around here. There's some pork chops in the refrigerator that'll go good with some mashed potatoes and gravy."

D'Andra stopped and looked at the mother who was more overweight than she, then thought of Night's aunt, and concern overrode the animosity at being treated like a short-order cook.

"Mama, you know why I'm baking instead of frying. Both of us need to lose weight; it's a healthier choice."

"You trying to lose weight don't mean I'm trying to. I've always been fat and am always gonna be fat, and so are you. Cassandra's the only skinny one in the family, got her daddy's genes. A little grease never hurt nobody girl; whether that food is baked or fried, you're still gonna be fat. So you might as well cook it how it tastes good.

"Kayla, go bring Big Mama that bag of chips on the table. And look in the refrigerator and get one of those sodas."

"Yes, ma'am," Kayla said, giving D'Andra an understanding look as she passed. Kayla had obviously become Mary's legs when D'Andra wasn't around.

D'Andra tried, but washing off her mother's caustic comments was not as easy as removing the sweat from her workout. She'd endured taunts her whole life. If it wasn't her family, it was her classmates. She thought she'd grown beyond the envy she used to feel at her mother's obvious favoritism toward Cassandra but her younger sister moving in had brought it all back to the surface.

The first time D'Andra noticed their being treated differently was when she was six years old and Cassandra was three. Her mother had purchased dresses for them to have a family portrait done at Sears. Cassandra's dress was a beautiful yellow concoction of satin and lace. D'Andra's navy blue sailor dress with the dreary red ribbon paled in comparison. When they got to the photography studio, Mary and the photographer made a fuss over Cassandra while D'Andra was treated as an afterthought. Her feelings showed on her face, evidenced in her frown amidst Mary and Cassandra's happy countenance. No matter how hard the photographer tried, he couldn't get D'Andra to stop scowling. It wasn't until Mary threatened a whooping that she pasted a fake smile on her face. D'Andra was eternally grateful when a busted upstairs water pipe in their childhood home had soaked and ruined everything below it, including the grouping of family pictures Mary had on the wall. Even thinking her ardent wishes to have the picture gone caused the pipe to burst wasn't enough to make D'Andra feel bad it had happened.

The second major incident that led to her feeling inferior and less loved happened when D'Andra was nine. She overheard her mother talking on the phone with Sam, Cassandra's father. He was married at the time Mary got pregnant, and while he provided for Cassandra financially and visited her once or twice a month, he had refused to leave his wife. On the other hand, D'Andra didn't know anything about her father aside from the few photos of a medium-height, golden-brown man holding her when she was a baby, and a name, Orlando Dobbs. Her mother would shut down every time she inquired about him and after a while, she stopped asking. Especially after eavesdropping on a conversation she wished she'd never heard.

"If I'd met you first, you would have been the father of both my girls. Cassandra is the pretty one, looks more like you every day."

Sam must have said something because her mother was quiet a moment.

And then: "Orlando? I don't know where he is. He can be dead for all I care."

D'Andra's hopes of ever meeting her father, at least with her mother's help, faded to black.

"Humph. I don't care how long it's been, she's still a bitch."

D'Andra's mouth fell open. Even at nine, D'Andra knew that *little bitch* was not a term of endearment. She ran to her room and hid in the closet crying.

That's where her mother found her hours later, asleep. "D'Andra! D'Andra, wake up! What in the hell are you doing sleeping in the closet?"

For a moment, D'Andra forgot what had brought her to her favorite hiding place. "I-I-I don't know." She chewed nervously on her lower lip.

"And stop gnawing on your lip. You look like your crazy ass da—just don't do that."

Her comment brought the memories back; her father, how her mother felt about him in contrast with Cassandra's father, and in turn her, the reason she'd hid in the closet. Had she thought to ask, she would have learned that the *bitch* Mary referred to was her true love's wife.

As soon as her mother left the room, D'Andra raced and grabbed the picture on the nightstand. It was one of a handful she had of her father and her. In this one he was holding her; she was about two years old. She looked to find the part of her that looked like him, the part her mother didn't like. Aside from them both being big, she didn't see much. Her mother was big too, so was that even a trait that Orlando Dobbs had passed on to her? D'Andra didn't know, and even now, all these years later, she still wanted to find out.

By the time D'Andra cooked dinner, cleaned the kitchen and put her nieces and nephew to bed she was exhausted. She pulled out the sofa bed, her new sleeping quarters since Cassandra and family moved in and, at her mother's suggestion, claimed D'Andra's bedroom for their temporary stay. The thought of taking in a movie or shopping at the mall had long been forgotten, and even an apartment search on the Internet was too much additional work for the night. The special way Night had made her feel and the satisfaction that had come from working out was a distant memory as well. And though her mother knew she'd joined a gym and scheduled her first workout today, not one question had been asked concerning it. Without Elaine's encouragement or Night's support, D'Andra had lost the battle to resist her own good cooking, and before she knew it had finished off two large pork chops, a mound of potatoes and two helpings of greens. At least she'd passed on the gravy and hoped that counted for something.

I'll just go to the gym an extra day, she thought as she tried to find a comfortable position on the lumpy, pullout mattress. She was trying not to beat herself up as the book Elaine had given her on relationships encouraged.

"You've got to love yourself before you can love anybody else, or before anybody can really love you. Remember that," Elaine had reminded D'Andra just last week.

D'Andra was willing to make what would undoubtedly be a long journey to self-love. She knew it wasn't a trip that one made overnight, and that sometimes it was an entire life's journey with forks in the road, or as this evening had so aptly illustrated, a fork in hand . . . one full of greens and potatoes and good old-fashioned southern fried pork chops.

5

D'Andra planned to do a bunch of nothing when she woke up the next morning. Sometime during the night she'd changed her mind about working out and decided Tuesday would be soon enough for her next exercise adventure.

Her family's plans quickly changed her own. It started with her nieces and nephew bouncing on her sofa bed and asking for breakfast before nine A.M. She'd just shooed them away with promises of afternoon tacos and turned over for more sleep when the loud sounds of soul brother number one, James Brown, seeped from under her mother's bedroom door. *I feel good* . . .

"Yeah," D'Andra mumbled as she rolled over and out of her bed. "You're the only one."

Shortly after learning that Cassandra's boyfriend was coming over for a game of Bid Whist, along with Mary's casino buddy Boss (who D'Andra suspected was also her mother's lover) and their cousin Jackie and her kids, she decided that there was no time like the present to work the pork chops off her thighs.

"We thought you could make a big pot of spaghetti,"

her mother offered as D'Andra placed workout clothes in a gym bag.

"You'll have to pull cooking duty today, Mama," she answered. "I've got work to do."

An hour later D'Andra was making it work, walking slowly yet continuously to the sounds of Jill Scott playing on her iPod. She checked her watch for a second time, watched the second hand to make sure it was working. Had it really only been five minutes? Then why was she so tired? Determined to focus on the finish line instead of the race, she removed her watch and placed it in the cup holder, then turned up the volume and started pumping her arms in time to the beat. Her rhythm was interrupted by a tap on the arm. She turned to see "walking goodness" standing beside her and removed her earplugs. She forgot he was supposed to be "walking dirt."

"Hey, Night."

"It's contagious isn't it?"

"What?"

"Working out."

D'Andra nodded. She didn't feel a need to disclose her pork chop motivation.

Night stepped up on the treadmill next to her, set a pace close to but faster than D'Andra's, and joined her in the workout.

"You give any thought to the project I told you about, being my spokesperson?"

"Poster girl was pressure enough but now you say spokesperson? Nothing like pressure to scare me away from the possibility."

"Pressure is what turns a rock into a diamond," Night countered easily. "And something tells me you're up to the challenge."

"So is this like, a job or something?"

"Of sorts. The first part is simply being a walking

testimony as to the success of my special workout plan. I work with you for free, you get fit, and I have living, breathing proof of what happens with *Night Moves*. I'm thinking of that for the name of my gym," he added.

"Hum." D'Andra was as attracted to his bulging thighs as the words he spoke. But what he was saying was important so she focused on listening.

"If things work out between us," he continued, "there could be the possibility for additional work later on. Like I told you before, mine will be a full-service establishment and part of that service includes health screenings and free classes for members about everything from nutrition to emotional well-being as important components of overall good health."

Had someone read Night the script for her dream job? What he described as part of his full-service goals was exactly the type of position she wanted. But would she be able to ignore her desire for him to put her in other, more intimate positions?

He may be fine, but D'Andra was determined to keep her focus. Making the major life changes she had in mind would take all her energy. She wouldn't have any left for empty imaginings.

"So what would I need to do?"

"It's simple really. I'd have a photographer come over and shoot you the way you look now, and in six months or so we'll shoot the new you. The posters will be used in marketing—"

"I don't know," D'Andra interrupted. She hadn't liked being photographed ever since she'd worn the navy blue sailor dress. "I'm not too good with photo shoots."

Night stopped his treadmill and signaled her to come down. She looked at the clock and was surprised to see that ten minutes had gone by. She'd walked for almost fifteen minutes! Still, she didn't let her excitement overrule her common sense.

"I'll help you with your program," she continued. "And I have a friend, Elaine, who'd be perfect as your spokesperson. She's had two kids and is losing weight . . ."

Night placed a gentle hand on her skin and the heat traveled up her arm, down her chest and settled in a slow burn just below her navel. She forced herself not to squirm under his intense gaze.

"I've found the perfect person," he declared softly. "From what I've seen so far you're a beautiful woman inside and out. That's important for anyone representing my establishment."

"I'll think about it," she said.

"Why don't you think about it while we ride bikes?"

She fudged on the pedaling a little bit and even stopped for a minute or so but when all was said and done she completed almost ten minutes of cycling and another ten lifting free weights. In between instructions on lifting techniques and which muscles were being benefited by which weight machine, Night regaled her with his grandiose plans about his gym, including plans to have it operate almost twenty-four hours a day, with a special, party-like atmosphere happening during the late night hours. She was impressed with how much attention he paid to details and in spite of her resolve to be cautious, found herself getting caught up in his excitement.

"I've developed your program and can email it to you today. That way you can get the green light from the doc and we can get started. Any questions, just give me a call. You do still have my card, right?"

"Yes," D'Andra said, glad she hadn't followed her impulse to throw it away.

"So, I'll see you on Tuesday?" he asked as she headed for the women's locker room.

The only thing D'Andra didn't like about his plans was using her for the photo shoot. She thought it would be easier to pedal one of those stationary bikes uphill. But he stood there looking so hopeful, so joyous at his plans coming together. How could she tell him no?

"I'll think about it," was as close as she could come to an answer before she ran for the showers.

D'Andra stepped from the confines of the gym into a picture-perfect day. The air held the slightest hint of a chill off the Pacific Ocean, tempered by a bright mid-January sun beaming directly overhead. For just a moment she missed Charles. On a day like today, when times were good between them, they would have gone for a walk on the beach or to see a movie. But that was before she'd seen his ass bouncing between a pair of legs that weren't hers.

She shook her head, hoping to rid it of these painful memories. Knowing that nothing could help her feel better than a trip to the mall, she went shopping. After a pantsuit, three tops, a new pair of tennis shoes, and a chef salad, she felt better and decided to keep the mood going by swinging through Wal-Mart, her favorite one-stop shop.

D'Andra stood in the middle of the aisle in this massive superstore, looking at a dozen different bathroom scales. She knew she wanted a digital one, the most accurate she was told, but had no idea that outside of that there was a plethora of other choices: lithium or no, body fat analyzer, body fat and body water tracking scale, weight tracker, scale with memory, daily calorie counter and more. She finally settled on a heavy duty, lithium scale with none of the extras. The mirror could track her weight just fine and if she wasn't counting calories she didn't need a machine to do it. She added the scale to a basket filled with a case of Slimfast, a case of water, low-cal popcorn, toiletries, and a varied assortment of Just My Size workout clothes. At the last minute, she veered to the toy aisle and picked up Hannah Montana gear: a guitar for Kayla, a doll for Tonia, and a Transformer set for Antoine. She thought about buying an outfit for each of them, then decided to wait until they were with her. Instead she chose a couple kid-friendly DVDs. Just as she was about to turn into the center aisle, she heard a familiar voice.

". . . you should have tried to make the show. Tevin Campbell, Al B. Sure and Keith Sweat brought it back for real, but Bobby Brown was a hot mess. He was up there spilling his business, putting Whitney on blast. He needs to forget about her and concentrate on getting his own act together."

"But did he sing my jam, 'My Prerogative'?"

Chanelle. Even with the painful events that caused their separation, D'Andra smiled at the memories hearing her former best friend's voice evoked. Bobby Brown and "My Prerogative" is how they became best friends at Marcus Garvey Elementary School when they were both ten years old. The school held a talent contest and what would later be dubbed the Fabulous Four—D'Andra, Chanelle, Connie and Dominque— created a fancy and fiery dance routine to their then-favorite R&B hit and favorite singer. Chanelle—who was nicknamed Nelly—especially had been in love with Bobby Brown. He'd even inspired her first romantic encounter with Phillip Jackson, if two ten-year-olds pressing closed lips together at the downtown skating rink can be called romantic. The only reason the kid got play at all is because he had his hair cut in a fade just like Bobby Brown.

> "Ooh, I saw you kissing Phillip. You like him."
> "So."
> "So you like him, that's so."
> Chanelle had giggled childishly. "You think he's cute?"

D'Andra had nodded. Of course he was cute. His hair was cut like their idol. He even looked a little like him: tall, skinny, his skin a Bobby-colored brown. But D'Andra would have found little wrong with what Chanelle did or who she liked. She'd been the first person who made D'Andra feel pretty, in spite of her weight. This had also happened during the making of what would become the first place dance routine, when they tried to learn the Running Man.

D'Andra had fallen on Chanelle's bed, dejected.

> "I can't do that stupid move."
> "Yes you can."
> "Uh-uh."
> "Why you think you can't do it D'Andra?"
> "Cause I'm too big, that's why."
> "Girl, you ain't big," Chanelle said with a serious face, even as her eyes bore into D'Andra's jelly belly stomach. "My mother is twice as big as you. She can't even cross her legs, they so big. Can you cross your legs?"
> D'Andra sat up, pushed herself to the edge of the bed and promptly crossed her legs.
> "See? If you can cross your legs, you ain't too fat, you just got cushion for the pushin'."
> Neither girl knew exactly what that meant but Chanelle had heard her mother refer to herself that way. "Plus you've got pretty eyes. I wish my eyes were that color."
> "Really?" It was the first compliment D'Andra received

from a peer and it moved Chanelle to the front of her
friend line. Especially since everyone thought Chanelle
was one of the cutest girls in their class, with her mocha
brown skin, wavy hair and lean limbs.

"Uh-huh. Now come on, let's watch the video again
so we can do that part just like Bobby does."

Filled with newfound confidence, D'Andra had
danced as if her life depended on it. They'd rocked
the Running Man, the Alf, the Smurf and a floor ma-
neuver that involved a roll and a twist that D'Andra
had at first felt impossible for her to achieve. D'Andra
really gained points when it turned out she was the
only one who could Moonwalk. The rest of the girls'
movements were jerky, they more or less walked backward. But D'Andra fairly glided across the floor.
When they won, the other girls were convinced it was
because of D'Andra's Moonwalk. She'd been a mini-
celebrity at Marcus Garvey for the rest of the week.

Chanelle was also the first among her peers to recognize she was smart. Whenever there were instructions or directions or anything lengthy in word count,
Chanelle would summon D'Andra over with a "Hey
girl, what's all these words?" Aside from her teach-
ers, and an every-now-and-then compliment from her
mother, it was her only early, grade-school praise.

D'Andra's smile faded as she turned her cart and
headed in the opposite direction from the voices.
Those happy moments were a long time ago, happier
times separated by more recent, less happier ones.
Months had passed, but D'Andra was in no hurry to
encounter her former best friend who'd been willing
to throw almost twenty years of friendship away over
some walking dirt.

* * *

When D'Andra returned home, all was quiet, a rarity since Cassandra had moved back in. She wondered for just a moment where everyone had gone, then chose to make the best of her time alone. She decided to eat a quick bite and then get on the computer.

Moments later she sat with the best semblance of a healthy meal she could make from what was available in the kitchen: a small amount of the spaghetti sauce her mother had fixed, spread over a piece of baked fish instead of pasta. She'd grated a small amount of Parmesan cheese, a commodity that used to cover everything on her plate if Italian was the food choice. She'd opted for wheat crackers instead of butter-soaked French bread and sparkling water replaced the soda she loved. Still reveling in a quiet house, not to mention being able to control the remote, impossible when Mary Smalls was home, she munched on a cracker and flipped on the TV. She was just about to decide that there was nothing on when she landed on a channel in time to see a big woman's naked backside as she proudly stood on a balcony with her hands in the air.

"What in the world?"

D'Andra clicked on to the cable guide and saw that the show she was watching was called *Monique's Fat Chance P.A.R.I.S* and the woman on the balcony was naked because as part of a beauty contest, she would be photographed in the nude. D'Andra sat transfixed as she watched five women struggle with whether they could go through with the photo shoot. All five of them and also the host, Monique, voiced the same concerns and attitudes she had about her own body. One contestant, a virgin, said no one else had seen her adult body. Another hesitated for religious reasons, afraid of how appearing nude might affect her children. A third, speaking with new confidence, said she'd worked for every roll on her body and she was going to own them. The woman she'd seen on the balcony, who she later found was named Marcia, didn't want to pose nude because she'd always been known as the "clumsy queen," with a very negative view of her body image.

Monique empowered them by telling them the choice was theirs, that no one had to pose if she didn't want to, and that she was going to pose with them.

"If I'm going to talk the talk, then I've got to walk the walk," Monique said.

Tears came to D'Andra's eyes as one by one the plus-size models faced their fears and decided to pose for the camera, with body paint their only covering. Marcia had stood on the balcony in celebration of her decision to be free.

That's when D'Andra decided. Monique was right. If she was going to try and help other people get healthy and feel better, D'Andra knew she was going to have to start with herself. She put down her plate and picked up her purse. After finding Night's card she reached for her cell phone. It was time to face her fears, all of them. She was going to do the photo shoot. She wouldn't strip completely like the beautiful women in the contest had done, but at least she wouldn't be afraid to show some thigh. That, she decided, was a start.

"Night, I'll do it."

"D'Andra?"

"Oh, yes, I'm sorry. I'm just trying to get this out before I change my mind. I'll be the spokesperson for your big girl campaign and do the photo shoot."

"That's beautiful, doll. What made you change your mind?"

D'Andra told Night about the television show and the nude modeling.

"You know," he said, dropping his voice an octave, "that too can be arranged."

"Not in this lifetime. That'll never happen."

"Never is an awfully long time. Besides, seeing you in all of your beautiful glory would be a powerful motivator to your sistahs out there." His voice held the purr of a cat, a very big cat, one that was king of the jungle.

"Yeah, well maybe the show is on DVD. If not, my sistahs will have to get their glory and motivation by looking in the mirror."

They finished the conversation with D'Andra giving Night her email address and agreeing to meet on Tuesday. They decided to schedule the shoot during what would become her regular Tuesday workout time. His plan was to work with her for forty-five minutes on Tuesdays and Thursdays, and for her to work out on her own two additional days of the week. This unsupervised time would include work on the treadmill, stationary bike and, as she became stronger, the Stairmaster and elliptical machine.

Their conversation left her excited and energized. She didn't even begrudge her family for leaving the kitchen a mess, and cleaned it while her thoughts raced a mile a minute. She felt good about the positive changes she was making in her life and decided that she might as well continue while she was on a roll. Just one wrong word or bad incident and she knew she could lose momentum.

As soon as she turned out the kitchen light, she hurried to the desk in the corner of the living room. She knew if she thought about what she was getting ready to do, even for a moment, she'd change her mind.

Quickly turning on the computer, she typed in the Web site for Google, then stared blankly at the box used to search. She didn't know what to type. So she just typed her desire: *find someone.*

Thousands of Web sites jumped on the screen. D'Andra picked one randomly: Peoplesearch.com. She read the information on their Web site and with only a slight hesitation paid the small initiation fee to begin the search. After the charge went through another box popped up. She took a deep breath, faced her fear and typed the name: Orlando Dobbs.

6

"Wow, all this in two days? You've been busy," Elaine said after hearing a recap of D'Andra's weekend. She was told about D'Andra's escapades in working out, the spokesperson opportunity, the decision to go apartment hunting, and the decision to try and find her father.

"I don't think I've ever heard you mention your dad," Elaine said softly. She'd been a daddy's girl since she was old enough to say "da"—still was—and couldn't imagine growing up without him. "When did you see him last?"

D'Andra offered a bittersweet smile as she finished off her low-cal Subway sandwich. "According to an old photo, when I was about two. But I don't remember."

"What does your mother say about him?"

"Nothing, Elaine. That's just it. In all these years, she's refused to say much at all. Except that he was an asshole that I was better off not knowing. But I still wonder about him, you know?"

Elaine didn't know but nodded anyway.

"And now, well, it's not just the need for a nostalgic walk down memory lane or a potential date with my sperm donor. I need to know the history from his side of the family for my health; whether there are patterns of diabetes, heart disease, cancer, stroke. I am a part of who he is, whether I want to be or not. So I need to know."

There was silence as they replaced their trays and left the cafeteria.

"So what are you going to do?"

"I don't know."

She told Elaine about the three listings for Orlando Dobbs she'd found via the Peoplesearch.com Web site. One listing was in Chicago, one in Florida and the last in New Jersey. Each had an address and phone number, along with additional information for a higher fee.

"I don't know," she repeated, as they entered the medicine room, grateful that soon she'd be too busy to think about it.

It was time to pass meds, a task for which full focus was required. The last thing she wanted to do was give someone the wrong type or amount of medication. She checked the patient report sheet and signed into the computer on the med cart.

Time to get back to work, she thought, the one area in her life where D'Andra thrived. When it came to doing her job, she was outstanding. It was good to have a place where she felt respected and in control, and this was it. She wheeled her cart around and opened the door.

"Don't think you've gotten off the hook," Elaine said, readying her own cart to work the opposite wing.

"About what?"

"The personal trainer, that's what. I saw how your eyes lit up when you mentioned being his spokesperson, even if you did try to sound all cool and casual."

"Girl, please. He's just walking dirt, nothing to tell."

"Uh-huh, just as I figured. He's a hunk and you're in love."

"In heat is more like it . . . details at eleven."

They both laughed and walked off in opposite directions. Fortunately, passing meds would keep *walking dirt* off her mind.

"There's my angel," Tom said as D'Andra entered the room.

"That's right, here I am. How's my favorite patient today?"

"Better now that my honey's here." Tom Broomfield's seventy-year-old blue eyes sparkled with mischief.

D'Andra laughed. "Yeah, I bet you say that to all the girls." She took his vitals and continued to chitchat. "You ready to start the rehab on that hip today?"

"The sooner we get started, the sooner I get that dance you promised."

"Well all right, handsome," D'Andra said, winking at him as she rechecked the computer and gave him his medication.

"You'd better get some sleep so you'll be ready when Bryan comes in later."

"It's hard for me to sleep, dear. But I'll still be ready for my therapy and before you know it, we'll be dancing off into the sunset to the Tennessee Waltz."

"Tennesee? I told you we're going to do some two-stepping, Chicago style. Now try and get some sleep."

By the time the night was over, D'Andra felt like she'd made up another dance: the patient shuffle. Aside from a patient with Alzheimer's walking off site, old Gladys Smith throwing her used bed pan, Jessie hiding his roommate's glasses and old man Pervis pulling out his willy and scaring Harriett, her patient she loved to hate—Mrs. Frieda Lee Miller—was full of herself all night long. She rang her button incessantly and refused to let anybody but "Grace", the name she insisted on calling D'Andra, take care of her.

D'Andra couldn't figure out why she had a soft side

for Frieda, whom D'Andra called Miss Daisy. Perhaps it was that she believed her patient's cantankerous ways were a result of loneliness and pain, physical as well as emotional. Miss Daisy had no relatives who lived close by and therefore no visitors. Perhaps Frieda thought that even negative I-know-I've-gotten-on-your-nerves attention was better than none at all.

The house was quiet when D'Andra returned home from work, almost three hours past the time she was supposed to have gotten off. She took a quick shower, put on her pajamas and had just pulled the covers over her head when the phone rang. She considered letting it go to voice mail but since her cell phone rarely rang these days, curiosity won out.

"Hello?"

"Hey, doll."

Night! "Oh, hey."

"It's ten in the morning, girl. Did I wake you?"

"No," D'Andra said yawning. "I haven't been to bed yet."

Night wasn't expecting the pang of jealousy that went through him. He didn't care about her like that. Did he? "Oh, it's like that. Well, sorry for interrupting."

"It's not *like that*, whatever that means for you." D'Andra snapped, testy because she was exhausted. "I work nights."

Silence.

"Yeah, you should feel bad," she continued. "Either *I'm sorry* or *my bad* will do just fine."

"My apologies, doll."

The smile in his voice brought one to D'Andra's face, even as the deep tone warmed her all over. Even through her exhaustion she could feel heat rise. It wasn't good to talk to him while lying horizontal, she decided.

"I won't keep you then, just wondered if you could

make it at three-thirty instead of four today. My photographer has to be across town at six and I want to make sure we finish with the shoot."

The shoot. With all the hoopla at work last night, D'Andra had forgotten, both that it was happening and why she'd thought it a good idea.

"I don't think so, Night. It's almost eleven A.M. now and I work again tonight. Maybe I'd better cancel."

Night had a feeling if they cancelled, the shoot wouldn't get rescheduled. "No, I don't think that's a good idea. How about we make it later, around eight? I know someone else who might be able to get the shots we need."

"Why don't we do it another day?"

"Because we're doing it tonight, at eight. You've got my address. I'll see you then."

The click of his phone hanging up served as good-bye.

He's too pushy, D'Andra thought as she repositioned her pillow and curled up on her side. But even so, her last thoughts before sleep were of him, and there was a smile on her face.

The sultry, wet sauna produced a thin sheen of sweat on both of them. D'Andra watched Night lick his lips as his eyes followed one large bead from the fold in D'Andra's neck down her cleavage. Her nipples hardened as he continued staring, watching the rise and fall of her breasts. The room got hotter still.

"Here, let me," he said, gently taking her towel as he came to sit beside her. He began to dab at the droplets on her face, neck, arms and legs. Then he took his finger and followed the trail of yet another bead of sweat as it ran down her arm and puddled in the palm of her hand. Night lifted her hand ever so gently; his dark brown eyes boring into hers, and kissed each finger.

D'Andra followed Night's lead. She inched closer to his brawny frame, taking his hand in hers and kissing each digit. Then, never taking her eyes off his, she opened her mouth and sucked in his long, middle finger. Her tongue swirled around and around from knuckle to tip. She smiled slightly at Night's quick intake of breath, even as she repeated the action with his other hand.

"I want you D'Andra," Night said huskily.

"What? Right here, right now?"

"Yes."

"But what if people see us?"

"The gym is closed; nobody's here."

D'Andra looked around. How long had they been in the sauna?

"Nobody's here," Night repeated, just before his lips pressed against hers.

The kiss seared her body like a branding iron. She craned her neck to give him all of her, even as she opened her mouth to his probing tongue and let him inside. Their tongues swirled in the age-old dance, their hands moving, exploring, touching new territory. D'Andra gasped as she felt Night's hand slip below her athletic bra. She was surprised at his gentleness, even as he massaged each nipple into a hardened peak within seconds.

"Now, I want you now." Night began to take off her top.

"No, Night, I don't want you to see me."

"I want to . . ."

Before she could protest further the top was over her head and off her body, flung to the corner of the room. Her bra quickly followed. Night buried his head in her double Ds before caressing then kissing each nipple in the same manner he had her mouth.

"Get naked for me."

D'Andra's eyes widened as she looked around. She rose from the bench, her hands over her still throbbing breast.

Night's smile was that of a predator who had tracked and trapped his prey. "There's no escape, doll," he drawled as he too rose from the bench and came toward her. "Do you need me to help you?"

"No, I—"

"Here, allow me."

With the skill of a surgeon he tugged the elastic of her shorts away from her waist and pulled down. D'Andra tried to cover herself.

"Don't. Let me see. I want to see all of you."

D'Andra was horrified. "No, Night. There's too much of me."

"Uh-uh," he said, as his tongue began a journey toward her personal paradise.

"Yes," she breathed. "Yes, there is. Don't look at me Night. I'm fat."

Night quickly straightened, took her chin firmly but gently in his hand and stared unflinchingly into her eyes. "You're fabulous," he said as he moved his hands over her curves, caressing her folds as if they were satin and squeezing her thighs as if they were silk. He reached around and smoothed his hands over her ample behind, jiggling it lovingly while his tongue once again found hers. His breathing quickened. After a thorough plundering of her mouth he stepped back, his eyes never leaving hers, and he stripped out of his shorts. His readiness was evident as his engorged manhood stood at attention.

"Now, do you want this?"

D'Andra looked down at nine-plus inches of ebony genius. No words came out; she could only nod.

"Well, come get it." His words belied his actions. He backed D'Andra up against the hot wood, lifted her as if she were weightless and pinned her against the wall. One of D'Andra's feet was balanced on the bench, the other dangling in the air with Night's arm under her knee. He glided in slow and easy, feeling her full, and set up a rhythm that threw her into a frenzy.

"Night," she moaned his name over and over. "Night, Night, Night . . ."

"Aunt DeeDee! Wake up, Aunt DeeDee!"

D'Andra fought sheets and little hands for air as she came out of what felt like a deep fog. She lay barely opened eyes on three sets of wide-eyed brown ones with expressions that ranged from quizzical to comical.

"You were dreaming, Aunt DeeDee," Kayla said matter-of-factly.

"Yeah," Tonia said. "And talking, too."

D'Andra frowned, still trying to wake up.

"In your sleep," Kayla added patiently, as if she were the adult and D'Andra the child.

"Yeah," Antoine echoed. "Talking in your sleep."

D'Andra rubbed her eyes and yawned, determined to gain her bearings. Hadn't she just been dreaming?

"You kept saying Night," Kayla continued.

"Night, night," Antoine echoed.

"Was it nighttime in your dream?" Kayla asked, looking pointedly at the stream of sunshine flowing in from the townhouse's east window. "Cause it's sunny now."

Night. The dream came rushing back in full clarity. They were in the sauna, it was dark, the gym was closed and she and he were . . .

D'Andra sat up to flee the dream. She squinted her eyes toward the clock on the wall. It was a little after three. No wonder she was so groggy. The kids had awakened her from a deep sleep and from a troublesome dream. She couldn't decide whether they'd done her a favor or not.

"Aunt DeeDee is going upstairs to finish sleeping, okay? I'm going to lock the door so come on up and get the toys you want now, 'cause I'm not going to open the door once I close it. Do you hear me?"

The kids nodded and dutifully followed her upstairs. After picking out a couple games for the Xbox and a DVD, they felt prepared to get through the next three hours. D'Andra hoped she could get some more sleep, but fragments of the dream kept floating around her head like wisps of smoke. Nothing would ever happen between her and Night. They weren't each other's type and the timing wasn't right. She determined to bring these wandering, non-productive thoughts under control and forced herself to think about Night in different terms, as her personal trainer and employer of sorts, nothing more. Mind made up, she rolled over, went to sleep, and dreamt of him.

When she awoke, it was a little after six, just enough time for her to eat, prepare her clothes for work and head over to Night's house. Not relying on his promise to take care of everything where her look was concerned, she put on the new workout clothes she'd recently purchased, a pair of denim-look, cotton stretch pants paired with a baby-doll-styled T-shirt sporting blue and white stripes, the vertical kind that were supposed to make her look slimmer. She viewed herself in the mirror. *Yeah, whatever.* Forgoing a lot of makeup she settled for simple mascara and lip gloss, and put her shoulder-length curls back in a ponytail. Looking in the mirror once again, she fought the desire to disparage her appearance. *Sexy is inner confidence.* That's what one of the women on *Monique's Fat Chance* had said. She'd try and keep thinking that until she believed it. She looked in the mirror once more and smiled.

Self-pep talk over, she placed her uniform and other essentials for work in a garment bag and stowed her midnight munchies, a bag of fresh veggies—carrots, celery, radish, and red peppers—along with her Lean Cuisine, a bag of popcorn, and sparkling water in an insulated carrier. She took her cell phone off its charger, found her purse between the covers and was off.

* * *

D'Andra hesitantly rang the doorbell. Between her reservations about being anyone's spokesperson and the images of Night in her erotic dream, she was a nervous wreck. Her face was flushed before the doorbell was answered.

When it opened, a kindly gentleman with graying hair and a humbled spirit greeted her.

"You must be D'Andra. Come in."

Her relief that Night wasn't the first person she faced was evident in her greeting.

"Hi," she gushed, a little too breathy.

The man narrowed his eyes as he looked at her, and then spoke.

"My name is Frank. I'm the photographer. You're a little early. Night just finished a workout session. He's in the shower. Come on into the living room where we're set up.

"My, my, my," he continued, looking back at D'Andra as he walked. "Night was right, you're a fine one. We're going to get some nice pictures here, yes indeedy."

D'Andra followed Frank into a nicely decorated and decidedly masculine living space bathed in hues of deep blues and browns. A suede navy blue sectional anchored the space on the room's far wall, while two chocolate brown leather recliners framed a cocktail table made of ebony wood. These colors, along with brighter hues of rust, grays and tans were reflected in the rug and accent pillows placed strategically on furniture around the room. Stainless steel accessories, including lamps and picture frames, furthered the masculine concept as did the abstract black-and-white photos encased in those frames: the clean body lines of abdomens, arms, legs and backs. Frank's camera equipment was set up in the corner across from the large picture window.

Frank's sunny personality immediately put D'Andra

at ease. As he fiddled with and readied his camera equipment, he kept up a lively monologue. She learned he was a semi-retired photographer who'd been a friend of Night's family for decades. His photos had landed in several national magazines, including *Jet, Ebony, Black Enterprise* and *Life*. This job he loved had taken him to dozens of states, several countries in Europe and across the plains of Africa. By the time he was ready to shoot his first roll, D'Andra felt she'd known him a lifetime.

"Okay, doll, just place yourself over by that plant," Frank said, "and act natural."

So this is where Night gets that corny word, she thought, even as she breathed a sigh of relief that the photo session was beginning without Night's presence.

"Just relax, doll," Frank said, "and show me those dimples."

D'Andra walked over to where he had pointed and struck a pose as stiff as wood. She held it and waited.

"Smile for me now, and move those curves around." Frank clicked a few frames.

D'Andra placed her weight on the other leg, placed a hand on her hip and one behind her head, trying to imitate the girls on *Fat Chance*. It wasn't working.

"Wait a minute," Frank said. "We need to get you in the mood."

He walked over to Night's entertainment center, which among other things held stereo equipment and a massive collection of CDs. After careful examination, he pulled one out.

"Oh, yes; we're getting ready to see some sexy now. I want you to feel this music babydoll, and *move!*"

After a couple seconds of silence, a rock and roll legend blasted out of the stereo speakers. *Oh, Maybellene, why can't you be true? You've started back doing the things you used to do.*

Before D'Andra could react to the loud, obnoxious and unexpected blaring, Frank grabbed her hand and began twirling her around the room. Both were agile and light on their feet, surprised at each other's skills. After one particularly dizzying spin, Frank released D'Andra, grabbed his camera and started barking instructions to the beat of the song.

"D'Andra!" He crooned, interchanging her name with Maybellene. "You are fabulous, you are the cat's meow, you are the most beautiful woman in the room! Get it, girl. Show me what you're workin' with!"

D'Andra twirled and danced and laughed and posed. Frank's joy was contagious, his words convincing. She was fabulous, beautiful, the cat's meow. And datgummit, she would show him what she was working with, and then some!

Frank urged her on as the camera flashed. "You keep on like that, doll, and I'm gonna have to sop you up like a biscuit with molasses."

A freshly-showered Night stood in the hallway, mesmerized, the heated conversation he'd just had with Jazz about dissolving their business partnership forgotten. Who was this confident kitten stirring it up in his living room? Gone was the uncertain, self-deprecating wannabe. In her place danced a poised, self-assured woman who was sexy as hell! He watched as her body, large and in charge, swirled to the sounds as the CD went from *Maybellene* to *Johnny B. Goode* and found himself reacting physically to her low, throaty laugh and coy expressions. No one was more surprised than he. D'Andra's happiness was contagious, her beauty tangible. Her attractiveness didn't fit society's narrow standards, but came from an attribute that could not be bought in a clothing store or at a makeup counter.

D'Andra tossed her head back and laughed, uninhibited and free. The sexy heels she wore with the tight denim pants and baby doll top emphasized her curves in all the right places as well as her well-formed calves. The top dipped to show ample cleavage and when she turned around, baby had enough back to cause a heart attack—juicy and round, prime choice pound for pound. When she placed her hands on her hips and stood with head held high, legs firmly planted beneath her and a look of triumph on her glistening face, Night knew he had his shot.

He sauntered into the room as soon as the flashes stopped and Frank announced, "It's a wrap."

D'Andra fairly glowed as she ran over and hugged Frank. "I've never had so much fun in my life!" she exclaimed. "Who is that crazy man singing on the CD? He plays a mean guitar."

Frank halted his actions as if he'd been shot. "Who is it?" He looked at Night. "Did baby doll just ask me who is playing on this here CD?"

"I believe she did," Night solemnly answered.

D'Andra's smart comment was swallowed as she noticed Night for the first time. *How long has he been standing there?* she thought. *Did he see me acting crazy?* D'Andra suddenly felt self-conscious and vulnerable. He looked like an African angel, his stark white drawstring pants flowed over his hips like water, tied just below that rock hard sculpted abdomen and inverted navel. He wore no shoes or shirt.

She tried with little success to pull her attention away from what she could have easily mistaken for a chocolate lollipop. How was she supposed to keep her mouth from watering when all she wanted to do was take a lick?

Frank helped her out of her dilemma. "Girl, stop eyeing that boy like he's a rib slathered in barbeque sauce!"

"I wasn't," she said, licking her lips.

Frank chuckled, even as he noticed D'Andra's discomfort. He took off his glasses and cleaned the lens with a handkerchief.

"Girl, I'd have handled it better if you'd cussed an old man out. To answer your previous question, that's Chuck Berry, Mr. Rock and Roll himself!"

"Oh, right," D'Andra mumbled, trying to regain her composure. She wanted nothing more than to glide her hands over the rock-hard chest of the man standing in front of her. Instead she refocused her attention on Frank.

"Thank you, Frank. I don't like to take pictures, but you made it so much fun."

"That's my job, baby doll," Frank answered. "It's easy when I have a fine specimen like you in front of the camera." With a wink, he turned and began placing his camera equipment back in its box.

Night's eyes scanned D'Andra's body. D'Andra warmed at his innocent perusal. "You were great," he said, after a moment.

"You saw me?"

"Yes, I did."

Their looks lingered on each other for only a moment, one that was charged with unreleased sexual tension that neither of them understood.

"Are you ready—"

"I should go—"

They both spoke at once, and shut up simultaneously.

"I should go," D'Andra began again, her eyes downcast, her countenance demure. She looked at her watch. "I have to be at work soon and still need to get changed." Actually, she didn't have to be at work for two more hours but didn't trust herself to be alone with Night once Frank left. *And he expects us to exercise*

*one-on-one, with him touching me? D'Andra . . . what have
you gotten yourself into?*

Night couldn't explain the dejection he felt at the
thought of her leaving. He wasn't at all comfortable
with the feeling and worked to rid himself of it. "I
thought we'd get a chance to work out but all right then.
Go on to your job. I'll see you Thursday, four o'clock
sharp."

D'Andra smiled and shook her head. "Are you
always this bossy?"

"Yes," both Night and Frank answered simultaneously.

"Don't hold it against him, child," Frank continued. "Been like this as far back as I can remember,
and I've known him since he was knee-high to a grass-
hopper."

At D'Andra's curious expression, Night interjected.
"An old southern saying that means since I was
young."

"Oh." D'Andra enjoyed the obvious camaraderie
that existed between Night and Frank, and in an unexpected moment of emotion, she missed the father
she never had.

"Well, I'd better go."

Night walked her to the door. "Thursday, four
o'clock, be ready to work out."

When Thursday came, D'Andra was more than
ready to work up a sweat. She'd been through the
wringer on her job, where the employees continued
to bare the brunt of higher-ups and their unwise ad-
ministrative decisions. One of the head nurses had
quit, along with a clerk, lab technician and nurse's
aide. D'Andra loved working at Heavenly Haven, but
didn't need the added stress. Fortunately, as a nurse,

she could always get a job somewhere else. If things continued the way they were at the nursing home, that's exactly what she planned to do.

Adding to the stress were the close quarters on the home front, compounded by Cassandra's frequent male visitors. When home, her mother spent much of her time in her bedroom, and Cassandra entertained her guests upstairs. Unfortunately D'Andra's "room" was the living room, the room one had to walk through to reach any of the others.

Less than ten minutes after Night answered the door, she was down in his home gym, sweating.

"Okay, you're going to lie down, place your feet under the roller and then pull the roller up as close to your butt as you can. Like this." Night pulled the leg weight up to demonstrate the controlled movement, deftly touched his butt with his feet and slowly brought the weight down. "Not like this." He brought the weight up quickly, using gravitational force instead of muscle to lift the weight. "See the difference?"

D'Andra nodded, even though for her the difference was minimal. Whether his legs moved fast or slow, Night had one of the roundest, tightest, best-shaped pair of buttocks she'd ever seen. His legs were sculptured works of art, his back a dazzling display of sinewy, rippling muscles. She could have watched him work out all day. But Night had other plans.

"Okay, your turn."

D'Andra was self-conscious as she lay face down on the bench of the leg curl machine. After ogling Night's perfect physique she was more than a little self-conscious of sticking her large gluteus maximus in the air. She did it anyway, reasoning that she didn't have time to be shy when it came to her personal trainer. She was with Night for one reason and one reason only, to lose weight. The more she stayed focused on this and the less she focused on his ass-ets, the better off they'd both be. Sure, Night often flirted. But D'Andra knew he viewed it as harmless fun.

"Are you going to lay there daydreaming all day, or are you going to try and work these leg muscles?" Night's question was pointed but not said unkindly.

"I'm sorry," D'Andra answered. She slowly curled her legs into the air and towards her butt.

Night studied D'Andra's execution and her "apple" as well. For all of her excess weight, she could still make an outfit look good. Her body's curves were in all the right places and he guessed that more men than she knew had appreciated the view as she walked past. Night was experiencing this same appreciation as D'Andra raised and lowered the cushioned bar slowly, mimicking Night's movements and, as he'd instructed, keeping a tight hold on the hand grips.

"Stay focused," Night said, even as he tried to stay focused on D'Andra's leg movements and not the large, luscious booty that tightened with each lift. "You're almost finished, just one more set of ten. Then we'll turn over and work on your quads."

As she neared the end of the third set of ten lifts, thoughts of Night's butt had been replaced by those of the pain in her muscles. She wondered if she'd ever used these particular butt and leg muscles before.

". . . nine, ten. Okay, good. Turn over."

"Ooh," D'Andra said as she sat up. "That hurt."

"No pain, no gain, doll," Night answered, even after he reached down and kneaded D'Andra's lower legs. He resisted kneading the other area he guessed was hurting.

"Come on, let's work those quads."

They did three sets of leg lifts on D'Andra's quads, followed by sets on a leg sled, inner/outer thigh machine and lat, for her arms. By the time they got to

D'Andra's stomach, one of the areas she wanted most to firm up, she was exhausted.

"Night, I'm tired. I don't know if I can do the rest."

"That's okay. *I* know you can do it. Now let's go. Get down there and give me twenty sit ups."

"Twenty?! At the gym I only did ten."

"Yeah, but that was two days ago. Let's push it."

"No," D'Andra answered softly.

"No, what do you mean no? You are remembering to do these every day, right?"

"I forgot."

"What do you mean you forgot?"

The truth of the matter was after getting laughed at by her mother, sister and her sister's kids when she tried sit-ups at home, D'Andra abandoned the effort. She knew their mocking was no excuse and that she could have gone to the gym, but she'd chickened out.

"Look, let's get something straight right now, D'Andra. My normal personal training sessions are a hundred dollars an hour, minimum. My time is too precious to waste on someone who isn't serious about what I'm doing. This isn't extracurricular for me; this is my job."

Night was normally cool under pressure but being fit was the one area where he didn't mess around. Though his voice was soft, his seriousness was unmistakable.

"I offered my services to you because you seemed to have the determination needed to make real change in your life. If I was wrong about that, let's stop this right here, right now. I'm putting one hundred and ten percent into your workout; I expect no less from you. Now give me twenty, let's go!"

Night's chiding caught D'Andra unexpectedly and immediately pissed her off. Who was he to have expectations of what she should and shouldn't do? And who was he to talk to her like that? She took it from her family, and she'd taken it from Charles. This fool didn't even know her. She couldn't get off the floor fast enough.

"Look, nobody asked you to take your precious time to teach me anything! I was minding my own business when you stepped up to *me* at the gym." She snatched her towel and water bottle off the nearby bench press, brushed past him and headed toward the steps.

"Damn, that's as fast as you've moved all day," Night said from his position behind her. "Looks like you've had plenty practice running away."

D'Andra kept moving. *I don't need this asshole trying to get in my business! He doesn't even know me!* She rushed up the steps and to his front door and slammed it behind her. She was almost to her car before she realized she'd left her keys on the coffee table in the living room.

"Damn," D'Andra said, busted. *What am I going to do now?* She had an extra car key but it was on top of her dresser at home. She would have taken a cab to go get it rather than look at Night's face again tonight but her purse was locked in her trunk.

She crossed her arms in a huff and leaned against the car. "Come on out with my keys and the smirk on your face," she said to Night's closed front door.

He'd come up the steps behind her and couldn't possibly have missed seeing her large key ring with a rubber Betty Boop decked in fluorescent yellow, pink and green. D'Andra stomped her feet even as she consciously kept her breathing slow. "This fool ain't worth my pressure rising," she warned herself.

D'Andra checked her watch, waited a couple minutes, and then checked it again. She looked up and down the street for who knew what, and then inside her car, as if the keys would magically appear in the ignition. Even if they did, her car was locked. As chagrined as she was, there was no delaying the inevitable. She had no choice but to add an encore to her dramatic exit. She had to go back and get her keys.

"I knew you had too much heart to stay away," Night said with a smile as he opened the door. "I'm going to add ten more minutes to your workout though since your heart rate has probably slowed some." He paused when she made no move to enter the house. "Then again, maybe not."

"I left my keys on your coffee table."

"Oh, and you think I'm going to give them to you before you finish your workout."

"I'm through working out; at least with you. Look Night, this was obviously a bad idea. I'm too lazy for your workout and too old for games."

"Who said you were lazy?"

"If you'll just get me my keys, please, I'll make sure not to take up any more of your *precious* time."

Night made no move to get her keys or move away from the door so she could get them. Instead, he incensed her further by leaning casually against his door frame and casting his famous megawatt smile.

"I'm not going to let you quit on me."

"Give me my keys, Night."

"Give me ten minutes."

"Look, I'm not playing; give me my damn keys or I'll call the police."

"And I'll tell them I don't know who you are or what you're talking about; not until you give me ten."

"Ooh, I can't believe this," D'Andra yelled. Now she was mad for real. "What business is it of yours if I work out or not?"

"You made it my business when you agreed to let me be your personal trainer. I've started this job and I'm going to finish it. Good health should be a habit, not a hobby!"

"Look, Mister Know-It-All, you're not the only one who's trying to be healthy. I've decided to get in shape and I'm going to do it. I don't need you preaching to me, and I don't need you to reach my goals. I know you wish you'd been able to save your aunt but she's dead and gone; helping me won't bring her back!"

Anybody watching would have sworn that time stood still in this moment. The pain that slowly made its way across Night's face was palpable enough to touch. He slowly backed away from the door, turned his back and waited for her to get her keys and leave.

D'Andra wished the floor could have swallowed her up. She regretted the words before they were fully out of her mouth. But it was too late to change them and too late to take them back. She rushed up behind him.

"Night, I'm so sorry; I didn't mean that. Night?" she said, placing a hand on his shoulder.

He reacted as if her flesh was fire. "Get your shit and get out."

"Night, please, I'm really, really sorry. That was way out of line and I . . . I don't know what possessed me to say something so mean."

Before she knew it months of pain, encased in tears, began spilling out all over Night's hardwood floor.

"I'm not trying to excuse what I said, Night, but I am truly sorry. I should be the last person in the world to say something to hurt somebody else. Words have been used against me all my life."

Night was as still as a statue. D'Andra figured that as long as he wasn't talking he wasn't kicking her out. She went on in a voice barely above a whisper.

"I'm more like your aunt than I want to admit. A couple weeks ago, I, well, I ended up in the emergency room at MLK Medical. I've had Type II diabetes for almost two years now and some family drama's been going down that caused my blood pressure to shoot sky high. It was borderline high anyway . . . guess it didn't take much to send my numbers into the stratosphere."

Night's only movement was to cross his arms, his back still toward her. He didn't say a word.

D'Andra slowly walked over and retrieved her keys, then over to the front door. But she couldn't leave, not without trying once more to make him understand her pain.

"That's not the half of it though, the reason for my anger. My ex-boyfriend was a real asshole, Night—"

"I'm not your ex-boyfriend. I thought we were becoming *friends*." He finally turned to face her.

"We are, at least I hope we still are after the horrible way I've acted. But I took all kinds of crazy shit from him and now I'm taking it from my family and I guess your snapping at me . . . it just caught me wrong, that's all. I know you don't understand. I can imagine things have always gone well for you. You probably have no idea what it's like to—"

"To what?" Night asked, fixing D'Andra with a penetrating stare. "To get pissed off? To be mistreated? To not be liked? To get dogged? You think you've cornered the market on feeling bad, D'Andra? You think when you cut me I don't bleed?"

He fired these questions at her as he walked to within inches of her face.

D'Andra was at the door and couldn't back up. For the first time since this argument started, she tried to lighten the mood.

"Come on, Night, you can probably count the times on one hand that someone's treated you badly. I mean, look at you. You probably can get almost anything you want."

Night looked at D'Andra for what seemed an endless moment. She wanted to flee but couldn't, frozen as much by his probing gaze as by the door's proximity.

Suddenly she was aware of everything about him: the heat that seemed to radiate from his body, the curl of his thick lashes, the small dimple on the left side of his mouth, the beginnings of a five o'clock shadow on his chin. She licked her lips subconsciously, barely daring to breathe.

Night followed the flick of D'Andra's tongue as it moistened her generous lips. He took in the subtle floral scent from her clothes that threatened to intoxicate him, the dilated pupils surrounded by hazel irises, the soft glow of sweat that still clung to her neck and down her generous cleavage, the slow rise and fall of her breasts as she awaited his response.

"Anything I want, huh?" he asked breathlessly.

D'Andra nodded, not trusting herself to speak.

"Well then get down those stairs and give me twenty *and* ten extra minutes." He moved in closer still, his hard chest grazing her chest. "Let's go!" he said softly, daring her to not obey his command.

For the next ten minutes, the only words spoken were Night's resolute directives: *push, tighter, higher, one more.* D'Andra's only sound was moderate and sometimes heavy breathing as she did sit-ups, squats and work with straps and an exercise ball. She was determined to finish the workout if it killed her; even as the reason for her doing so was because she wanted to live.

Finally he indicated they were ready for the cool down. "I knew you could do it," he said, his first gentle verbiage. "It may sound like I'm being hard on you but it's not personal I assure you; it's all for your good."

"I know," D'Andra said.

Night directed her to the mat on the other side of the room. "We're going to cool down with light stretches. Remember stretching after the workout is as important as stretching before. You want to keep your muscles long and supple; make your body line fluid and tight. He joined her on the floor, his legs in a v-shape in front of him.

"Spread your legs as wide as you can and grab my hands," he instructed.

"Your legs are so long." D'Andra became self-conscious again as she worked to widen her legs that refused to spread. "That's as far as I can stretch them."

Night placed a foot just inside each of her knees, leaned forward, grabbed her hands and began to push gently. "Trust me, D'Andra; I'm not going to push you too hard." He applied slightly more pressure. D'Andra's legs parted another inch on each side.

"Ooh, Night, that hurts."

"Hurts so good, doesn't it?"

"Not . . . really."

"So tell me about this ex that had you biting my head off." He spoke conversationally as he continued to coax her legs farther apart.

"There's nothing to tell. He cheated on me with another woman and is out of my life. I'm better off without him."

"Good job," Night said. "No, you stay down, and lie back. I'm going to finish stretching you." Night took D'Andra's leg and pressed it gently up and over her head. "What was so bad about him?"

"Everything. I really don't want to talk about him. I'm trying to put the past behind me, focus on myself. It's all about me right now."

Night chuckled. "I hear ya."

"Yeah, I bet you do." D'Andra's words were tempered by a smile.

"Oh, so it's like that; you think I'm one of those conceited, self-centered jocks with a BlackBerry full of numbers and ice running in my veins."

"Pretty much."

They both laughed at that one; D'Andra didn't

really believe it even though with his looks it could be totally true.

"Well, Ms. Smalls, once again, you'd be wrong." He switched to the other leg and continued stretching her muscles. "Like you, I'm trying to focus. It's all about me right now; me and opening my gym."

D'Andra knew she shouldn't venture down intimate avenue but couldn't resist. "Well, I know your woman is in your corner. She must be very proud of you."

Night smiled at D'Andra's obvious probe. "Yeah, my woman is very proud of me."

D'Andra didn't know why the information bothered her. She knew he had somebody, probably several somebodies.

"That's good," she said, and tried to sound like she meant it.

Night reached for D'Andra's hand and helped her up. "But mothers are like that when it comes to their sons . . . proud."

A thrill shot through her heart as she hid a smile. *Am I to believe this man is unattached?* She immediately berated herself for the thought and the feeling. Who he had was none of her business. If she wasn't careful, her muscles weren't the only ache he'd leave her with.

"Make sure to take a hot shower when you get home; even better if you can soak in a Jacuzzi," Night said, as they made their second, and much more peaceful, ascent up the stairs. "Good work today."

"Thank you," D'Andra said, and she meant it. "And please, please forgive me for the comment earlier. It was totally out of line and I apologize."

"It's already forgotten. What time are you going to Bally's this weekend?"

"Um, I don't know." *Whatever time you're not there.* Seeing him two days a week was torture enough, especially in the private confines of his home. She had accepted that for the foreseeable future she'd be alone, until she got herself together. There was no use pretending she wasn't attracted to the man. No use flirting with danger.

"Then I'll see you for sure next Tuesday."

"Yep, see you then."

"I look forward to it, D'Andra. Looks like we're in similar places in our lives; you're focused on getting healthy, and I'm focused on making people healthy with my own gym. And I don't know about you, but I could use a good friend right about now. What do you say?" He lifted his water bottle in a toast. "To friendship?"

D'Andra lifted hers in response. "To friendship." She refused to examine the heaviness that replaced the thrill in her heart. Because she knew if she looked into truth, she'd have to admit that she wanted Night to be more of a FWB—a friend with benefits. And personal training wasn't the benefit she had in mind.

7

D'Andra awoke to a steady thump, thump sound followed by a drone of chatter. At first she thought it was her neighbor, and then she realized the muted yet very discernible hip-hop beats were playing in her house. She threw back her comforter and stomped up the stairs to the bedrooms on the second floor. Her bedroom door was locked.

"Cassandra! Cassandra! Why do you have this door locked? Turn that music down and open this door!"

The music kept playing. D'Andra kept knocking. She was livid. Cassandra knew D'Andra slept between eight-thirtyish and three, and then took another short nap, if she was tired and could grab it, right before going to her eleven P.M. shift. The living room clock read two-thirty P.M. Their mother obviously wasn't home. Loud rap music was the one thing Mary Smalls didn't allow, not even from her favorite daughter.

"Cassandra!"

The music stopped abruptly. "There. Damn. Your knocking is ten times louder than the music was."

"You know this is my sleep time. Where's Mama?"

There was a pause before Cassandra answered.

"Cassandra!"

"She's at the casino, now leave me alone."

D'Andra jiggled the door knob. "What are you doing with the door locked, San? This is still my room with my stuff in there, remember? Why are you trippin'? Open the stupid door!"

D'Andra stood staring at the door as if it held some answers. It was petty stuff like this that kept unnecessary drama going on in the house. It was enough that her mother had asked her to give up her room for her sister and her sister's kids. But honestly, D'Andra hadn't minded that. Especially when she thought it was only for a month or so. But what little D'Andra had asked for in return—peace and quiet during the day, help with the housework, and not to be mistaken for a live-in babysitter on the weekends—was being ignored with more and more regularity.

At least the house is quiet, she thought, as she turned to walk back downstairs. Quiet enough for her to hear a bass sound that had not come from the stereo speakers. *No, that heifa is not screwing somebody in my room!*

D'Andra tried to stay calm as she walked back up the stairs. "Cassandra, I know you haven't brought a man into this house, in my room, on my bed."

"Whatever, D'Andra; get away from the damn door. I'm not going to open it. I've turned off the music, now leave me alone!"

Cassandra wasn't even trying to hide the fact that she was talking to someone, and he was not on the phone. "She's always been jealous of me just because I can keep a man and she can't. Gets on my damn nerves."

"Keep *a* man?" D'Andra yelled through the door, leaving the insinuation hanging in the air. "Your *mother* shares this house and your *kids* share that room. Show some respect."

As if to drive the point home, the front door opened and Kayla, home from school, bounded inside.

D'Andra blew out a long frustrated breath. "Your daughter's home," she said low enough so the child wouldn't hear. "Figure out how you're going to introduce her to your company."

By the time she returned downstairs, a headache was announcing its arrival, partly due to the stress, and partly due to the fact she hadn't eaten all day. She walked straight to her purse for the Tylenol, and into the kitchen for a glass of water.

"I've got to get out of here," she said to the yellow-colored kitchen walls.

"You leavin', Aunt Dee?" Kayla asked. "Can I go with you?"

D'Andra looked into the shining, excited eyes of her sister's spitting image. She prayed their physical appearance was all they had in common. It seemed so; Kayla was sweet and even-tempered, helping more around the house than her sister and mother put together. If not for her work schedule, she'd almost consider taking Kayla with her when she moved.

She bent down and gave her niece a hug and kiss. "No, sweetie. I'm not going anywhere. Not right now."

"Can I go with you when you leave?"

"I'll be going to work then, Kayla. Work is for grown folk, remember?"

"I can work," Kayla boasted proudly. "I help you cook, and the other day I did the dishes all by myself."

Yeah, probably because your trifflin' Mom was up in my bed screwing, is what D'Andra thought. "That's a big girl, Kayla. I'm proud of you," is what she said.

D'Andra had just poured Kayla a glass of orange juice when she heard bodies coming down the stairs. She braced herself for the confrontation. Instead, she heard the front door close.

Oh no she didn't, D'Andra thought. "Kayla, go with your mother."

"Where is she?"

D'Andra grabbed her niece's arms and scurried to the front door. "Run, baby, go with your mother."

As she'd expected, Cassandra wasn't alone. She and a tall, good-looking man with baggy jeans and a hat on sideways were getting into a shiny, black Infiniti. Kayla ran up to her mother, who tried to send her back.

"She's going with you," D'Andra yelled. "You know I've got to work and I am not going to watch her. I'm not playing, San. Take your child!"

"We're just going to Mickie D's!"

"Good, get Kayla a Happy Meal!"

D'Andra slammed the door on Cassandra's comeback, plopped down on the sofa bed and pulled the covers over her head. She was so angry she could hardly think straight. Her sister had thought only about herself as far back as D'Andra could remember. Cassandra thought she was the sun and the world revolved around her. And for most of her life it had, with D'Andra being just one of the planets twirling at her bidding. But no more.

Cassandra's whine preceded her inside the door. "C'mon, DeeDee. Watch Kayla for me. Just fifteen minutes, I swear."

"No."

The childhood nickname Cassandra used, the one that used to melt D'Andra into doing whatever was asked, had no effect.

"Girl, you know you love your niece. We'll pick you up something at McDonald's. What do you want?"

D'Andra looked at her sister as if for the first time. This woman had nerve like Kobe had game. *Did she not just screw her man in my bed, lock me out of my room and curse me for wanting to get in? Now she wants to bring me a sandwich?*

D'Andra took the covers away from her face. "Where are the twins?"

"With Jackie."

"Then take Kayla over there."

"I can't."

"Why not?"

"Cause I haven't told baby boy out there about the twins. He thinks I only have Kayla."

"You're a trip, San."

Cassandra was losing patience and it showed in her voice. "Are you going to watch her?"

"What part of the word *no* don't you understand?"

"Forget you, you old cow. Soon as baby out here gets paid you're gonna wish you'd have done what I asked you."

"No, soon as *baby out there* gets paid you can get your nasty butt out of my room. And while you're at it, count how many times you've done what I asked you!"

D'Andra turned over in a "talk to the butt" gesture. Cassandra was momentarily stunned. D'Andra never said no to her. "Bitch," she mumbled, as she walked out of the house.

"Yeah," D'Andra whispered with a smile on her face. *But this bitch is in the house without your kids.* Standing up for herself felt good. She could get used to it.

Try as she could to get back to sleep, after an hour sleep still eluded her. D'Andra got up and went over to the computer to log on to her e-mail account. Along with the usual spam, a couple forwards from Elaine and a promotion from Bally, was an e-mail from Peoplesearch.com. D'Andra's heartbeat quickened as she clicked on the link:

Improve the chances for your search success by upgrading now to our premium package, only $99 for 30 days of unlimited access to the information

you need. With the premium package, you get not
only the name and address of that long lost friend or
relative, but you also get . . .

D'Andra deleted the mail without finishing it. She
hadn't done anything with the information she'd already been given. She tried to convince herself it was
because of the stress of the job compounded with her
new workout routine, but she knew she was lying. It
was fear, plain and simple, behind the fact that the
printout containing information on Orlando Dobbs
was still stashed away in a zippered compartment of
her purse.

She reached down for the purse beside her and
pulled out the paper. Staring at it for one long moment, she reached for the phone. Before she could
think or change her mind, she punched in the area
code and phone number for the Chicago address. A
somewhat dry female voice was on the answering service, instructing the callers to leave their name and
number at the sound of the tone. D'Andra left a brief
message and then dialed the Florida listing.

"Hello?" a gruff voice answered.

"Uh, hello. May I speak to a Orlando Dobbs?"

"Who's calling?"

"My name is D'Andra Smalls." D'Andra gave her
last name figuring that if the person on the other end
was indeed her father, it would mean something.

There was a short pause, during which D'Andra
didn't breathe.

"This is Orlando," the voice said finally.

"Orlando Dobbs?"

"Is this some bill collector or something because if
it is, I don't owe you nothing!" The man grumbled
unintelligibly, then belched.

D'Andra hurried on, afraid he'd hang up. "No, not at all. I'm sorry that I'm nervous. You see . . ."

Her voice trailed off. Suddenly D'Andra was second-guessing her actions. Did she have the right to waltz into someone's life and potentially turn his world upside down? Was she sure she wanted to know the man who was her father? Then she remembered the very legitimate, valid reasons for finding this side of her family. She took a deep breath and pressed on.

"My mother's name is Mary Smalls and she dated Orlando Dobbs about thirty years ago. I believe that man is my father and I'm trying to find him."

There was a pause on the other end. "Mary who?" he asked when he finally spoke.

"Mary Smalls."

"She live here in Jacksonville?"

"No, she lives in Los Angeles. That's where they dated, and where I was born and raised."

The sigh on the other end was audible. "Well, no, then that ain't me. My name is Orlando, and I dated a woman named Mary long time ago. But the only time I was in California was when I served in the Navy and was stationed in San Diego. That was almost forty years ago, and I ain't been back since."

"Okay then. Well, thank you for your time."

The gruff voice softened unexpectedly. "No problem. I hope you find your daddy."

The call to New Jersey met with yet a different result.

"I'm looking for an Orlando Dobbs? My name is D'Andra Smalls, and he was friends with my mother, Mary."

"What the hell I know about who Orlando was friends with?" the testy woman on the other line exclaimed. "Only thing one of his friends can do for me is pay me back the five hundred dollars I spent to get his ass out of jail two months ago. Drinking and driving, his second D.U.I. I told his ass I wasn't gonna keep bailing him out. The only reason I did it this time was because I needed my car fixed. It might take him a fifth of Tanqueray and a case of Budweiser but that man sure can fix a car. Now who you say you was?"

D'Andra quickly relayed her story.

"Well, now, I ain't trying to burst yo bubble but if'n Orlando is your daddy, the best thing he did was leave you alone, child. His ass ain't been nothin' but trouble since I met him and we been together almost twenty years. Got four kids here he don't half see. He find out somebody in California asking about him, he liable to show up on your doorstep with a mouth full of lies and a wallet that ain't got shit, trying to con you out of what you got."

It was a long shot, but D'Andra gave her contact information anyway, along with her mother's name and the time frame when they would have dated. The woman had her wait while she got a pen. D'Andra only hoped she actually wrote something down. If this no good, Tanqueray-drinking, car-fixing jailbird was her father, at least she'd know.

That piece of work done, D'Andra clicked on a few apartment sites and printed out a couple possibilities within her budget. She hadn't broached the subject of moving with her mother yet, and hoped she would be a bit more encouraging than she was about her exercising, or finding her dad. Not that her mother's opinion would change anything. The wheels of change had started rolling downhill, and D'Andra, though a little scared and a lot confused, was enjoying the ride.

8

D'Andra entered Bally Fitness, and after only two weeks felt more the member and less the stranger. The familiar sounds of the gym greeted her and the sparse evening crowd made her smile. D'Andra felt she worked out better without an audience.

"Hey, D'Andra."

"Hey, Marc."

"Got a hot date with the treadmill?"

D'Andra laughed. "Something like that."

"Well, enjoy."

D'Andra swiped her card and went through the turnstile, wondering if Marc lived at the gym. It seemed that every time she'd come so far, no matter what day or time, he was there. She'd also noted that even though she saw him flirting with every other skirt in the building, there was a wedding ring on his finger. *Looks like dogs come in all colors, shapes and sizes,* she thought as she walked to the women's dressing room to secure her purse and gym bag in a locker. Moments later she was on the treadmill, doing a medium-paced walk to Jill Scott's "Living My Life Like It's Golden."

D'Andra kept up this pace for the next ten minutes and was pleased to note that her breathing and stamina had improved. She patted her face, took a swig of water and set the timer for five more minutes as India Arie reminded her that she was not her hair or her skin but the soul that lived within.

After the treadmill, D'Andra felt energetic enough to try the Stairmaster. She walked over to the row of machines and boldly stepped on one, but couldn't figure out how to set the timer or adjust the incline. Marc strolled over, more than happy to help out.

"You're looking good there, D'Andra," he said with a wink. "Those workouts with Night must be paying off."

D'Andra was taken aback by the comment. "How do you know about my workouts with Night?"

"Night's my partner, didn't you know? We go way back. He told me he was working with you, whipping that body into shape."

"He said that, huh?"

"Well, maybe not those words exactly but . . . you lucked out getting Night for a trainer. He's one of the best."

D'Andra couldn't argue that point and still regretted having argued with Night. He was taking valuable time out of what was probably a busy schedule to train her for free. And what had she done? Acted like she had no "brought-upsy", no manners at all. It would have served her right had Night cancelled the sessions. Sure, she may have continued losing weight. But she knew it was happening much faster thanks to Night's workout regimen, not to mention his encouragement and personal attention. At Night's suggestion, she hadn't stepped on her scales since the day after she bought them, but she was pretty sure she'd lost weight. She didn't know how much, but her nurse's smock seemed to fit a bit looser. Night suggested she weigh herself sparingly, focus more on inches lessened than pounds removed.

"Hey, what's going on here, Marc? You trying to take my client?"

D'Andra's heart did a little flip flop at the sound of Night's voice. What was he doing here on a Saturday night?

"Hey, man, we must have talked you up," Marc said as he playfully punched Night in the arm.

"All good I hope."

"It was. D'Andra was just going on and on about what a great trainer you were."

D'Andra's head whipped around at Marc's comment. "I didn't say that."

"Oh," Marc continued, knowing he was starting something. "You're saying he's a bad trainer?"

D'Andra smiled. "No, I didn't say that either."

"Well, doll, what did you say?"

"Nothing. Marc was saying what a great personal trainer you are and I hadn't had time to respond. But if I had," she continued in what despite her best intentions was precariously close to a flirt. "I would have agreed with him."

Night tried to hide the pride evoked by her flattery behind a modest shrug. "I try," was his simple reply.

"I told her she'd feel like a new person with her body in shape."

A group of people walked up to the front desk. "Be right back," Marc said, and was gone.

"Is Marc your best friend?" D'Andra asked.

"One of them," Night responded. "I'd trust him with my life. Now let's get you going on this Stairmaster."

In less than five minutes, D'Andra stopped the machine. Her thighs were burning. "I'm not ready for this yet," she said.

To her surprise, Night simply nodded. "Probably take another month or so of building up your muscles. Once you do, this is a great device for toning."

He stopped his machine and climbed down just as Marc walked back over.

"What do you say we do some weights, hit the sauna, and by then you'll be off, right, Marc?"

"Yeah, man, but I got a hot date tonight."

D'Andra couldn't stop from rolling her eyes.

"Aw, see, there you go; a typical female thinking the worst about men. The date is with my wife. It's her birthday and we're taking a red-eye flight to Vegas."

Marc had called her out correctly. "You're married?"

Marc held up the ring D'Andra had previously spotted.

"I saw the ring. But the way you flirt . . . I couldn't tell."

"Flirting is cool as long as you look but don't touch."

"If you say so," D'Andra responded.

"I say so. But you guys go on and have a good time."

Night turned to D'Andra. "So where are we going?"

"Actually, I'd better get home. Lots to do tomorrow," she added in response to his raised eyebrow.

Going out in a group would have been one thing but going out solo with Night felt too much like a date; even though it would be a spontaneous, casual one. Knowing how physically attracted she was to him didn't make that sound like such a good idea. Better to keep this friendship on familiar footing, in a gym or around workout equipment.

"It's just as well," Night said, watching Marc head back to the front desk. "I promised my mom I'd go to church with her tomorrow. Might as well make it an early night."

Since this is exactly what D'Andra wanted, it made no sense that his comment was disappointing. But it was. She wanted to be with him; she didn't want to be with him. She longed for romance, but didn't want to admit it. She wanted a man but knew she didn't need the hassle right now. It's just the way it was.

"I didn't take you for the church-going type," she said.

"I'm not really," Night answered. He turned and walked toward the weights. D'Andra followed.

"But they're having some type of family day tomorrow. Mom makes me feel guilty if I don't go, especially since I didn't go on Christmas, about the only other time I walk among saints."

"And all the other time who are you walking around . . . devils?" D'Andra asked playfully.

"No," Night replied as he wriggled his brows. "Dolls."

D'Andra and Night worked out with the weights and then she went home, more hungry than ever for something that wasn't on a restaurant menu.

9

"Aunt DeeDee, come on, you promised," Tonia said, shaking her aunt's shoulder for emphasis. "Today is Sunday and you promised we'd go to the beach!"

"Promised," Antoine echoed. He was the baby of their family, even if it was only by seven minutes.

"You said if we were quiet until ten o'clock you'd take us," Kayla said, pointing to the clock.

"Look!" she added triumphantly. It was ten o'clock exactly.

"Get off me you little rugrats," D'Andra said, trying to push them off her bed the way she was trying to push last night's dream, another one with Night, out of her mind.

"Are you gonna fix us pancakes, Aunt DeeDee?"

"Uh-uh, I want waffles, with bacon!"

"Are we still going to the beach, Aunt DeeDee?"

"Ooh, yeah, the beach, please!"

A chorus of pleases followed her into the bathroom, shut out by the door in their faces. The kids had a habit of talking to her simultaneously and just as crazy, she had a habit of being able to hear them all.

Her head was cloudy from the liquor she drank last night, but the evening with her family had been fun for a change; when all three of them, she, her mother and sister, had gotten along. That in itself was a surprise, but the first one was that Cassandra was there at all, alone, on a Saturday night.

"What's up?" she'd asked when D'Andra came through the door.

"Nothing. What are you doing home?"

"I live here, remember?"

How can I forget with you and your kids in my bedroom and me on the couch? "Of course not," she said. D'Andra had had a good time with Marc and Night. She didn't want to spoil her good mood.

"Hey, Jackie is on her way over. You want to hang out, play some Whist or something?"

D'Andra's mind whirled with possibilities. While married, Cassandra never invited her to anything, and had only done so once since getting divorced. "What's the catch—why are you being so nice?" she asked directly.

"Dang, why does there have to be a catch?" Cassandra started to cop an attitude but then shrugged and went into the kitchen. "Can't I just be nice to my sister, for a change?"

D'Andra joined Cassandra in the kitchen. She poured a glass of water and removed a can of Slimfast from the refrigerator.

"She's bringing her kids with her," Cassandra said, reaching past D'Andra into the refrigerator for a liter of cola.

"Bebe's kids? Aw, hell no." So that was it. The spawns of Satan were coming over. Jackie's kids were destroyers. They'd hit anything that moved and break anything glass.

"You shouldn't want your kids around them. They're a bad influence."

"You should be more understanding; they've got

ADD—attention deficit disorder," Cassandra said, as if she was telling D'Andra something she didn't know. "Plus, they're cousins."

She looked on the counter and felt on top of the refrigerator. "Where's that coupon from Pizza Hut?"

D'Andra walked over to the drawer by the refrigerator and handed Cassandra a folder of coupons. "No, they don't have ADD, they have NAW."

"What's that?"

"The antidote for ADD: Need Ass Whupped."

"Ooh, Dee, you know you're wrong. We don't hit our children these days. We talk to them."

"Yeah, talk with the hand, and if that don't work, a belt. That's what I'm gonna do if those kids break my stuff. See if they understand that language."

"Don't worry, she got 'em fixed; they're on Ritalin or some shit."

"Dang, for real?" D'Andra didn't know which was worse; that the kids would act like banshees or zombies.

But the night had been fun. Jackie had a zany sense of humor and the man she'd brought with her, Todd or Teddy or Thomas or something, was actually decent, if a bit on the nerdy side. She hated to admit or in any way advocate drugging children but little TayTay and Benjamin were much better behaved than the last time she'd seen them.

The young ones had watched DVDs while the adults gathered in the dining room around a rowdy game of Bid Whist. Mary Smalls came back from the casino and she and Boss joined in the fun as the partners took their turn at the table. The winners stayed at the table while the losers had to *rise and fly*. As the liquor flowed, so did the trash talking and finally D'Andra gave into Jackie's prodding to have a Shady Lady, Jackie's favorite drink.

The drink's grapefruit juice and melon liqueur had

hidden Patrón's power and when asked, D'Andra felt she could handle another round. Midway through her second glass she too was slamming her cards down on the table. The funniest time of the night happened when her mother, a Shady Lady or two in the wind herself, turned to D'Andra, her playing partner, and said, "Baby, can you go upstairs and get me my suitcase?"

An inebriated D'Andra sincerely asked, "Why, Mama?"

Mary slapped her ace of spades down so hard it spun on the table. She and D'Andra had taken all thirteen books. "Cause somebody's headed to Boston!"

D'Andra laughed out loud at last night's antics as the shower's hot water helped to clear her head. The previous evening was a reminder that sometimes her family actually liked each other.

As D'Andra stepped from the shower, last night's dream came back into her mind. Her face flushed as she remembered the details: Night's long, thick, slightly curved manhood poised over her. She wondered if it really looked like that even as she wondered why she kept dreaming about him. She'd never dreamt of Charles, in fact had never before had an erotic dream that she could remember. But her memories from their phantasm encounter had her longing to see the real thing.

"Aunt DeeDee!" a trio sang out.

"C'mon, Aunt DeeDee, we're hungry!" Antoine whined.

"Hurry up, Aunt DeeDee!" Tonia demanded.

"Can I help you cook?" Kayla asked as soon as D'Andra opened the door.

D'Andra and company whipped up a semi-healthy brunch of blueberry pancakes (with flaxseed added to aid in digestion), egg-white omelets (which everyone complained about yet ate), and turkey bacon.

Mary offered a rare compliment, saying she was surprised at how good the eggs were without the yokes.

"That's where all the bad cholesterol is," D'Andra explained.

"Well, I like my eggs yellow," Cassandra added.

"Well, next time you can make 'em that way," D'Andra retorted.

Cassandra looked at D'Andra surprised. Her sister was starting to let fewer and fewer of her barbs go uncontested.

"I'll do the dishes, Dee," she said, to everyone's surprise. "What? Like I don't clean?"

"No!" was the unanimous answer.

Forty-five minutes later, D'Andra and the kids were at Dockweiler Beach, a long glorious stretch of ocean in Playa del Rey. They'd gathered an array of beach accessories: umbrella, blankets, beach chairs, arm floats, beach balls, sunblock, shovels and pails. D'Andra carried a bag filled with bottled water and low sodium snacks. She also had a mini first-aid kit, just in case. And in a move that would have made Johnnie Cochran proud, she'd chanted a verse in hip-hop fashion while they were en route that Tonia was bossily reminding Antoine of as he ran down the slope.

"Antoine, get back here! If you want to stay, you must obey!"

D'Andra hid her grin and chided both the twins. "Tonia, I'm the boss around here. Antoine, bring your little skinny butt back up here until we're ready to go down."

They found a spot away from the diverse Sunday crowd, the loud music and the Frisbee throwers and set up camp. Kayla helped D'Andra spread out the blanket and put up the umbrella, even after she'd told her little helper to run and play.

She handed Kayla a bucket and one of the shovels. "Go find some shells to put in the fish tank."

"What fish tank, Aunt Dee?"

The one that's going in my new place when I move. "I'm thinking about buying one. You can help me decorate it with the shells you find."

D'Andra positioned her chair to be shielded from the sun. It was unusually hot for early February, which explained the dense crowd. She remembered how Chanelle's cousin from Michigan always teased them when she came to visit.

"Y'all get on my nerves," she'd say whenever one of them complained about rain or a fifty-degree chill. "Come to Detroit, handle ice and snow, and *then* talk to me about cold weather."

Chanelle's cousin was right; Californians were spoiled. It had rained for probably five whole minutes the two days prior. The way people were soaking up the sun you'd think they just endured Jack Frost.

D'Andra reached into her beach bag and pulled out the reading material she'd brought to occupy her while the kids ran around. The book's title, *Love Like Hallelujah,* had caught her eye as she passed by the book section on her way to the DVDs in Wal-Mart. D'Andra bought the book because she hoped to have a love like that.

She pulled out a bottled water, reclined her chair and opened the novel. Before she'd finished the first chapter she was in love with one of the main characters, Cy Taylor, who fit the description of the man of her dreams. In the book's beginning, he was in love with his fiancée and shopping in Victoria's Secret for her honeymoon surprise.

D'Andra hoped men like Cy came in fact as well as fiction. Still, it did a sistah good to dream. As long as it was about somebody fictitious and not the personal trainer she would see in two days. She'd tried to forget her dreams but every time her mind wandered it was to the naked man who stood before her, poised and ready, in Bally's sauna . . .

D'Andra placed the book on her chest as she rested her head back on the chair. Maybe reading a novel filled with *romantica* wasn't such a good idea after all. The things the Cy character thought of doing with his fiancée were the same things Night had done in the dream.

There she went again. D'Andra hurriedly put the book back in her bag, determined to get away from anything that reminded her of Night. She shielded her eyes to see where the kids were. As to be expected, Kayla was holding court down by the ocean's edge, with about ten white, black and brown children, including the twins, gathered around her. No doubt she'd have a pile of shells for D'Andra to choose from, and no doubt she would have delegated the gathering of such shells to the minions around her. On that count, getting her hands dirty, she was more like Cassandra. She'd rather not.

Satisfied that all was well with her charges, D'Andra took in the scene around her. There was a vast array of sights and sounds: bicyclers and roller bladers, joggers and walkers, families and couples. Far down on the beach she saw a Black man playing with a group of young boys and smiled. *That's an image rarely seen on television,* she thought, a brothah with his children. It felt good for her to see it, and made her think that maybe there were some good men out there after all, other than the fictitious Cy Taylor making his woman scream hallelujah.

After lying back and resting her eyes a moment, D'Andra decided her legs needed a little sun. She rolled her wide-legged palazzo pants up to mid-thigh and repositioned the umbrella to allow the rays to reach her sun-deprived skin. Anybody who thinks that Black people don't tan should see my arms, she thought, as she noted the contrast between them and her legs. She reached for the sunblock in her bag then frowned when a cloud passed over the sun, blocking out her light.

Only this cloud had two muscled legs and big feet. Her breath caught at the display of manliness showing itself from the waist down. She was suddenly conscious of her exposed thighs and noting their chubbiness, remembered she'd forgotten to weigh herself this morning. She was sure she'd lost at least ten pounds, maybe more. But manly or no, this guy was pretty bold; standing there and staring without a hello.

"Excuse me, but you're in my sun," she said with playful attitude.

"Oh," the man said, squatting down to see her face. "I thought I was looking at it."

"Night! What are you doing here?"

"Same thing as you, catching some sun. I know, you probably don't think I need it but my skin loves this heat." He looked at the bottle of sunblock. "Allow me."

D'Andra was thankful for her sunglasses; that way Night couldn't see her reaction to the same words he'd uttered in her dream. She squirmed, suddenly aware of her bare legs, and of the fact that Night was staring. She lowered her eyes to break the contact. Wrong move; her gaze landed squarely on his crotch, or more specifically the bulky bulge that made up his crotch. *Just like in my dream . . .*

"What are you doing here?" she asked again, for lack of anything better to say. Her mind had a tendency to turn to mush around Night. She was going to have to change that.

He's a friend, my trainer, walking dirt, nothing more! For once she thankfully let Mary's voice enter her mind.

I ain't raised no fools. Now straighten up and act like you've got some sense!

Just then a group of boys ran over, knocked Night to the ground and started pouring sand over him. Laughing, he caught the nearest one by his foot and returned the favor. Soon the boys were off, chasing each other toward the water. With no hesitation, Night followed them right into the ocean, their sand fight changing to a water one without breaking momentum. She noticed Antoine running toward them to join the fray.

Resuscitating a five-year-old with water in his lungs wasn't on her schedule today. D'Andra jumped up and ran towards her nephew.

"Antoine! Get back!"

Night turned and saw the source of D'Andra's frustration stop cold just at the water's edge. He smiled at the child, then ran over, grabbed him and placed him on his shoulders.

"He's okay," he called out to D'Andra. "I've got him."

Once again D'Andra was struck by Night's kindness. Too bad she wasn't in the market for a man right now because, if she were, he'd be a good candidate for an LTR: a long-term relationship. But this time was all about her. After she got herself together, if he was still around and available, maybe she'd see what was up.

D'Andra noticed a young boy of about eight or nine clinging to Night. She'd never wondered whether or not he had children but now the question niggled her mind. Was that his child? The boy looked a lot like Night and many men his age had children. D'Andra had never even considered "baby mama drama" when it came to Night's life. But then she had to remind herself that Night's life was none of her business. *Just walking dirt.*

"Hey, let's take a walk along the beach," Night said, coming up and spraying water on her.

"Night! My hair!"

"Your hair is fine," he said laughing. "C'mon, let's get some exercise."

"I don't like walking in the sand. It's dirty . . . and wet."

"Newsflash D'Andra. You're at the ocean; sand and water are a part of the deal. Besides, walking in sand is good for you."

"Yeah, right."

"I'm serious. You ever heard of reflexology?"

"Yes."

"Well, walking in the sand provides a natural reflexology; the sand forms itself to your feet and the granules massage your pressure points with each step. So you're not only burning calories but you're releasing toxins. C'mon, let's walk."

"I have to watch the kids."

Night turned to his group. "Kimani, come here."

Sixteen years of walking testosterone loped over. "What up, Night?"

"You're in charge of the group for the next fifteen minutes. Can you handle that?"

D'Andra could have sworn she saw hair grow on the boy's chest; he was that proud. "Sure I can."

"Those kids too," Night said, pointing to D'Andra's three.

Kimani nodded.

"We're just gonna stroll up the beach a ways."

"Ai-ight."

Night turned to D'Andra. "Let's go."

"Did you know you can be pretty bossy sometimes?"

"I've been told that a time or two; but that's primarily an asset in my business."

The two chatted comfortably as they walked along the shoreline. At certain points, Night directed D'Andra to do lunges, holding the pose for as long as possible before changing legs. At other times, they did squats.

"Is that boy your son, the one in the cutoff jeans?"

"Why do you ask?"

"He looks like you."

Night smiled. "I've heard that before. No, he's not but I wish he were. He's my second cousin, Aunt Jewel's grandson."

"Oh."

"So you want kids, huh?"

"Of course."

D'Andra didn't trust herself to say anything more so she remained silent a moment before changing the subject.

"I want to thank you again for taking the time to work with me, Night. I think it's really helping."

"I think so too; you've lost weight."

"You think so? I haven't weighed myself again, like you told me."

Night flashed a satisfied smile, then returned to his ever-present role of trainer.

"Be more concerned with how you feel than what you weigh," Night instructed. "Your body will let you know when it's the right size. It's too easy to get caught up on a number when different body types weigh differently. Women of color have denser bodies so on most of those charts they come off as overweight, when that may not be true at all."

"You told me this Night; you don't remember?"

"Yes, and I'm telling you again. It's cool to weigh yourself every now and then, as long as you don't let the number dictate how you feel about yourself. I want to make sure you get that."

She quelled the urge to salute. "I've got it."

They walked more, sometimes talking, sometimes enjoying companionable silence. There were a million questions D'Andra wanted to ask but didn't. She was afraid that the more she got to know him the harder it would be to keep up the wall. So they kept the conversation limited to health and fitness.

"I made a big decision yesterday," she said after a pause.

Night's question was in his expression.

"I decided to go back to school, take some classes at El Camino."

"Excellent. What field?"

"Nutrition."

D'Andra told Night about the statistics she'd read on the Internet, the unhealthy habits that led to her own health crisis and her plans to help educate the community.

"That's exactly my plan with the classes I'm structuring—teaching people to eat to live instead of living to eat."

"I think you'll get a great deal of interest and hopefully participation. More and more information is available on the importance of diet and exercise, and the older you get, the more important it becomes."

"How old are you, if you don't mind me asking?"

"Getting ready to hit the big 3-0," D'Andra answered readily. She wasn't one of those women who felt uncomfortable with her age. To her, it was just a number.

"What about you?"

"Thirty-five."

"I would have guessed younger than that."

Night stroked his chin. "Yeah, it's the baby face."

"Hum, no doubt. I'm sure you've gotten more than your share of attention with that face." D'Andra said this matter-of-factly, without sarcasm.

Night cut his eyes at D'Andra to see if she was teasing. She wasn't. "You'd be surprised," is all he said in response.

A piercing scream cut off further conversation. It came from where they were headed and the group of kids who'd been left in Kimani's charge. Night sprinted ahead as D'Andra ran as fast as she could in the gripping sand. When she reached the circle, Night was kneeling over a squalling Tonia. The first thing D'Andra noticed was Tonia's lack of tears.

"Stop crying, Tonia. Where does it hurt?" Used to handling health crisis, D'Andra's demeanor was cool, calm and collected.

Tonia's answer was another wail.

"Tell her Tonia!" Antoine urged, not wanting his twin's pain to spoil his fun. "If you want to stay you must obey!"

That remark brought a smirk from Night, a snicker from some of the kids, a scowl from D'Andra and yet another howl from Tonia.

"Move back, kids," D'Andra ordered. Either Tonia had worked up a little water or something was really wrong with her. D'Andra moved the tiny hand that was clutching the equally tiny foot and immediately noticed the red welt forming on her niece's heel.

"Carry her over here for me, Night," D'Andra said commandingly as she pointed to her beach umbrella. "She's been bitten."

Night followed D'Andra's orders without comment, even as he hushed Tonia's howls with a whispered edict that only the little girl heard: screaming makes the bite hurt more; humming softly helps it feel better. The entire circle moved as one to D'Andra's belongings. Night laid Tonia on the blanket while D'Andra retrieved her first-aid kit.

"Looks like a jellyfish bite," she said matter-of-factly as she alternately used sand and a scruffy towel to remove the prickly tentacles remaining in Tonia's foot. She examined it closer once the area had been sanitized. Fully in nurse mode she diagnosed the situation. "Doesn't look too venomous though; there's no swelling and limited redness."

Once done she activated a small bag of dry ice and instructed Tonia to hold it on her foot. Lastly she pulled out a vial of clear liquid and using a cotton swab, dabbed it on the inflamed area.

"Does that feel better?" she asked her.

Tonia nodded slowly, and continued humming.

"Why are you humming?"

When Tonia's answer was simply to hum a little louder, D'Andra shook her head and looked at Night, who shrugged his shoulders.

D'Andra shook her head, perplexed. "Well . . . at least she stopped screaming."

Excitement over, the rest of the group ventured back to the ocean's edge. Soon Tonia joined them, playing as if nothing had ever happened.

"Here, give me that." Without waiting for an answer, Night took the bottle of sunblock from D'Andra's hand and as methodically as she'd applied the ointment to Tonia's heel, began to rub the cool cream on to D'Andra's legs.

"I can do that, Night," D'Andra eked out around the breath caught in her throat. His nimble fingers on her ankles and calves were causing all kinds of feelings and thoughts to shoot through her body and mind.

"I know you can; but I get the feeling you're the type that takes care of everybody else. You came here fully prepared, first-aid kit and all. It's time someone took care of you."

D'Andra felt herself relax in spite of herself. Night gently kneaded her muscles as he rubbed in the lotion. She could get used to this, but no, she couldn't. It felt too good.

She drew her legs away from him. "Really, Night, I

can do it." She reached for the lotion, but Night had other plans.

"What is it; my sensual massage turning you on from the toes up?"

He'd hit the nail on the head and D'Andra didn't know whether to be frightful or flattered. There was no way someone like Night would understand how someone like Charles could make a woman distrustful of all men. She was sure that the man kneeling at her feet was used to being the heartbreaker, not the heartbroken.

"What are you doing?"

"I'm washing your feet so I can give you a foot massage."

"Didn't you hear what I just said?"

"And didn't you hear me? I'm taking care of you for a minute. You know how bossy I am. Shut up and take it, woman!"

He took one of the bottles of water and, pouring it over D'Andra's feet, washed off the sand. Then he sat down and placed her foot in his lap. Placing a small dab of the sunblock in his hand, he began to gently yet firmly massage D'Andra's feet. As he pressed and kneaded certain parts of her foot, he explained what organs were affected by each location.

"This area," he said softly, as he massaged the fleshy area beneath her toes, "corresponds with your lungs. So this," he pressed, kneaded, and massaged in a circular fashion, "helps the air flow through the lungs better."

He kneaded the outer part of her right foot. "This area corresponds to the liver and this"—he switched to the left foot and massaged the middle of her foot with his thumb—"works on your kidneys."

"Hum," D'Andra said, feeling blissfully indulged. Night's foot massage was affecting her whole body, including one particularly sensitive area probably not represented on her foot but getting wetter by the minute.

Night gave rapt attention to each area of her feet. He loved the feel of D'Andra's skin, its softness and suppleness. As he massaged each toe, and in turn stimulated the places each one represented: head, eye, pituitary gland, etc., he thought about other areas of D'Andra's body he'd like to massage, and decided he would love to touch her all over. He shifted before his suddenly hard member made its presence known to D'Andra's foot. Placing his palms against them, he kneaded her heels, the last part of her foot to get attention.

The action sent a shiver up D'Andra's butt; so much so that she giggled.

"Ooh, Night," she whispered. "What part does the heel go with?"

Night smiled, knowing what had just happened because he'd done it on purpose. He squeezed a couple more times, knowing this action was taking the place of his massaging the real thing.

"Night?" D'Andra prompted again to mask her growing ardor.

Night took his hand away and calmly wiped it on a towel. "Your ass," he said in a professional, matter-of-fact tone, similar to the one D'Andra had used when tending Tonia's foot.

D'Andra's hazel eyes flew open to meet deep, chocolate brown ones.

"My what?"

"Uh-huh, you heard me, and you felt it." He licked his lips unconsciously and D'Andra thought she'd have an orgasm. She jumped up from the beach chair.

"It's time to get the kids."

Night turned and watched the topic of their conversation bounce seductively with D'Andra's stride. His shaft twitched its agreement to his approving stare. He took another swallow of water, trying to cool down. "Uh-huh," he said again.

10

D'Andra finally stopped lying to herself. She had developed feelings for Night. He made her feel so good at the beach, so special, so cared for, that she didn't get too upset upon once again seeing a pile of dishes when she returned home. According to Mary, Cassandra's intended good deed had been usurped by an unexpected visit from Anthony, her pro baseball player boyfriend. Trying to wrap him around her finger certainly topped being a woman of her word, D'Andra had deduced as she stacked dishes with hardened syrup and pancake remains into soapy water. And Mary? Mary hadn't cleaned house ever since she birthed two maids to do it for her.

D'Andra's sleep was fitful Sunday evening and later that Monday, as she ran errands before reporting to work, her thoughts were still of Night. She was torn in her emotions regarding him, afraid both of what would happen when the workouts were over and he left her life, and what might happen if he stayed. One thing she couldn't deny, his workouts worked. She'd finally remembered to step on the scale this morning and to her surprise and delight she had indeed lost ten pounds.

Another night of hell at Heavenly Haven, D'Andra thought as she eyed the stack of new admissions. The workplace was still in turmoil and the staff was stretched thin. One nurse had been replaced but two more had left.

"Miss Daisy's in rare form tonight," Elaine said as she came around to the nurse's station. "Don't say you weren't forewarned."

D'Andra laughed at Elaine's use of her nickname for Frieda.

"I think I can handle her," she answered. "I'll just threaten her by saying I'll stop Bryan from coming by. You know she's got a thing for the PT."

"Who doesn't? He could give Brad Pitt competition and that's not an easy thing. He's hot."

"And gay."

"No way."

"Yes, way. Can't you tell?"

"No, and you can't either."

"Well, maybe not. But his nails are manicured and his hair looks better than mine. Plus he's always talking about his best friend, Wade."

"So what? Oprah's always talking about her best friend, Gayle, and she's not gay."

D'Andra fixed Elaine with a look. "She has Stedman; who does boyfriend have?"

"He can have me if he likes kids. Max will just have to get over it."

"Girl, please; Max knows he doesn't have a thing to worry about. They'll be prying wood from under your fingernails after he dies; that's how hard you'll be holding on to his casket before they pull you away!"

"That's morbid. You have no sense."

"You neither; that's why we get along."

D'Andra hesitated, wondering if she should admit to Elaine what she'd only today admitted to herself. But she had to talk to someone and her current options were limited.

She continued to key information into the computer as she strived for a casual tone. "I ran into Night this weekend—twice."

Elaine was immediately all ears. "Do tell!"

"Well, Saturday night I saw him at the gym. Then I took the kids to the beach yesterday and he was there with his cousin and some other kids."

"Interesting," Elaine said, implying several messages in the singular response.

"Why do you say it like that?"

"How many beaches are there in the LA area and what are the chances you'd be at the same one, at the same time, if fate wasn't working her magic."

"Oh please, it was just coincidence."

"Whatever it was, I think you should go for it. You know you like him. How long are you going to let a jerk named Charles ruin your happiness? You deserve a good man, D'Andra, and you know that's what you want. It wouldn't hurt to let your guard down a little bit, see if there's any fire where that smoke is."

"Easy for you to say; it didn't happen to you."

"I know, kiddo," Elaine said, releasing an understanding sigh. "But what did you tell me Night said to you the other day? No pain, no gain? That advice may apply to your heart as well as your hips. He sounds like a keeper, girl. You'd best get to keepin' before somebody else finds him and leaves you weepin'."

"If that's your attempt at poetry, don't quit your day job, Elaine."

"And don't you try and change the subject. If he is indeed unattached as you believe, he won't stay that way for long. If you want something to happen, you just may need to be the one who gets the ball rolling."

"I could care less if he's seeing someone."

"Yeah, try that lie on Miss Daisy, not someone who knows you as well as I do."

With that, Elaine sashayed into the chart room while D'Andra walked down the hall to begin her rounds.

As soon as she turned the corner, she found Elaine had been right.

"Grace!" Mrs. Miller yelled in her shrill, high-pitched voice. "Grace, come here!"

"Right away, Miss Daisy," D'Andra responded. *Finally*, she thought. If only for a moment, here was someone to get her mind off Night.

11

She stood at the door a moment before ringing the bell, calming her usual pre-meeting jitters. She'd only seen him two days ago, had seen him regularly—Tuesdays and Thursdays at four P.M. sharp—for more than a month. D'Andra knew that continuing to react this way at the prospect of seeing him was silly. However, this would be the first time she'd seen him in the light of truth, the truth that she was falling in love with him.

The door opened unexpectedly. "Are you going to stand there all day or come inside?"

Night's forceful question hid his nervousness. He'd thought of D'Andra the rest of Sunday and all day Monday and today: her soft skin, health-oriented goals, the kindness she displayed at entertaining her nieces and nephew and skill she showed when attending Tonia's bite. In her were all the things he wanted, if he were looking for someone, which he wasn't. Right now he needed to focus. He was close to seeing his dream realized and Jazz had shown him better than anyone how easily one could get distracted.

"I've got good news," D'Andra said as they sat stretching before the workout. "I've lost ten pounds."

"How is that news? I told you that Sunday that you'd lost weight."

"That was your guess. I confirmed it by weighing myself."

"If I tell you a chicken chews tobacco, look under its left wing."

"What in the world does that mean?"

"It means if I say something, it's gospel. I could tell by looking at you that you'd lost."

"And so the part of my weight loss story where the tobacco chewing chicken comes in is . . . where?"

"An old Southern saying, don't try and figure it out. At any rate, I'm proud of you. In fact, this *news* calls for a celebration. What do you say I put together a little something; a light dinner to follow our workout. You game?"

"I don't know; can you cook?"

It was Night's turn to harrumph. "Please, is the sky blue, does a bird fly? I can hang with the best of them."

"We'll see; 'cause you're looking at one of the best."

"What, you want to do a little Iron Chef cook-off? Or would it be more like a Throwdown?"

"Oh my God, you watch the Food Network."

Night looked embarrassed. "My secret's out. But I have an excuse. That was my first job; busing tables and then helping Uncle Robert in the kitchen at Jewel's. I did that for almost six years, until I left for college."

"So your Aunt Jewel owned a restaurant?"

Night nodded. "But I enjoyed her cooking skills long before that. Our family relocated to L.A. when I was ten years old. Aunt Jewel and Uncle Robert had already lived there five years by then, and had talked about owning their own business from the time we arrived. They realized their dream a few years later and I worked for them until I left for college."

"Then I guess since you've spouted your cooking credentials, you're on!"

Night's voice dropped as he continued. "Under one condition."

D'Andra's heart sped up as she awaited the answer. "What?" she breathed.

"It has to be low-cal, low-sodium, low-cholesterol, and delicious."

D'Andra smiled. Little did her trainer know that those were exactly the types of meals she'd been fixing for over a month. *This is going to be fun,* she thought.

But there was work before pleasure. Night seemed especially focused tonight, paying attention, at least in D'Andra's opinion, to every muscle in her body. Sculpting, he called it. Well, she had another name: torture.

"Look, Night. I'm not trying to have Janet's abs."

"That's not what I'm going for. But this right here," he said, placing a large hand lightly on her midsection, is your core. If it's strong, the rest of your body is going to line up. In about five months, you'll thank me, trust me."

"Five months! I'm not trying to wait that long to see results."

"Unless you're blind, you're already seeing them." He looked at her appreciatively. "I know I am."

D'Andra thought about what Elaine said and stuck a toe in amorous waters. "Would that be a flirt, Mr., what is your last name anyway?"

"Didn't you know? I'm a one-name wonder, like Tiger, Kobe, Diddy . . ."

"You mean Tiger *Woods*, Kobe *Bryant*, and Sean 'Diddy' *Combs*?"

D'Andra's quick wit turned Night on as much as her thick thighs. "Simmons. JaJuan 'Night' Simmons."

"I love your first name . . . JaJuan. Does anyone call you that?"

"My mom, when I'm in trouble. But never mind

that. You're just trying to distract me from the task at hand—tightening that butt. Get up."

He helped D'Andra to her feet and led her to the other side of his basement's home gym.

"Now as you push the roller back, away from you, I want you to control this muscle, control this here."

Night lightly squeezed the area just below D'Andra's buttocks. He did so clinically, detached, as a doctor might.

"This is the muscle we're working on and along with the squats, we'll end up with a firm contour on what is already a nicely shaped frame."

D'Andra looked to see if there was any teasing in Night's eyes. His face was neutral, business-like.

She decided to interact with him in the same way. "How many of these do you want me to do?" she asked, bending over the cushion on the Glute Blaster, a vertical leg press machine, and placing her foot under the metal lift as Night had instructed. She grabbed the handles and wiggled her butt to get more comfortable as well as to push Night's buttons.

"Let's start with ten," Night said, forcing down his libido. For a man who saw upturned butts for a living, he was a bit disconcerted that this one could turn him on so forcefully. Granted it was a fabulously round mound on a beautiful woman, but she was his client. This was his job.

His voice was harsher than intended as he worked to refocus his thoughts. "Push, higher! No, keep your movement controlled. Concentrate D'Andra. Focus on the muscle you're trying to work. If you don't do these ten properly, we're going to do ten more, *plus* the other two sets. Now, do it right!"

Turning from *Gigolo JaJuan* to *Sergeant Simmons* got them through the workout.

D'Andra felt self-conscious as she entered the

kitchen in Night's oversized shirt and baggie shorts. Secretly, she was happy to be in his clothes, and to know that they were loose on her. She surreptitiously admired his sculpted legs and back in his loose-fitting shorts and tank top as he stirred a delicious-smelling concoction at the stove.

"I like your bathroom décor," she said by way of greeting. "Thanks for suggesting the shower; it was a good idea."

"Didn't think I'd want your funky butt in my kitchen, did you doll?"

D'Andra swatted him even as she laughed. "Forget you!"

Night smiled. This is what he loved about their friendship, the easy camaraderie he'd never experienced with Jazz, or anyone else.

Their conversation was easy as D'Andra made herself at home in Night's well-stocked kitchen. It was obvious he cooked and by the look at the spices and other ingredients that stocked his shelves, he knew what he was doing. For his contribution, Night had tackled the main course, a baked herb fish he'd perfected with a zesty blend of parsley, chives and rosemary topped with a lemon-yogurt sauce. D'Andra worked on the perfect complement: a vegetable stir-fry of lightly breaded zucchini, yellow squash, eggplant and fresh tomatoes tying into the fish dish by using some of the same spices Night had used along with a curry spice she'd found in his spice rack designed to, as her favorite chef Emeril would say, kick it up a notch. The concoction that had tempted her taste buds was a clear consómmé soup for their first course.

"Wow, candles and everything," she exclaimed, when coming around the corner she noticed Night lighting the tapers on the dining room table. "I'm impressed."

"This is a celebration, isn't it?" Night asked, his eyes sultry upon her.

"If you say so," she answered. She could feel herself go warm and was thankful that in the subdued lighting her blush wouldn't show.

Night went into the kitchen and came out with a light sauvignon blanc. "Just a glassful for each of us to celebrate your victory," he explained. "Normally I try and stay away from what I call empty calories, but your workout tonight deserves a reward."

Both were quiet as they reflected on what shape, no pun intended, the reward could take on.

"To an amazing personal trainer," D'Andra said, when they lifted their glasses for the toast.

"To an amazing woman," Night responded.

They stared at each other, mesmerized as they sipped the delicious vintage. D'Andra didn't know whether it was the wine or Night's presence that made her dizzy. She tried to fight the thoughts even as they scrambled for a spot in her conscience. Night was kind and thoughtful . . . and fine. He was smart and goal-oriented and on top of that, the man could cook. For the second time in as many days she admitted the inevitable: she was falling in love.

"Are you seeing somebody?" Her mouth blurted out the question before her mind had a chance to censor it.

Her blunt inquiry caught Night by surprise and made him feel good at the same time. Maybe he wasn't the only one with an interest beyond the weight room. An interest he was still in the process of denying, even as he answered.

"Not anymore."

"But you were? How recent?"

"Several months ago."

"Was it serious? I'm sorry, it's really none of my business."

"No, it isn't," Night said smiling, "but I don't mind talking about it." He took another bite of the vegetables before continuing. "This is delicious."

"Thank you; so is the fish."

"Thanks."

"Anyway, I found out that it's going to take a very special woman to be beside me in this business. It's my job to be around women, some of them quite attractive, 24/7. Along with the intimacy of ongoing physical closeness comes an added attraction that women feel by being helped. I'm dealing with something very personal to them—their bodies. It takes someone trusting, secure in her own skin and in the strength of our relationship to be able to deal with that. Jazz couldn't, so she left."

"Why do you think she, Jazz, couldn't deal with it?" D'Andra asked the question wondering if they would be the same demons she'd fight.

"She was jealous and insecure, and had no reason to be. Jazz is gorgeous with a near-perfect body. I did nothing to give her a reason to doubt my love for her or question my trust, other than help other women lose weight. Not only were we together romantically, but had planned to be business partners as well."

"I can see it from her point of view," D'Andra said. "Having women all up on your man all the time, flirting, touching, sweating . . ."

"Hum," Night said, stroking his chin and looking at D'Andra pointedly. "I could enjoy that, with the right client. That's why I don't date the people I'm training . . . as a rule."

D'Andra hoped her disappointment didn't show. "I see."

"But if you'll remember what I said when I met you, I don't always follow rules, even my own."

D'Andra lowered her eyes and continued eating

silently. Both knew the relationship had shifted, and where it went from there was up to D'Andra. Night had just made it clear that he was interested in taking what they had to another level, even as he'd left D'Andra an escape route if she so chose.

D'Andra felt she was being pulled in two directions. On the one hand, she was flattered that someone like Night found her attractive and wanted to be with her. On the other, she also knew how falling in love with someone like Night only for him to dump her would devastate the bit of pride she had left, the bit that Charles hadn't destroyed.

But Night wasn't Charles, she thought as she continued to be conflicted. Night was everything she wanted, but was he what she needed right now?

Night watched the various emotions play across D'Andra's face. He wondered about and simultaneously wanted to throttle the man who'd brought the pain he saw etched in her expression. But he also saw the determination with which she tried to mask these emotions so he wisely didn't question her.

"I'd better go," she said abruptly, rising from the table at the same time she spoke. "This was absolutely wonderful, Night, but I have to work later so I'd better try and get a little rest before then."

Night eyed D'Andra without speaking. *She's used to running away,* he thought. *And I'm used to catching what I chase.*

"Let me," he said, rising from his chair and taking over D'Andra's work of clearing the table. "Get your rest. I'll do the dishes, no problem. I really enjoyed sharing dinner with you. Congratulations again on the weight loss; you look good."

He knew he should let her go, but he wasn't ready for the evening to end. "What time do you have to be at work? I mean, do you have time for dessert?"

"You made dessert?"

"Just a simple fruit medley I made earlier today," he said slowly, "marinated in its own juices," he continued. He licked his lips, trying to use charm to mask his nervousness. He felt like he was back in junior high asking his neighbor to the school dance.

"Okay, but just a little for me."

"Make yourself comfortable in the living room. I'll be right out."

D'Andra settled herself into the plush suede, navy blue sofa, and looked around. Everything about the room suited Night, from the dark, rich colors to the fabrics, suede and leather. The square Osaka coffee table was sturdy and purposeful, like its owner, and the stainless steel accessories, lamps, bookcase and table ornaments lent a crisp, clean quality to the surroundings. The large picture window was framed by silvery curtains, a touch that lightened the manly room. There was a grouping of pictures on the table just under the plasma TV, but Night entered the room just as she was about to give them a closer inspection.

"A gourmet fruit cocktail for milady," Night announced in a horrible English accent.

D'Andra giggled as she took the dessert bowl and napkin Night offered. He feigned hurt as he sat down beside her.

"What, you're not mistaking me for an English dandy?"

"Uh, not at all, not for a nanosecond even. Don't quit your day job." She took a bite of the fruit mixture. "Um, this is good."

"I'm glad you like it."

"This is just fruit; nothing else?"

"Well, I did add a little sumpin' sumpin' to the mix; but there are some things a chef keeps to himself."

"Oh, really?"

"Oh, yeah. The bananas are my favorite."

"Bananas? I don't think I have any." D'Andra poked her fork through her bowl's contents.

"Oh, you've got to try the bananas. My secret ingredient really works great on them."

He placed a piece of banana with a syrupy substance onto his spoon and turned to D'Andra.

She opened her mouth for the bite. "Oh my goodness, Night; that's delicious." She closed her eyes and chewed, lost in the taste of gooey goodness.

Night watched D'Andra as if she, not the fruit dish, was the dessert. Her lips had intrigued him from the first day they met. And now he imagined joining his with hers, sweetened all the more by his maple syrup secret.

D'Andra's eyes opened to find Night's fastened on her lips. She licked them self-consciously.

"You missed some," he said, taking his finger and wiping a trace of juice from the side of her mouth. "Here." He placed his finger next to her mouth.

She couldn't resist. She turned her head slightly and tentatively licked the tip of his finger.

"I don't think you got it all," he whispered, as he gently forced his finger into her mouth.

She couldn't pull her eyes from his as she gently sucked his large index digit. Even as she did so, her dream, where he licked the moisture from her sweat-drenched body, came into her mind. She knew she should, but she couldn't stop. Neither could he. Weeks of thinly restrained sexual tension demanded attention and would not be denied.

Soon his tongue replaced his finger and he ravished her mouth. A rush of heat showered them both; hot and wanting. Night's hand found its way under the shirt that D'Andra wore and under the bra that held treasure. D'Andra's intake of breath was his reward at finding and massaging a pleasingly plump nipple that quickly hardened in his hand. Suddenly his finger was not enough; he wanted to taste her. With one quick movement, he removed her top, and with a singular sense of purpose, unhooked her front-latching bra. The sight that greeted him almost took his breath away.

"You're beautiful," he said before taking one nipple into his mouth while kneading the other. He showered her with kisses; from her breast to her temples, down her cheek and her neck, all the while touching, kneading her silky soft skin. He wanted to plunge himself inside her, his months of celibacy now painfully obvious, his lack of sexual release making him reckless with want. He guided D'Andra to a lying position, even as he continued to plunder her mouth with his tongue. D'Andra was a big girl, but he handled her as if she were a ballerina.

D'Andra was hot all over, moaning with every lap of Night's tongue. He felt so good; used his mouth so well. Her hands couldn't get enough of the smooth skin over hard muscle. She gripped the butt she'd admired from the first and was not disappointed. It was firm and round and powerful. Already it was leading the way into the familiar dance of love and D'Andra's hips joined in immediate sync. Night rubbed his hands over D'Andra's belly roll in a way that made it feel sexy to her, even as his hand tugged at her shorts, looking for a soft thatch to land. D'Andra's hands followed of their own volition, followed to the hard piece of muscle pulsating against her upper thigh. She tugged at his shorts, and then she remembered.

"Night, stop, I-I-I can't do this." She turned her head to deflect his kisses. They landed softly on her ear and the side of her neck. "Please, Night, I'm sorry, please."

Somewhere in the distance, Night heard a voice. *Stop? Sorry? Can't?* He shook his head as he tried to wrap his mind around a negative sounding word on an excruciatingly positive experience. He felt as if he were on his way to heaven and D'Andra's body was the cloud; soft and cushy, warm and inviting. His manhood jumped in anticipation, even as he felt D'Andra's hands on his shoulders, trying to push him up and off her.

"I'm sorry," she said again.

Night was silent as he sat up, closed his eyes and tried to regulate his breathing.

"Oh my gosh," D'Andra exclaimed. Her hands were not big enough to hold all she was trying to hide—her naked torso.

"The window, Night! Where's my . . . your . . . where's that shirt? Where's my bra?"

Looking at D'Andra try and decide which side of her breast she was going to try and cover with which hand was the levity he needed to bring the blood back from his lower head to his upper one. He laughed as he pulled the shirt out from where it had been scrunched beneath him and handed it to her. A quick search found the bra on the floor. D'Andra hurriedly put both on.

"Don't worry, doll; those are one-way windows. No one can see your loveliness . . . besides me."

D'Andra couldn't believe that she'd let happen what had almost just happened. She needed to get outside so she could breathe and think. "I'm sorry," she said again.

"Why do you keep apologizing? The only thing I'm sorry about is that you're leaving."

D'Andra explained as she reached for the gym clothes she'd changed out of and her purse. "I, we shouldn't have done that. I'm focused on getting myself together on several levels and you're focused on your gym. I appreciate your helping me work out

and your friendship. Anything more will only compli-
cate things."

"All right, then," he said as he walked a hurrying
D'Andra to the door. "I'll see you Thursday?"

"Yeah, see you then." She didn't trust herself to
even look back as she spoke, afraid her body would
betray her and make her words a lie. She wanted
nothing more than to finish what they started, to
spend forever in Night's strong arms.

Night watched D'Andra scurry into her Suburban
and head down the street like somebody was chasing
her. His eyes narrowed even as a smile appeared, then
widened. *Yeah, you'd better run.* Because somebody was
after her; and somebody was determined to catch her
and make her his, complications be damned. It was as
simple as that.

12

"You were right. There's a definite attraction going on between Night and me." D'Andra had purposely waited until her lunch break in the nearly empty cafeteria so her conversation with Elaine wouldn't be overheard.

Elaine dropped her fork. "I knew it! I knew there was something there." She leaned forward in her chair, eyes twinkling with excitement. "Well c'mon chick; out with it. Did you screw? Was it good? Was he big, like the cock you saw in your dream?"

D'Andra laughed at her friend's inquisitiveness. From someone else, she may have been offended, but aside from the soaps, reality TV and an occasional movie, her job at Heavenly Haven provided the spice to Elaine's steady, predictable life.

"Put a pause to your pen, Nora Roberts; that chapter has yet to be written."

"Oh, for goodness sakes, D'Andra, what are you waiting for?"

The microwave dinged, giving D'Andra time to gather her thoughts while she retrieved her Subway sandwich. She'd been asking herself the same question all evening. For all her "it's all about me" talk,

D'Andra wanted to be with Night; to hell with the consequences. For the past few hours, none of her reasons for choosing to be alone made sense.

"I'm waiting until I've accomplished my immediate goals," she said, pausing again to take a bite of her chicken sandwich. "I'm working hard to get in shape—"

"But there's something hard you're not working," Elaine interjected.

D'Andra ignored her. "I'm looking for a place to move. *And* I made another major decision I haven't told you about."

"There's more?"

"I'm going back to school."

D'Andra briefly filled Elaine in on the research she'd done which led to the decision to return to school and become a certified dietician.

"With my associate's in nursing and this BSN, the sky's the limit to what I could do. There's counseling, teaching, training, lectures, seminars, writing; all ways I can help educate our community, well, women in general and Black women in particular, to the dangers of heart disease and other illnesses brought on largely by diet and stress."

"Those are excellent goals," Elaine said sincerely. "You know I've always admired your tenacity and your drive. I still do. But I also worry about you. You're always looking out for other people; I guess I feel the need to look out for you.

"All I'm saying is while you're on the road to this new you, leave room for someone else to travel with you. You've wanted a good man and you deserve to let that happen. But since that fiasco with Charles, you've been so leery about opening up, even a little bit . . . just don't fail to see the forest for the trees, that's all I'm saying."

"And I hear you, girl. It's just not so easy, you know? That situation with Charles and the company which shall remain nameless, that was some mess for a sistah to go through."

"But don't you see that as long as you deny yourself, they're still putting you through it?"

"But I'm not . . . okay maybe I am but for a reason."

"I know, it's all about you."

"Exactly. You don't understand what it's like; you haven't had to deal with this kind of drama in a decade or more."

"Listen sister, married life is not without drama, trust me on that count."

"Please; what type of drama have you and Max experienced lately?"

Elaine paused, in serious thought for a moment. "Well, there was that stopped-up drain he took forever to fix."

"Oh my God," D'Andra said dramatically.

"And those two weeks he spent on the couch last year when I found out he'd looked up his high school sweetheart on Classmates.com."

"Call the popo, I think you're gonna need backup," D'Andra countered sarcastically.

But she appreciated Elaine's positive attitude, especially knowing of more serious tests to her friend's marriage than had been brought up at the table. Like the two miscarriages Elaine had before little Seth was born. Or the horrific battle with Alzheimer's disease that put strain on everyone before Max's father died last year.

"All right, I give," Elaine conceded. "You've made your point. I am a lucky girl, and I'm thankful for that every day. I just want you to be lucky too."

"Maybe I will be."

"I'm crossing my fingers."

D'Andra's heart warmed as she watched her loyal, red-headed, freckle-faced friend head back to the nurse's station. "From your lips to God's ears," she whispered.

And to yours, God whispered back.

13

D'Andra pulled up to Night's house with a new attitude. She'd taken Elaine's advice to heart, and while she wasn't ready to go in and seduce the man straight out, she had promised herself to stop hiding behind excuses and fear, to live life a little more dangerously than she had in the past. What had Elaine said as they left work this morning? Nothing ventured nothing gained?

D'Andra reached for her towel, water bottle and purse, and headed up the walk to Night's front door. She hadn't seen or spoken to him since their impromptu rendezvous two nights before and her heart beat with a mixture of nervousness and excitement. Would he greet her as if nothing had happened on Tuesday? Would he be sorry their friendship had gone to that level? Would there now be discomfort in their dealings as client and trainer? Would he refuse to open the door?

Night had watched the clock since noon, willing the hands to move faster toward his four o'clock workout session with D'Andra. He'd thought of little else, and certainly no one else, since their session two days ago. He'd replayed their tryst in his head, time and again, and all he wanted to do was see if the real thing was as sweet as he remembered. He didn't even give her time to ring the bell before flinging the door open.

"Get in here, doll," he murmured, reaching for D'Andra's hand and closing the door quickly behind her. Then, backing her up against the door, he proceeded to kiss her like a thirsty man needing water.

"Oh . . . my," she said when they came up for air. So much for her wondering about Night's reaction to seeing her again. "Uh, good afternoon."

"Good afternoon, D'Andra. You look beautiful, as usual."

"Night," she said, ducking her head under his arm and going around him toward the stairs. "I look the same as I always do."

"I said 'as usual'. You want anything before we begin our workout?"

Yeah, you, is what she thought. "No, I'm cool," is what she said.

They went through their usual warm-up exercises, a combination of stretching, callanetics and pilates. Night was professional even as he was attentive, with prolonged touches and lingering looks filling the space between counts.

Ten minutes into the exercises, D'Andra had worked up a sweat. She took off her warm-up jacket and was immediately conscious of the baby doll style T-shirt she wore underneath. The top was flattering in that it emphasized her breasts and de-emphasized her stomach and hips, stopping at the top of her thighs. D'Andra had put the top on underneath to soak up sweat as much as anything; and now all it was soaking up was Night's attention. The sexual attraction between them was palpable and as much as D'Andra wanted to keep her mind on working out, she knew both she and Night were thinking of working her over in a way more fit for the bedroom than the weight room. If she was going to continue working with him, she had to clear the air.

"Night, we need to talk about what happened the other day."

"Okay."

"I'm obviously attracted to you, but like I said before I'm trying to stay focused on me right now. I went through a painful breakup with my ex and I don't think I'm ready to go down that road again."

"Which road . . . pain or love?"

"Is there a difference?"

"There can be. Look, D'Andra, this is new for me too. I have a rule not to date my clients, and I also said I'd put all my focus into opening my gym. But some things just happen, and sometimes . . . I think we should let nature take its course."

Everything D'Andra wanted was standing right in front of her. Why was she so afraid of taking a chance? . . . *As long as you deny yourself, they're still putting you through it.* Elaine's words swirled around in her head along with her doubts.

"Let's just be friends for right now," she said finally. "Is that okay?"

"Is that friends with benefits?"

"Night!"

"All right, all right. But don't ask me to keep away from those lips of yours because a brothah can only have so much discipline."

"Maybe a kiss or two, every now and then; until I'm ready."

"Girl," Night sighed as he stepped to her and indulged her in a lazy, thorough kiss. "I think you're going to be worth the wait."

* * *

Jazz frowned as she entered Bally Fitness. She could never understand what Night saw in the place that made him like it so. On several occasions she'd tried to coax him into joining one of LA's more upscale gyms, like Equinox or Crunch, where she worked out. A perfect size four with almost no body fat, Jazz hadn't joined the gym, Equinox, for fitness purposes. She'd joined it to network, to meet celebrities, athletes and progressive businessmen for her public relations business. It had proven an excellent move. Using her stacked body as well as her sharp mind, she'd gained seven prominent clients since joining the gym a year ago, putting in more time since her breakup with Night.

Those attributes, body and mind, were the same ones used when she set her sights on Night, four years ago. It was at a Santa Monica beach, on a bike trail near her house. He was riding, she was walking her dog, Power. She took one look at the dark, smooth skin and tight, toned body of the rider coming toward her and stepped right in his path.

"Is that bicycle the only thing you ride?" she'd asked brazenly.

A tan isn't the only thing she took from the beach that day. Night came over, and they barely left her bed all weekend. By Monday he was smitten with her sexiness and she was hooked on his hammer. The love came later, such as it was.

Jazz was all about making it, and Night was the perfect complement to her well-orchestrated life. It bugged her to no end that she couldn't get him to leave his common friends and stay solely in her world of the elite. He'd compromised in some areas, attending various parties and social functions in the designer duds she chose for him and when he wasn't training clients, spending most of his time at her sleek, two-bedroom condo in tony Santa Monica, instead of the ghetto neighborhood of Inglewood where he lived.

But in other things, Jazz remembered, he wouldn't budge; like distancing himself from his countrified mom whom she'd been forced to endure almost every Sunday, along with the calorie-laden monstrosities that he and his mother erroneously referred to as "good eating." And in refusing to leave this gym, where he worked in management right after graduation from college and where one of his best friends still trained and pumped iron. Zeroing in on that best friend, Jazz looked down her nose at the woman at the counter asking for her ID card, and walked around the turnstile to where Marc stood.

"It's all right, Mitzy," he said to the chagrinned employee whom Jazz had ignored. "What brings you down to mix with the little people, Jazz?"

"You know the only thing that could bring me here, Marc. Where is he?"

"Doesn't work here full-time anymore."

"Really?" Jazz was elated at this bit of news; maybe there was still hope for them after all.

"Nope. His gym will be opening in a few months and he's been busy with that. Most of his other clients right now have gyms in their home and the few who don't, he trains at his house."

Jazz wondered about those clients, the bane of their existence that had led to her leaving him. Looking back, it had been one of the few times she'd made a poor choice. Night tried to get her to trust him, but she hadn't. And now she was paying the price of his being out of her life, not to mention the emptiness of his being out of her bed. She'd tried to replace him in that area, but no one came close. Others had money, power, looks; but Night had mad loving skills.

And he'd loved her from his heart. She knew that now. That's why she was determined to get him back.

"Is he still training that singer, what's her name?"

Marc knew fishing when he saw it, and he wasn't going to bite. Any information she wanted about Night, she was going to have to get from him.

"I'm not sure who all he's training now. I think a couple pro ballers though, and yeah, a couple celebrities. Night doesn't come cheap, you know. But he's the best; that's why he can command that long paper."

"He is the best," Jazz agreed. She knew what Marc said was true as sure as she knew he was withholding information. Time to try another tactic.

"Hey, how's the wifey? I haven't seen her since, well, since me and Night broke up."

That's because in your mind she's beneath you. "Oh, Lindsay? She's great; just celebrated a birthday. We went to Vegas."

Where'd you stay, Circus Circus? "That sounds so sweet, Marc. Tell her I said hello and that we should get together sometime soon."

Why, so she can choke on your fakeness? "I'll do that."

Good, maybe I can give Pug Face a much needed makeover. Lindsay had been too white bread America for Jazz's taste. The fact that she was in as good a shape as she didn't sit well with Jazz either. She'd endured them both only because they were Night's friends.

Sidling up to Marc, she flashed her most come-hither smile. "So . . . who's my man seeing these days?"

You're so transparent. "I don't know," he said, looking at her pointedly. "You'll have to ask him."

"C'mon, Mark, you're his best friend."

"That's why I'm telling you that if you want to know something about Night, then go to him. Don't try and pump his best friend for information."

Jazz fixed him with a look that Marc knew meant

she wasn't leaving until she felt she'd gotten what she came for.

"As far as I know, he isn't seeing anybody. He's been all wrapped up in opening his gym."

"You think he's really ready to do it? I mean, where'd he get the money and the space?"

Jazz considered Night's plans to open his own business a pipe dream, especially since her name and stellar credit rating were no longer available to him.

Thankfully, Marc's client walked up at that moment. "Ready to work out?" he asked the attractive blonde. She nodded. He heaved a grateful sigh. "Take care of yourself, Jazz."

That's exactly what I'll do, she thought as she maneuvered her Caspian blue SLK Roadster down Century Boulevard. Night's modest two-bedroom home was only minutes from Bally's, giving her little time to second-guess her impromptu decision for a surprise visit. She pulled up behind his black GMC Acadia parked in the driveway at the side of his house and cut the engine. After staring at the neatly trimmed shrubbery that lined the walk for a moment, she reached for her compact. They hadn't seen each other up close in a while; she wanted to put her best face forward to make his re-acquaintance.

"You sure you don't want to take a shower and have a quick meal?" Night wasn't ready for D'Andra to leave.

"Tempting, but no, I have a couple errands to run and will try to sleep a couple hours before going to work tonight."

"It was another good workout, D'Andra. I'm proud of your progress, and your focus."

"Thank you." Coming from him, this was high praise. Night's body was as perfect a one as she'd seen; she could only hope that with his help hers would look half as good.

She was almost to the door when Night stopped her. "Aren't you forgetting something?"

D'Andra looked down. She had her gym bag, her water and towel. Her keys were in her right hand and her warm-up jacket over her arm. "What?"

"This." Night's lips were soft as cotton candy as they descended on D'Andra's. He teased and nibbled a moment before plunging his tongue into the crevices of her mouth, searching hers out for an oral dance. He pressed his body against her and before long she felt his desire press against her.

"I'd better go," she breathed.

"Yes, you'd better."

She opened the door.

"Hey, what do you say about a movie this Saturday? I heard about an independent one I'd like to check out."

"Why, Night Simmons, that sounds like a date!"

"How about it?"

Her hesitation was brief. "Sounds great."

"I'll call you later with the details."

D'Andra would have been hard-pressed to wipe the smile off her face or the song from her heart. She was going to follow both Elaine's advice and her intuition. Night was a good man; she could feel it. And while she planned to take it slow, she definitely planned to take it.

"Oh, excuse me!" She'd been so deep in thought D'Andra nearly bumped the twig of a woman who was walking the opposite way up the walk into the shrubbery.

"Yes, excuse you," Jazz snarled in return. Little did it matter that she was equally at fault. She checked her purse for condoms as she neared the entrance.

D'Andra just stared, taken aback at this woman's rudeness, and her beauty. She looked about as big as a minute, with wide, slanted eyes, ridiculously long eyelashes and the kind of bee-stung mouth men loved. Her shoulder-length black bob framed high cheekbones and a long slender neck. She wore a tight-fitting dress and sandals with straps that wrapped around slender calves. Her toes were French-manicured. D'Andra saw all of this in the two seconds it took for the woman to huff, roll her eyes and sashay around D'Andra towards Night's front door.

D'Andra held her head high as she walked to her car, even though her high spirits had been cut low by Miss America's withering glare. The woman had the same haughty countenance as Cassandra sometimes donned when she thought she looked particularly cute—and did. Her sister would have given the stranger a run for her money, maybe even pushed her butt off the sidewalk. D'Andra was nobody's pansy, but neither was she the type to get in your face.

What was important in her mind as she started her car and headed off Night's block, wasn't so much how the woman looked but who was she to her trainer. And as immediately as she had the thought, she dismissed it. Night said himself that he was surrounded by beautiful women, trained them on a regular basis. D'Andra remembered that being one of the reasons his girlfriend had left him. For a moment, D'Andra felt a bit of camaraderie with his ex, or at the least some understanding. One had to be made of stone to let her man around that kind of glamour all day and not worry a little bit. D'Andra had witnessed firsthand the power of sweaty seductions, and how hypnotic a gym in close quarters could be. She could just imagine the woman's surgically enhanced breasts bouncing invitingly as she lifted and flexed. D'Andra would bet money those titties weren't real. They were too big on a woman that little. D'Andra forced her thoughts away from the woman and from Night as well. If she were to have any type of future at all with him, she had to be trusting, and she might as well start now.

"Hey, handsome!" Jazz exclaimed, throwing herself into Night's arms as soon as the door opened. She kissed his stunned lips and cupped his cheek gently. "I've missed you."

Night was momentarily too surprised to speak. How long had it been, almost eight, nine months since they last spoke? What was she doing here? What did she want? And did D'Andra see her come to his house?

"Who was that chunky monkey that almost knocked me off the sidewalk?" Jazz asked, answering his unasked question. She snuggled against Night from behind, missing the look of fury that crossed his face as a result of her insult.

"Her name is D'Andra," he said, unfolding her arms from around his waist and turning around. His crossed-arm, wide-leg stance bore that of a warrior. "What are you doing here, Jazz?"

"I couldn't stay away any longer, Night. I've been a total fool and torn an unbeatable team apart. Well, I'm back, and willing to do whatever you tell me. Ready to help you get the business going, solicit impressive clients . . . and I think I've got another financial backer for us."

For a moment, Night was pulled in by some of Jazz's traits that he found most attractive: her ambition, drive and tenacity. She was beautiful and he'd loved her dearly. Whatever perfume she was wearing was driving him wild.

He turned from her. "What we had is over, Jazz. Didn't you get the dissolution papers regarding our partnership?"

"Baby," she cooed, lightly scanning her hand over his backside, enjoying the reaction when he clenched it under her touch. "Those pesky details we can take care of later. I ran into Marc and he said you're still opening the gym. I didn't think you were, I mean, with us no longer together . . ."

"You didn't think I could make it without you, is that what you're saying?"

"No, Night, it's not what I meant. But my part of the partnership was securing finances. I just wonder how you were able to buy the property."

"You're not the only one with connections."

Night breathed a silent prayer to Aunt Jewel, who'd left him a sizeable amount of money in her will. He worked to rein in his anger at Jazz's assumption that he couldn't succeed without her. "What do you want?"

Jazz didn't know what kind of welcome she'd expected, but this wasn't it. She had Night wrapped around her fingers, putty in her hands. At least that's how it used to be. Sure, he always exuded strength, but not with her. Not like this.

"Come here, Chocolate," she whispered his pet name through moistened lips, batting her lashes and approaching him again in a way that dared him to deny her. She rubbed her Zuni silk mini across his bare chest and licked it. He tasted sweaty, salty, like he used to after intense lovemaking. She could feel his heart beating, hard and fast. She knew he wouldn't be able to resist her.

His intent was to push her away but almost of their own volition, Night's hands came up to cup her round, fleshy bottom. She smelled like flowers and felt like butter. At one time, she'd been his world.

But that was then; this was now. He moved his hands from her bottom to her hips and pushed her gently but firmly away from him.

"I've got things to do, Jazz. It's good to see you. I

hope you're well. But what we had is over." He walked to the door and opened it. "Don't come by again."

"You don't mean that."

"Does it sound like I'm playing?"

"Night, I made a big mistake breaking up with you."

"I broke up with you, remember?"

Jazz ignored the comment and went on. "And I've paid for it every day your arms haven't been around me. Please, baby; I'll do whatever I have to, whatever you say, to make up for how I left you. It wasn't fair, I know. But I was weak, jealous; afraid I'd lose you. So I left first, thinking it would hurt less. It hasn't."

Feeling she was making inroads into his heart, she continued. "I've changed, Night. I know I can trust you now; that you'll be faithful even with all the other women around. Please say we can try again, Night. Please?"

Night's resolve wavered a bit. At her best Jazz was beautiful, smart, funny and sexy as hell. At her worst she was belittling, insensitive, jealous and conceited. He remembered what his mother had said after Jazz made fun of a homeless man. *Ugly sure comes in a pretty package.* He remembered the comment she'd made about D'Andra, a woman who was beautiful inside and out. His moment of wavering was over. He'd made his choice, and it wasn't Jazz.

"I wish you well, Jazz," he said as he ushered her to the door. "Please don't come here again."

Angry didn't begin to describe Jazz's mood. She never considered for a moment that Night would refuse her. It wasn't often she was turned down for anything, especially by a man.

It just means I'll have to work a little harder, she thought, as she backed out of Night's driveway. Jazz Anderson always got what she wanted. Her next plan of seduction was hatched before her car reached the end of the block.

14

"Where are you going?" Mary Smalls, who was sitting on the couch devouring a slab of barbequed ribs and a mound of fries, eyed her daughter suspiciously.

"I have a date," D'Andra sang back.

"What, you?"

"Dang, Mama; you don't have to act so surprised."

"And you don't have to act like you go out every day. I ain't seen you on a date since Charles left."

"I left *him*, Mama."

"Whoever left who, he ain't here. This one any good?"

"Yes." D'Andra wasn't ready to share Night with her family. They'd be able to do their damage soon enough, if what was building went that far.

"You want some of these ribs?"

"No thanks, Mama."

"Oh, that's right; this food is too rich for your blood. I can see you're losing though."

This was the first acknowledgement of D'Andra's nearly fifteen-pound weight loss. "I'm working on it."

"Next thing you know, you'll be as small as Cassandra."

"I'll never be her size; and I'm not trying to be. I'm just trying to be a healthy weight for me. You should come join the gym with me, Mama; we could do the treadmill together."

"Girl, I'm not trying to put my big fat ass on something moving under my feet."

"Well we could do something else then. Go walking at the beach maybe, or the park."

"Look, everybody ain't trying to lose weight. I'm fine just the way I am. Besides, Boss loves me this way."

It was a rare, fairly civil conversation, one that D'Andra didn't want to have turn into an argument. So she changed the subject. "Why aren't you at the casino?"

"Humph. Them bitches been taking too much of my money," her mother replied, referring to her favorite vice, the nickel and quarter slot machines.

D'Andra laughed. "I thought those were your girls?"

"That's when they're paying me; when they're robbing me, they're bitches."

The fact of the matter was Mary hadn't been feeling well lately. She'd been tired, sluggish. This past week she was in a building where the elevator was out of service. She barely made it up two short flights of steps to her appointment. Her daughter was probably right that a little exercise would be good for her. Maybe she'd join her one day. She affirmed that thought by grabbing another juicy rib soaked in sauce and followed the bite of meat with half a slice of white bread.

"Looks like Cassandra might be close to getting married," Mary said.

"To whom?"

"What do you mean, to whom? Anthony, the ball player."

"What about the rapper?"

"What rapper?"

D'Andra hadn't told her mother about Cassandra's

romp between the sheets in the house they all shared. Obviously Cassandra hadn't either.

"I thought I heard her mention a rapper."

"No, Cassandra's gonna marry that ball player so we can get paid. He took her and the kids to Magic Mountain. Once the man starts entertaining the kids, you're close then."

D'Andra wanted to ask if that were the case with Cassandra's father, if he'd ever taken Cassandra anywhere. If he had, D'Andra didn't remember. But then, she could barely remember her own father, and that may have been best. Instead, she decided to head towards Pacific Theatres where she was meeting Night. It was early, but she could walk around, maybe visit a store nearby. She was too excited to sit still, and didn't want her mother to say anything to spoil her mood.

"See you later, Mama," she said. She came over and gave Mary a quick peck on the cheek.

"Try and keep him if he's a good one," her mother said. "And make sure he has some money!" she added, just before D'Andra closed the door.

Coming to Manhattan Village shopping center early had been a good idea. It was a perfect evening, announcing the coming of March, with a nice breeze that ruffled D'Andra's freshly permed curls. D'Andra made a leisurely stroll down the row of shops, and in just short of an hour she picked up two pairs of earrings, a short, flirty spring dress, a couple of her favorite baby doll tops and a bottle of Vera Wang cologne. Now she headed to Pacific Theatres, where she and Night would be seeing a much-talked-about independent film. It was such a delight to learn that Night liked offbeat movies the same as her. Chanelle used to always say about a subtitled movie, "If they can't say it in English, then I don't need to know."

Night and D'Andra had agreed to meet in front of

the theatre by the ticket counter. D'Andra arrived about
five minutes before their scheduled meeting, and took
the time to make sure she was presentable, as if she
hadn't checked ten times before leaving the house and
once again in the dressing room at Macy's where she'd
done her earlier shopping. It wasn't that she was nervous, not exactly. But try as she might she hadn't been
able to forget about Miss America, the woman with the
perfect body and drop-dead gorgeous face. She knew
she couldn't compete with her; knew it was crazy to
even try. So she'd gone for casual chic in black Capri
pants and a belted jersey top. She felt her slingback sandals flattered her calves and ankles, worth the discomfort brought on by sixty minutes of walking around in
new shoes. Pleased with what she saw when she looked
in the mirror, she pulled out her Raisin Rapture
L'Oreal lipstick, and after applying it added a thin coat
of gloss. She puckered her lips at the mirror and
deemed them just right . . . perfect for Night's lips when
they met hers later on that evening. She couldn't wait
to see him.

Night was running late. It had been a crazy day.
Night's hip-hop artist client came into town unexpectedly and wanted a workout. Then the realtor called
with good news about the property for his gym. The
buyer who'd swooped in after Night had to pull out
had fallen out of escrow. Night had to move fast if he
wanted to secure it, but now, with the ability to offer
a higher down payment than he could have with Jazz,
the bank would work with him. He hadn't thought
twice about putting his name on the dotted line. The
space was as good as his. He couldn't wait to share the
news with D'Andra about being that much closer to
realizing his dream.

Once home, he'd barely had time to shower and shave and hoped his casual attire of jeans and a starched shirt would be okay. Jazz was always critical of his attire if it wasn't perfect. For a moment he hesitated, thinking to change his clothes. Then he remembered it wasn't Jazz he was meeting but D'Andra, who had accepted him for who he was from the first. He couldn't wait to see her.

Just as he was setting his home alarm, the phone rang. Night thought about answering but decided against it. He was late enough as it was. His cell phone started ringing before he got to his car. Probably Mom, he thought, without looking at the caller ID. He figured he'd call her back once he got on his way. There was a spring in his step as he bounced to his car and hurriedly backed down the drive. Before he was able to drive off the block, his phone rang again.

He answered without looking at the caller ID. "Hello?"

"Yes, may I speak to . . . a JaJuan Simmons?"

Night's heartbeat quickened immediately. No one called him JaJuan but his mother. Almost no one outside his immediate family even knew his real name. He'd been called Night by everyone—student and teacher, adult and child, friend and foe, men and women alike, since he was six years old.

"Yes, this is JaJuan Simmons."

"Mr. Simmons, this is Martin Luther King Medical Center calling. You need to get over here right away, sir."

"Martin Luther Ki—" Night's hands turned clammy. "Why, what's going on?"

"It's your mother, sir. There's been an accident."

D'Andra didn't worry, at first. It wasn't unusual to run a little late with L.A. traffic. Plus she knew previews would run for about ten minutes. They still wouldn't miss the movie.

Twenty minutes later and she thought to call him. But she didn't want to appear over-anxious. She figured she would give him ten more minutes and smiled at the thought of watching six feet of fine man walking through the theatre's double glass doors.

Ten minutes passed and still no Night. She called his cell, the only number she had, and got voice mail. She thought about calling the gym and asking for Marc, but that seemed a little overboard. After all, this wasn't business, it was a date. She refused to think anything negative. He'd have a perfectly good explanation when he drove up, which she knew would be any minute now.

Forty-five minutes passed before D'Andra admitted the obvious; Night wasn't coming. She'd called his cell phone again twice with no results. A niggling fear set in. What if something had happened to him, an accident of some kind? She thought about going to his house, but just as quickly dismissed the idea. If he had been in an accident he wouldn't be at his house. After an hour she could no longer hold the doubts at bay. Nor could she erase the image of Miss America, in all her glory, stopping by Night's house and changing his plans. That image melded with the one of Charles, and the horrible incident that had led to their breakup. The pain rushed up unexpected, clouded her mind and lodged in her throat.

She made it to her car without breaking down. Navigated the traffic as if nothing was wrong. But once she reached her house, the blue Toyota parked in front of the black Infiniti rubbed salt in her wounds. She didn't see her mother's Buick, and doubted that the kids were home. D'Andra couldn't help but draw the obvious conclusion: Cassandra had been dropped off by Anthony and immediately called Hollah, the rapper, who was no doubt fucking her brains out in D'Andra's bed.

The insistent bass of an unknown tune was D'Andra's greeting as she opened the door. Otherwise, the house was still; no one else in the downstairs area. As loud as the music was, D'Andra could still hear creaking bedsprings and lovers' moans. She walked into the kitchen, slammed a few cabinet doors, and when the lovers' sonata continued, walked into the living room, turned on the television and blasted CNN.

The amplified drone of Anderson Cooper's "Planet In Peril" had the desired effect. Within minutes the creaking stopped, and then the music. A slamming door alerted D'Andra that she would soon have company.

"What the hell?"

"Oh," D'Andra asked innocently. "Is this too loud?"

"You know good and damn well it is!"

"Not really; didn't know what you could hear over the music and the bedsprings."

"Damn, D'Andra; you could have just knocked. I thought you were out on a date."

"I was . . . where's Mama?"

"Hollah gave her some money to go to the casino."

"I thought you had a date with Anthony."

Cassandra looked anxiously towards the stairs as she stepped toward her sister.

"Girl, don't be mentioning his name like that," she hissed, looking over her shoulder again. "Hollah's my man right now. He's getting ready to sign a record deal with Snoop's label."

"Guess baseballer didn't get up to bat fast enough," D'Andra countered sarcastically.

"At least I've got a man," Cassandra shot back. "Don't be mad at me because of whatever happened tonight that has you back before ten o'clock. And don't try and mess up my shit. I'm trying to get paid and come up. I've got kids."

"Kids? Plural? So you finally told him about the twins?"

"Yes, not that it's any of your business. He took me to drop them off at Jackie's."

D'Andra snorted and Cassandra, in a rare moment of sharing, let her sister peep into her world.

"I've got to get it where I can DeeDee," she said softly, her eyes on the stairs. "You were always smart; you can handle things yourself. I've always known that my looks are my ticket and I'm okay with that. But the truth of the matter is I'm not getting any younger; and I've got three kids. It's either Hollah or Anthony that will help me get where I need to go and yes, may the best man, and the man who gets there the fastest, win. Right now, Hollah's got the paper; that's why he's here."

"If Hollah's got the paper, why aren't you at his house? Or the Marriott, the Hyatt, someplace private?"

"And why aren't you with your man? Mama said you had a date. Don't come in here thumbing your nose at me, big sis. I'm handling my business."

"Yes, in my bed."

"Whatever . . . I'm handling it. And if all goes well I'll be out of here in another month or so."

"With your children?"

Pushing Cassandra's "baby button" was not the button of peace.

"At least I've got kids," she snarled. "What have you got besides a fat ass and a piece of paper that allows you to wipe an old person's behind? Don't get so high and mighty on me, D'Andra. Because the truth of it is you're cleaning up shit and living with your Mama. You ain't all that." Cassandra turned toward the stairs.

"I don't want to hear y'all fucking."

"Why? Will it remind you of what you're missing?"

"Oh, please. There is *nothing* missing from my life!"

"Yeah; keep telling yourself that, sister. Maybe one day you'll believe it."

Moments after Cassandra stomped up the stairs she came back down with a carry-on bag, Hollah by her side.

"Yo, D'Andra," he drawled, nodding his head knowingly.

What did he think he knew? D'Andra thought. She dared not ponder the answer. It was no telling what Cassandra told him to get him to spring for a hotel room.

"Hey," she said simply, not wanting to be rude.

As she watched them walk out the door, she wondered about Cassandra's friend, Hollah, and his real name. She pondered men with nicknames, why and how they stuck. Looking back it seemed interesting and a tad odd that she'd only recently learned Night's full name. Her first thought was that he was being secretive, but she knew that reasoning was simply paranoia. Maybe she didn't know more about him because she hadn't asked. Belatedly she realized that aside from his cell phone, home address and love of all things fitness, she knew very little about the man who'd stood her up, and even now had her panties in a bunch.

The silence in the now empty house was deafening. Too late D'Andra realized that next to it, she preferred the bedsprings. She wished more than ever for a friend in that moment. The thought of calling Elaine was quickly doused. Saturday night was date night for Max and her, when the kids stayed with one of their parents' siblings. D'Andra didn't feel her situation enough of an emergency to interrupt their private time. Without thought, she went back to her old standby of comfort: food. She walked to the freezer and pulled out the quart container of Ben & Jerry's chocolate chip cookie

dough that hadn't been touched since she started
working out. Bypassing a bowl, she took a large spoon
from the drawer and walked into the living room. Just
as she was getting ready to take her first bite, the phone
rang.

Finally, she thought, already forgiving Night for whatever held him up. She didn't even look at the caller ID
as she answered.

"Well, it's about time you called. Your excuse better
be a good one and even then, you're going to owe me
big time!"

There was a slight pause, and a throat-clearing
sound.

"Night?"

"Dee, it's me, Connie."

Connie? Dee hadn't talked to her childhood best
friend in months, since about the same time she
stopped talking to Chanelle and Connie kept trying
to mediate a truce. But this was her girl, and she
sensed trouble.

"Hey, Connie. What's wrong?"

"It's Dominque," Connie replied between sniffles.
"She's gone, Dee."

"Gone? What do you mean gone?"

"She's gone, dead. They found her body in Griffith
Park. Nelly said it was all over the news last night."

The ice cream forgotten and melting, D'Andra
reached for the remote. "Oh my God! What happened?" she asked, reaching a news station and hit-
ting the mute button. Nothing stayed news for more
than twenty-four hours in L.A., but D'Andra kept the
TV on just in case.

"What happened?" she repeated, tears in her voice.

Connie relayed the short version: that their friend's
partially clothed body was found near a bike trail. An
initial autopsy revealed a possible drug overdose and

while there were no physical signs of trauma, foul play was suspected.

"You need to call Nelly," Connie concluded.

"Why?" D'Andra barked, anger quickly joining the mix of anguish and tears.

Connie sighed. "She's taking it pretty hard for one thing. And you two need to talk for another. Dominque is gone, Dee. We can't get time back. Life's too short to end a friendship on a misunderstanding."

"There is no—"

"I'm not going to argue with you," Connie interrupted. "I love you both and I've heard both sides of the story. I just think that you should too, and that's all I'm going to say about it."

Silence filled the air.

"I'll call Miss Ann," D'Andra said finally. She knew Dominque's mother would be beside herself right about now.

"Yeah, Nelly said she had to be sedated. I tried to reach her a little bit ago. No one answered. But keep trying, okay? I'll let you know when I'm flying in, which will be as soon as the funeral arrangements are made."

They said their good-byes and hung up the phone. D'Andra missed Night immensely. She dialed his number again, and once again, got voicemail. Life was too short for many things. Like playing games with grown ass men. It didn't matter why Night stood her up. The fact of the matter was, he did. And unlike with Charles, she wasn't going to wait around for a sorry explanation. She jerked her phone off the couch, scrolled down to Night's number, and pressed *delete.*

15

"You've got to call him again, D'Andra; go over to his house tomorrow. From what you've told me, he doesn't sound like a man who would stand you up without so much as a phone call for no good reason."

"It's been two days, Elaine. Unless he's dead, in a coma or had an accident where his fingers are broken and he can't dial a cell, there's no reason he couldn't have called me by now."

Elaine had to admit, it didn't look good. D'Andra had so looked forward to Saturday's date with Night, and to see her friend's face when she walked into the hospital had told her immediately things hadn't gone well. But why would he not show and not call? D'Andra wasn't just a friend, she was his client. It didn't make sense.

"Just cover all your bases before you jump to conclusions," Elaine suggested. "Go to his house, stop by the gym. Maybe somebody there will have seen him and you'll at least know he's alive."

D'Andra rolled her eyes. "Oh, please, he's alive. He just woke up and realized it wasn't me he wanted."

She didn't want to believe that; not after the camaraderie they'd experienced, the kisses they'd shared.

But what else could it be? And try as she might, the image of running into Miss America kept teasing the edges of her mind. Was the woman just a client, or more? She definitely looked more Night's type, and she definitely had serious attitude upon seeing D'Andra. Was there something going on there? And then there was what Connie had said, about life and misunderstandings. Connie was right. And so was Elaine: she needed to talk to her friend Chanelle, and she needed to find out about Night.

D'Andra headed straight to Night's house as soon as work was over. She knew it was early but after making the decision to try and track Night down, the need to sleep had, for the moment, disappeared. Still, she stifled a yawn as she turned the corner. Right away she noticed that his silver Nissan Z350 was in the driveway but his GMC truck was gone. D'Andra didn't know how to feel about that. Had he left early, or been out all night?

She pulled up to the curb in front of his house and turned off the engine. Reaching for her cell phone, she dialed his number again. His message box was full. Even though she knew he wasn't home, she got out anyway, walked to the front door and rang the bell. She tried to peek inside the window and found that just as Night had assured her as she lay sprawled half-naked on his couch, you couldn't see in from the outside. She heaved a sigh, part relief, part frustration. She didn't know whether what had happened to him was an accident or another woman, but something was definitely going on.

She was almost to her house when she thought about Marc. It was only eight-thirty but she hoped he was at the gym. If not him, perhaps Mitzy or one of the other regulars she'd noticed since coming there would have seen him. She had just gotten out of the car when her phone rang. Thinking it was Night, she couldn't pull her phone out fast enough, not even stopping to check the ID.

"Hello?"

"Girl, where you at; and what's wrong with you? You sound out of breath."

"Oh, hey Mama. I'm all right; I had to dig the phone out of the bottom of my purse, and didn't think I'd answer in time."

"Well, I was just checking on you; you're usually home by now."

D'Andra smiled. She knew in her heart that her mother loved her, cared for her, but Mary didn't show her emotions much. "I'm almost there; had some errands to run."

"At this time of the morning? Oh well, do me a favor and bring a gallon of milk home."

"Okay."

"And none of that two percent junk!"

D'Andra hung up the phone without answering, so that when she brought in the jug of two percent milk she could act as if she hadn't heard the warning. Her mother could clog up her arteries if she wanted to; but D'Andra wasn't going to pay for it.

"You're here early."

D'Andra turned around to see the object of her search coming in the door behind her. "Hey, Marc."

"I see you've got the bug; once you start working out, you can't get enough, can you?"

"It does feel good," D'Andra admitted. "But actually, I'm here because I was hoping to run into you. I'm looking for Night. Have you seen him?"

Marc frowned slightly, shaking his head. "No, I haven't."

"I'm not trying to get in his business," D'Andra said, trying to keep her tone light. "But we were sup-

posed to get together Saturday night and he didn't
show or call. His voice mail is full and I haven't heard
from him."

Marc's frown deepened. "Hum; he didn't return
my call either and didn't show to play basketball like
we do most Sundays. Did you try him at home?"

"I don't have that number, but I went by there. His
car is parked but his truck is gone."

Marc tried not to let his worry show. "He'll turn up;
he might be over to his mother's. Sometimes he helps
her out around the house. I'll try and reach him over
there later, and will tell him to call you."

"I appreciate that, Marc." As an afterthought she
gave him her cell number. "Just in case you hear anything," she said before leaving the gym.

D'Andra slept fitfully, and finally gave up the pre-
tense a little after two o'clock. Her first thoughts were
of Night, and within minutes of awakening, she reached
for her phone. There was a message! *Finally*, she
thought as she punched one to activate her voice mail.

"Hey, Dee, it's me . . . Nelly. I know you're shocked
to hear from me but please call me back. I know I . . .
there's something I want to . . . just call me, okay? Bye."

Chanelle—ever since her conversation with Connie,
D'Andra had expected the call. One of the Fabulous
Four was dead. That should have been enough for
D'Andra to want to talk to Chanelle. But time hadn't
totally healed the wound of the way their friendship ended and D'Andra wasn't sure if even death
could bridge the acrimonious gap now between them.
D'Andra admitted the lack of communication was
strictly on her; she'd refused Chanelle's calls repeatedly
and was both grateful and saddened when they stopped
coming. Now was her chance to reconnect with the
friend who, until now, she'd refused to admit she
missed so much. And in honor of Dominque's memory,

she'd call her. As soon as she solved the mystery of what happened to Night.

Chanelle's was the only message. Despite her promise to the contrary, she dialed Night's number again. His message box was still full. After a quick shower, D'Andra dressed and knocked on her mother's bedroom door.

"Mama, you want some lunch?"

"What are you fixing?"

D'Andra opened the door before answering. "Baked fish and rice, with a salad."

"No, that doesn't sound good. Anymore of that nacho dip in there? I'll take that with some Doritos."

"You're going to have to get up and fix that artery-clogging meal on your own," D'Andra countered with renewed resolve to not help her mother kill herself. She turned to leave.

"What did you say to Cassandra?" Mary asked.

"When?"

"Over the weekend, I guess. You haven't noticed the kids are gone?"

"I just figured they were over to Jackie's."

"They are, but that's not the point. I'm wondering why she's been gone for two days."

D'Andra sighed. "You'll have to ask her, Mama." And then, noticing the worry lines on her mother's face, she added, "She's a big girl, Mama. She's probably over at her boyfriend's house."

That brought a smile. "Ooh, Lord, I hope so. If she can get Anthony to put a ring on her finger, we'll all be better off."

D'Andra refrained from suggesting it was probably Hollah, and not Anthony, who'd be putting whatever on her sister; probably some good loving right now, judging by how long she'd been gone.

"What happened with that dude you met Saturday night? You didn't say anything."

The last thing D'Andra wanted was Mary Smalls' trying to shove her down the wedding aisle. Plus she didn't want to hear the sarcasm that would surely follow her revelation that she'd been stood up.

"It was all right," she said, deciding on a noncommittal answer. "We're just friends."

"You're not getting any younger, girl; better try and get a baby out of someone with some money. That'll take care of you for eighteen years at least."

D'Andra had no words to respond. Instead she simply closed the door and headed for the kitchen.

A couple hours later, D'Andra began to worry in earnest. She'd gone by Night's for their four o'clock workout and the place looked the same as it had that morning. Then she called Bally's and while Marc had left for the day, Mitzy said that as far as she knew, Night hadn't been in. D'Andra knew she should probably go to the gym and work out there since Night wasn't around; but she was too keyed up to exercise. Instead, she decided to use the time and go to Santa Monica. Night had suggested a natural superfood supplement to replace the diet drink he said was filled with additives, preservatives and other ingredients that were actually doing D'Andra more harm than good. He said the product was a mix of Chinese herbs, fruits and vegetables, a total of seventy-one ingredients. D'Andra couldn't imagine anything with that many ingredients, and green, tasting good, but she decided to give it a try. Seeing the results on both his and her body caused her to pretty much consider his word as gospel when it came to health.

She turned up the volume and let The Wave's contemporary jazz wash her troublesome thoughts away. After David Benoit covered Michael Jackson's "Human

Nature" and Wayman Tisdale "threw it down," the duo of Bryan Legend and Corinne Bailey borrowed a question from Roberta Flack and asked where was the love. That brought the thoughts she'd momentarily pushed aside back to the forefront. Where was the love? And where was Night?

D'Andra was surprised and grateful to get a parking space right in front of Dragon Herbs, the store with the supplement Night had suggested. Within minutes she was in and out, although she vowed to come back, maybe with Elaine, and take a lazy look at all the supplements, herbs, lotions, tonics and potions within the store's small and exotically decorated walls. She glanced to her right, aware that she was less than two blocks from the beach. For a moment she entertained a quick stroll down the path; water always seemed to soothe her and Lord knows her soul was troubled. But the beach would undoubtedly bring to the fore her last memories there, with Night and the kids. She decided against it and walked to her car instead.

That's when she saw her, less than ten feet away, walking a dog. She acted before she had time to think; otherwise, she never would have done it.

"Aren't you one of Night's clients?" she asked boldly, stepping in the woman's path as she awaited an answer.

Jazz tossed her hair to the side as she cocked her head. She knew what love struck looked like, and it was staring at her. It didn't surprise her and was part of why she'd never be totally comfortable with Night's decidedly female clientele. But she'd endure it because the man was worth it and she'd make damn sure that they all knew he was not available; and she figured she'd start with the cow in front of her.

"Client?" she asked with a laugh. "I am much more than his client."

D'Andra managed to absorb the punch without

flinching. But inside, her heart dropped. "Have you seen him?"

When Jazz simply stared at her, D'Andra continued. "I've been worried about him. He missed our appointment today and Marc hasn't seen him at the gym. I'm just wondering if he's okay."

Jazz kept her cool as she digested this news. She'd blown his phone up all weekend, filling up his voice mail. But that Marc hadn't seen him was a red flag. Still, she wasn't going to pass up this opportunity to shore up her boundaries where Night was concerned. . "I can assure you, Night's fine. He's been, uh, busy, if you know what I mean; sometimes he's simply insatiable! Your appointment probably slipped his mind. But what's your name? I'll pass along a message to call you."

Without another word, D'Andra turned and walked to her car. She managed to put in the keys, start the engine and pull away before the dam burst. Her worse fear had been realized; Night had stood her up for another woman, and from what it looked like, had been in this woman's arms all weekend.

What was it about her that made men betray her; throw her away like a paper bag? She'd wanted to believe Night was different; that he meant those things he said to her. She'd been thrilled to know he loved her big curves, and that he was determined to help her be her best self. But it had all been an illusion. Why? What did he have to gain from hurting her? She hadn't asked him into her life; he'd offered his help and almost begged for their relationship to go to another level. He'd invited her out to the movies. Why would he do all that with someone like . . . D'Andra realized she didn't even know the woman's name. It didn't matter. Night knew it, and what's more, Night knew they had a date Saturday night but it looked like he passed up her supersized company for a french fry snack. She was just revving up for an ugly cry when her cell phone rang.

"D'Andra . . . it's Nelly."

"Hey, Chanelle."

A gut-wrenching sob sprang up from D'Andra's soul before she could censor it. The sound of Chanelle's voice confirmed just how much she'd missed her best friend, the first one she would have called six months ago, the one she spoke to almost every day for twenty years . . . before catching her with Charles. But hearing her voice, thinking about Dominque, running into Night's woman, it was all too much. Sobs were the only conversation for several minutes.

"I know . . . it's crazy, Dee," Chanelle said, believing D'Andra's tears were for their lost friend. "I just saw her last month. She was over at Miss Ann's and they called me to come over. We had a good time; talking, laughing, reminiscing about old times. She was still too skinny but other than that she looked good!"

D'Andra hadn't seen Dominque for over a year, when D'Andra was seeing Charles and Dominque started dating Papa Stone, a notorious ex-gang member and known drug dealer. Everybody had tried to get her to leave him, especially after he'd supplied her with an endless supply of drugs washed down with the finest champagnes. She'd justified using them because even though they were being sold illegally, they were legal drugs: Vicodin, OxyContin and other painkillers. Dominque would alter these with amphetamines, which she'd use to wake up after a night of partying. Her once placid demeanor turned erratic and after her family and friends, including Chanelle and D'Andra, staged an intervention, Dominque had broken off contact.

"Where's her boyfriend?"

"He's MIA; the police are looking for him now.

They found her body down by Griffith Park, Dee. She'd been dead at least a week. But there were no scars or signs of struggle; that's why they don't know whether or not it was accidental."

"Nobody should die like that."

"Miss Ann keeps blaming herself. Connie's flying in on Friday. The wake is on Monday and the funeral Tuesday. Miss Ann wants us to help with the program and stuff. She said she doesn't know if she can, you know, pick out the clothes and—"

"I'll be there," D'Andra said. Whatever was needed, she'd give whatever she could. Connie and Dominque rounded out the Fabulous Four who'd won the contest back in fourth grade. They'd all admired Connie when she decided to move across the country to attend Howard University. They were even more impressed when several years after graduating she married her college sweetheart, now an attorney, and had twins, a boy and a girl. The last time they'd seen her was two years ago, when Chanelle and D'Andra had flown to DC to help celebrate Connie's husband's thirtieth birthday. That had happened not long after the intervention; Dominque had been the missing piece to the picture-perfect weekend.

Chanelle's voice broke. "Thank you, Dee. It will be so good to see you, I've got so much I want to say."

"This is about Dominque, Nelly, nothing else."

"This is about friends, D'Andra; and how quickly they can be taken away . . . forever."

"Where are we meeting on Friday?"

"Over at Miss Ann's."

Dominque's mother still lived where her daughter had grown up. Re-entering that house would be like stepping back twenty years. But at one time Miss Ann had almost been like a second mother. She'd do it for her, and for Dominque. "See you then."

16

"You need to go home, Night. Get some proper sleep. I'll watch over your mama." Robert added bass to his voice in an attempt at sounding stern.

Night shook his head. "Can't. Not until she opens her eyes."

His uncle placed a hand on Night's shoulder, nodding understanding. The jaws of life couldn't have pried him away from Jewel's side after her heart attack last year. Even after the beats had stopped and the line had gone smooth on the EKG machine, he'd refused to believe she was gone. Even after all the tubes were removed and her skin began to cool, he still stayed there just in case. Just in case by some miracle she opened her eyes. But she hadn't, and the agony of seeing her sister, Night's mother, lying in the same hospital was almost too much to bear, brought back images too painful to remember. But this was his favorite nephew and he wasn't going anywhere. He owed the boy that, and his mother that much more.

"Go on home, son." Now it was Carter Johnson's turn to try and convince Night to get some much needed rest. "You don't want to end up in a bed next to your mother, do you?"

Night looked at his stepfather and managed a smile. This man had been a stalwart of strength since coming into Night and his mother's life when Night was fourteen years old. He'd gladly given the man-of-the-house reins to Carter when he entered the picture, but right now, Night felt that he was the man his mother needed most. And he wasn't leaving her side.

"When she opens her eyes," he said softly. He then grasped the hand of the woman he loved more than life itself and continued the one-way conversation he'd been having for seven straight days.

17

"Hey there woman; since when don't you return phone calls?" There was more sass than bite to Elaine's words, as she gave D'Andra a sisterly hug.

"I meant to call you back yesterday, but when I thought to do it I knew you'd be sleeping. Thanks for the flowers, though. Even though it said Heavenly Haven, I know that was your doing. It was thoughtful and I appreciate it."

"That's what friends are for."

D'Andra couldn't help but think about the emphasis being placed on friendship these days. It had been healing for her to spend time with Connie and Chanelle. They made an unspoken pact to let bygones be bygones for the time they were together and for the brief days surrounding Dominque's funeral; it almost felt like old times. D'Andra knew Chanelle still wanted to talk about what happened, but D'Andra wasn't sure she wanted to hear the details. Still, she agreed to call her when her life calmed down. They'd left it at that, past the stalemate but not yet on the road to renewed friendship.

D'Andra ran these facts down quickly to Elaine before asking what she'd missed during her days off.

"Oh, this is a good one. The office is all abuzz about this guy who came in to check out our rehab unit. Half the women who saw him are already in love with him and the other half wished they'd seen him."

Still hurting from Night's disappearing act, the last thing D'Andra wanted to talk about was men. This obviously wasn't Elaine's problem.

"I must say he's extremely good-looking," Elaine went on. "He was just leaving as I came on for a double shift around three. Tall, dark and handsome almost doesn't do justice to a looker like him. I think his name is JaJuan."

D'Andra snapped to attention. "What'd you say?"

"JaJuan," Elaine said nonchalantly, then noticed D'Andra's changed demeanor.

"Do you know him?"

"Night's real name is JaJuan," D'Andra answered, sitting up straight. She couldn't imagine that fate would play such a cruel trick as having another JaJuan come into her life at this moment. "I wonder why he'd be looking at our rehabilitation facility." The equipment? No, D'Andra reasoned, that couldn't be it.

"His mother was in an accident and just came out of her coma yesterday. She was extremely fortunate; no internal injuries and hopefully no sustained brain damage. Looks like her biggest problem is a busted right leg. That's what he was checking out our rehab center for . . . they want to begin her treatment as soon as it has healed."

D'Andra digested Elaine's words in silence. So this is where Night had been and probably what he'd said when he'd finally left a message while D'Andra was at Dominque's funeral. She'd been so angry, she'd erased the message without listening to it. When would she learn not to assume? Everybody knew what they said about that word, that it normally made an ass out of "u" and "me." She hoped she wasn't too late to salvage yet another friendship, maybe the most important one of all.

"I have to go," she said, rising from the table at the back of the cafeteria where she and Elaine had sat for privacy. "I need to make a phone call."

Ten minutes later, D'Andra was back on her ward making the rounds. It hadn't surprised her that she'd gotten voice mail at three o'clock in the morning. But she'd done what she needed to do. Now all she could do was wait.

18

The blinding sunlight told Night it was late in the day. He rolled over lazily, stretched long and hard. It was the first full night in his bed for more than a week; his extended stay on a hospital cot with bird baths for cleaning had been harder on him than he realized.

Night thought of the moment and broke into a huge smile; the moment his mother, Val Johnson, had opened her eyes. It was just after one o'clock in the morning two days ago. He was by her side as he'd been for most of the time since her arrival. Not able to keep his eyes open for one minute longer, he'd laid his head on the side of her bed, his hand holding hers.

"JaJuan?"

At first he thought he'd fallen asleep and was dreaming. And then it came again.

"JaJuan, what are you doing in my room?"

Those were the first words his mother spoke since surviving a terrible car accident with a broken arm, a busted up leg and being in a comatose state for almost a week.

The room became a beehive of activity after that. Doctors were called, nurses came in, check after check was conducted to properly assess her state of mind and well-being. It was almost three o'clock before Night was finally convinced that his mother would live, that she was going to be fine. She'd need extensive rehabilitation for the leg, but no major organs had been injured and there was no permanent brain damage. Night wasn't known for being a man of prayer, but he sent a thousand thanks to God that morning.

The second set of thoughts after those about his mother was of D'Andra. His calls to her had gone unanswered. He could only imagine what she'd assumed when he was a no show for their date. He belatedly realized he should have called the night of the accident but forced himself not to worry, however. *As soon as she knows the truth*, he thought, *we'll be back on track*.

A few moments after stepping out of the shower, a smile was back on his face. He'd checked his messages after he got dressed and was thrilled to hear D'Andra's voice. He couldn't dial back fast enough. Just as the phone rang on the other line, so did his doorbell.

He flipped the phone shut and walked down the hall. His stepfather had been worrying about him and Frank, the photographer, about as close to a second father as anyone could ask for, had also left a message threatening bodily harm if he didn't get a return phone call before the sun went down. It didn't surprise him that the old man had chosen instead to do a drive by.

"Some people just can't . . . D'Andra!" Night hadn't looked through his peephole and was totally taken off guard. "I was expecting someone else."

D'Andra's heart sank. "Oh." She turned to leave.

"No, it's not what you're thinking." Night's firm grasp on her arm stopped D'Andra's retreat. "I was expecting Frank, or my stepfather, Carter. I'm so glad it's you."

His chocolate orbs bore deeply into D'Andra's

hazel ones, melting her in an instant. "I heard about your mother," she whispered. "I'm sorry."

The sincerity of her compassion went straight to Night's heart. "Come inside," he said softly.

As soon as he closed the door, they were in each other's arms. In a moment they realized how much they needed each other, had missed each other. D'Andra basked in the feeling of Night's arms around her. She felt protected and safe, like she could finally take off the mask of strength she'd worn for her family and friends the past week. She didn't even realize she was crying until Night wiped her tears.

"There, doll, it's okay." Night hugged her closer to him, relishing her softness and warmth. Where before he'd felt discomfited, he now felt anchored, as if his topsy-turvy world had suddenly righted itself. He pulled away just enough to see D'Andra's eyes. He could get lost in those eyes. His eyes moved to her lips, soft and inviting, pulling him like a magnet. He licked his own soft, plush lips before lowering his head to meet hers.

At first their kiss was soft and tentative. But when D'Andra reached up and wrapped her arms around Night's neck, it unleashed a hunger he didn't know he possessed. He probed her lips with his tongue and when she opened her mouth, plunged in with fervor. Their tongues dueled and danced as he crushed her breasts against his chest, massaging her back and generous backside.

"I need you," he said simply.

He took her hand and led her down the hall to his bedroom. No words were spoken as he turned to her and pulled off her baby doll top. He reached his hands inside the band of her pants and pulled downward, taking a moment to kiss D'Andra's thighs and stomach as he knelt. While he handled her pants, D'Andra undid her sports bra and let it join the pile of clothes

beside her. She stood in her "Vintage Flirt" hipster
panties and watched Night strip from his T-shirt and
pants. He wore no underwear and his engorged manhood sprang forth with the power of a python, and a
head just as large. She instinctively covered her breasts
but in that moment Night stepped forward and removed her hands, replacing them with his tongue, his
lips. He suckled first one nipple and then the other
before burying his head in her weighty mounds.
D'Andra gasped at the power she felt in that moment.

"I need you," Night repeated softly.

"Yes," was D'Andra's breathy reply.

Night guided D'Andra to the bed and laid her down,
before going to his drawer for protection.

"Let me," D'Andra said. She took the packet from
Night's hand and while lovingly massaging his massive
manhood took the steps to ensure both their safety.

Night joined D'Andra on the bed. Their foreplay
was slow and deliberate, each committing the other's
body to memory. Night feasted on D'Andra's plump
lips before continuing an oral journey down the
length of her body. After he'd paid full attention to
each and every part, he lapped the nectar from her
personal paradise as if it were his life's force. D'Andra
cried out in ecstasy as she gave way to wave after wave
of blissful release. She wanted to return the favor and
worship at Night's sexual shrine, but he had other
plans. He hovered over her for only an instant,
staring deeply into her eyes, before plunging to the
hilt, backing out and plunging again. They set up the
timeless rhythm of love, at first slow and methodic
and then rapid and intense. When they simultaneously met at the apex of ecstasy, the shouts were of joy
and triumph . . . and of feeling complete and whole.

A few hours later, D'Andra woke with a start. She
was disoriented and it took a moment of clearing

her head to remember where she was and what had happened. Then she shifted ever so slightly and came up against the hardness of Night Simmons. The smile on her face was instant and sincere. She had never been happier in her life. While hers had not been a promiscuous life by any means, she'd had her share of lovers. Without a doubt, none could compare to what she'd just experienced. Her body throbbed from the memory alone.

Night stirred beside her and opened his eyes. The peaceful countenance was soon replaced by anxiety.

"Oh no, what time is it?" he said, tossing back the sheet that covered them both and reaching for his cell phone. "Mom is probably wondering where I am."

D'Andra scooted up behind him. She massaged his neck and shoulders, then pressed her breasts against his back. "I'm sure she's fine," she cooed, giving him the same comfort he'd offered her earlier.

And she was. The phone in her room was continuously busy, but Night was able to reach a nurse who informed him that his mother had slept throughout much of the day and was entertaining guests at the very moment he called. Night knew those guests were probably Carter and Frank, and belatedly realized his mother's line had probably been busy because of her constantly calling and caring church friends.

His concerns quieted, he rested back against the pillow, pulling D'Andra with him. She nestled her head on his shoulders and swept her hand back and forth across the six-pack she'd admired from the first time they met. They lay in companionable silence for a moment and then Night asked an unexpected question:

"Do you want to meet my mother?"

19

In the thirty minutes it took Night to drive to MLK Hospital, he told D'Andra about his life with Val Johnson. How she and his father, John Simmons, had been an unbeatable team until he was killed in a freak on-the-job accident when Night was twelve. His mother had been compensated and with it bought the house where Night spent his teenage years and where Val still lived. D'Andra learned of the extremely close bond between mother and son, one that remained even after Val remarried a wonderfully kind man named Carter Johnson, when Night was fourteen. They'd been married for twenty-one years.

"You know, I've thought about you meeting my mother before," Night admitted.

"Oh, really?" D'Andra answered, pleased that she'd been on his mind. "What brought that thought on?"

"I can't remember," Night lied.

In reality it was the difference in D'Andra's kind demeanor compared to his ex-girlfriend, Jazz. Val was always kind to Jazz, while Jazz merely tolerated his mother. Theirs seemed to be a forced relationship. Things would undoubtedly be different with the woman at his side.

The nurses greeted Night with wide smiles and shy glances. They looked quizzically at D'Andra and one of them, a cute, light-skinned sistah with natural short twists, actually rolled her eyes. Night simply placed his arm around D'Andra's shoulders and proceeded to his mother's room.

"I brought you a surprise," he began. And then, "what are you doing here?"

Jazz covered her surprise with a smile. She was expecting, even anticipating, Night's arrival but hadn't expected him to bring the Pillsbury Dough Girl along with him. Her brow furrowed a bit as she wondered why he'd bring a client, but she quickly dismissed any discomfort with a toss of her long, straight hair and wide open arms as she rose from the chair.

"Night!"

She may as well have been hugging a tree for the response she got. Night stood stock still, his eyes pleading understanding as they gazed at D'Andra. For D'Andra's part, she didn't know what to think. They'd just made mind-boggling love for hours, only to run into his so-called ex in his mother's hospital room? All of the old insecurities rushed to the forefront. She took comfort in doing what came naturally.

"My name is D'Andra," she said, as she approached Night's mother. "You must be the famous Miss Val I've heard so much about."

D'Andra leaned over and hugged Val gingerly.

"Nice to meet you," Val replied. Her next words were replaced by a grimace.

"Are you alright?" D'Andra asked, instantly going into nurse mode. Without thinking she felt Val's head and reached for her wrist, taking her pulse in seconds. "Where's the pain?" She continued running a topical check on Night's mother without a thought that this wasn't her job nor the hospital in which she worked. "Your heartbeat's steady, and I don't detect a fever. Should we ring for the doctor?"

"No, baby, I'm fine." Val's eyes were lit with admiration as she eyed Night's new friend. "Just a little pain when I moved my leg."

"Sorry about that," D'Andra said once she realized she may have overstepped bounds. "I'm a nurse and old habits die hard I guess."

"And a very good one I suspect," Val answered. She turned to Jazz who was still clinging to the oak tree otherwise known as JaJuan "Night" Simmons.

"Thank you for coming, Jazz. And thanks for the flowers. Now I've kept you away from your busy schedule long enough. Give my best to your family." It was an obvious dismissal.

"Uh, sure, Val," Jazz replied. She walked up and offered a weak hug to Val's left side while resisting the urge to prove that she too could stroke a forehead and take a pulse. She turned to D'Andra with an outstretched hand.

"I'm Night's friend, Jazz."

"She's my ex-girlfriend," Night interjected, coming to D'Andra's side. "It was nice of you to check on my mom," he said, reiterating his mother's walking papers even as he wondered how Jazz knew about the accident. *Marc.* Of course. When Night didn't return Jazz's calls she probably went by the gym. He'd have to tell his friend in no uncertain terms that he was no longer to share any information on his life, personal or professional, with one Jazz Anderson.

"Again we meet," D'Andra said evenly.

Jazz wasn't sure how to respond to D'Andra's comment. Night hadn't taken her calls since before she'd spoken with D'Andra by the pier. The uncertainty made her all the more determined to get back into Night's life. She'd do whatever it took, including playing the money card.

"Can I speak to you privately?" she asked Night.

"Not now," he said. He walked over to his mother's bed and gave her a light hug. D'Andra walked over to his side. The family picture made Jazz want to puke.

"Make it soon," she said, barely keeping the venom from her voice. "It's about the financing for your baby, the gym."

Before Night could respond, she was gone.

Jazz didn't wait until she got to her car. As soon as she turned the corner from Val Johnson's room, she pulled out her cell phone and began to dial. Brad picked up on the second ring.

"Hey, beautiful. I've been meaning to call you. Escrow will be done in thirty days. I'm sure you'll be ready to celebrate—"

"Never mind that," Jazz interrupted. "Can you stop the sale from going through?"

"What?"

"You heard me. I don't want Night to get the building!"

"Why, what's going on?"

"Look, Night and I broke up a few months ago and our business partnership is dissolved."

Jazz changed her voice from demanding to demure. "You're my friend, Brad, and it's probably not professional to tell you this. But I—I caught Night with another woman." Jazz drummed up genuine tears as she embraced her lie. "It made me question whether he was with me for me, or because of my connections . . . to amazing people like you."

"I'm not sure, Jazz," Brad continued in a halting voice. He liked Jazz, had even desired to date her, but he'd worked hard on this sale and while he was wealthy and didn't need the commission, it was going to be a nice one. He was torn.

The sound of Jazz's heels tapping across the concrete pavement filled the otherwise silent moment. Finally Brad spoke.

"Give me a couple days. I'll see what I can do."

"Brad, you're the best," Jazz purred. "I'm going to have to think of a really special way to thank you."

There was a definite bounce to Jazz's walk as she reached her convertible, and her scowl had been replaced by a satisfied smile. She'd give anything to be a fly on the wall when Night found out his dream location had fallen out of escrow. She refused to feel guilty. It was his fault, not hers. He was the one who'd chosen a super-sized hamburger when he could have had Chateaubriand. She hoped Night's dumpy new girlfriend could comfort him when he found out he'd lost everything. Jazz's eyes narrowed as she pondered her truth: if he'd stayed with her he could have had it all.

20

Night was all smiles. His mother had gotten progressively better in the weeks since regaining consciousness. He and D'Andra were officially a couple, following his mother's accident, their missed date and her run-in with Jazz. He'd been right. His mother adored D'Andra and it seemed the feeling was mutual. D'Andra had visited Val a few times alone and told his mother not to make a fuss to her son about it. Of course she did.

"That's just the sweetest soul," she'd said when Night came to visit one day after D'Andra had left. "She brought me those books over there and gave me this special pillow for my neck. Very thoughtful."

That gesture had expanded D'Andra's place in Night's heart and her kindness, combined with her diet and Night's workout that was reshaping her body and the spell she cast on him when they made love—which had been almost every night since the first time—Night had fallen, and he had fallen hard.

"What are you smiling about?" D'Andra asked.

"You," was Night's simple reply.

"Yeah, I'm happy too," she responded.

They were both momentarily silenced by their own

thoughts of gratitude as they took in the beautiful March day and the sounds of smooth jazz coming from the stereo.

"Where are we going?" D'Andra asked after the beautifully played *Europa* by Gato Barbieri had ended.

"To see our future," Night replied. "Matter of fact . . ."

He reached for the phone. "I probably should have called Brad sooner. We made these plans a week ago, to pick up the keys to the gym."

"Figured out what you're going to call it yet?"

"I'm leaning towards *Night Moves,* because of the party-like atmosphere I'm going to create during the late night hours. But then again, I also like *Jewel's Gym* and even Frank's suggestion, *Night Works.* "

"I'm surprised he didn't come up with something with doll in it."

"Oh, you know he did and yes, *Dollhouse* was one of them."

D'Andra groaned. "See what happens when you listen to Bob Berry?"

It was Night's turn to moan. "*Chuck* Berry, doll, and please don't make that mistake around Frank. He'd consider it sacrilegious. Hey Brad, Night."

"Oh, hey Night."

"Just double-checking to make sure you're in the office. I'm checking out the space today and am coming to get the key."

Brad cringed at the sound of excitement in his client's voice. He was still battling with Jazz's request to stall the close, if not pull the sale altogether. Night was a good man. It was hard to believe what Jazz had said about him. But Jazz was a friend, and so deliciously sexy . . .

"Uh, yeah, Night. I guess you can, sure, come on by."

"Everything's still cool, right?" Night asked, sensing his realtor's discomfort. "I mean we are still set to close next month."

Brad cleared his suddenly clogged throat. He'd never been a good liar. "I'm, uh, running into a couple snags but, uh, don't worry. Come on and pick up the key."

"Snags? What kind of snags? I need to know right now exactly what's going on. I've hired contractors to start renovations next month and ordered equipment that will be delivered in May. I'm in the process of interviewing trainers. If there is anything that's going to throw me off from my opening on the fifth of July . . . you need to let me know now."

Brad loosened his tie and wiped a bead of sweat from his brow. "Actually, Night, I wasn't quite sure where things stood, since you and Jazz are no longer business partners—"

"Jazz? What's she got to do with anything? Her name isn't on the papers, my company's is." Night's sunny day was turning gloomier by the minute. It was obvious Jazz was up to her old, manipulative tricks. "What exactly has Jazz said to you?" Night asked bluntly.

"She just, uh, said you two were no longer partners."

"And why would you think that changed anything regarding my buying the property?"

Brad was in a hole without a shovel and he didn't like it. He didn't want to screw Night until he was sure of his facts. "Look buddy, I'm sorry I mentioned it. When will you be at the office?"

"I'm about ten minutes away."

D'Andra was all too aware of Night's drastic change in mood. She wanted to comfort him, but how? Remaining silent seemed the best choice. She simply placed her hand softly on Night's thigh.

He covered it with his own. After another moment, he sighed, brought D'Andra's hand to his lips and kissed it.

"It's hard to believe that at one time I thought Jazz was *the one,*" Night said.

"She's a very pretty girl."

"Yes, and on her good days she's funny, thoughtful and really smart. But on the other days she's self-centered, mean and manipulative. There started to be too many of those other days. That's why we broke up. That and the fact she didn't really like my mama."

"Ooh, no way Night. How could anybody dislike Miss Val?"

"Somebody who felt they had to compete with her for my love. You don't, you know," he said, glancing quickly at D'Andra. "I have enough love for my mom and my woman."

Moments after Brad let Night borrow the keys to do another walk-through, Night and D'Andra were back on the highway, headed to the Ladera Heights Shopping Center and Night's future gym. The conversation was once again lighthearted, as they continued to learn about each other. Night shared stories of his growing up, first in Texas and later L.A., and D'Andra told him about the "Fabulous Four." They were laughing at D'Andra's memories of moonwalking when her phone rang.

"Hello?"

"Hi, I'm trying to reach a . . . D'Andra, D'Andra Smalls?"

"This is D'Andra."

There was a slight pause. "You left a message on my machine several weeks ago. My name is Sylvia. Sylvia Dobbs."

D'Andra's mouth went dry instantly. She clasped her small cell phone with both hands. "You know Orlando Dobbs?" she asked tentatively.

"I might," was the reply.

D'Andra glanced over at Night before continuing.

"I'm looking for the Orlando Dobbs who lived in Los Angeles in the eighties and knew a Mary Smalls."

"What's your relationship to Orlando?"

D'Andra swallowed, her heart beat frantically in her chest. "I might be his daughter."

21

D'Andra had remained unusually quiet since getting the phone call about the man who could be her dad. They'd continued the ride to the gym space in near silence and even his excitement about the gym as they walked the space had elicited little more than monosyllable replies.

"Want to talk about it?"

"I don't know."

"You know I'm here for you if you do. I know what it's like to not have a dad and wonder about your father. My dad died when I was old enough to remember him well, but there are still questions. There's always something missing . . . so I feel you."

"My mother won't talk about him," D'Andra began. "She believes I should just leave it alone and can't understand why I want to know him. She never knew her father, and I guess never felt the need to know that I do. My sister knows her dad and while their relationship is limited at best, she _knows_ him, where he lives, his telephone number. There's a connection."

Night stopped and placed his hands on D'Andra's shoulders. "I don't agree with your mother. I think you should find your father. And I'm here to help, if you need me."

D'Andra's eyes watered but she refused to cry. "Thanks, Night. That means a lot."

She was still thinking of Night's kindness as she clocked into work that night. Her evening with him had been a blessing; it felt good to feel taken care of for a change. Work was busy but manageable, with nobody running off, throwing up or acting out on her watch. She and Elaine shared a quick bite and caught up on each other's lives.

"So, are you going to Chicago to meet your father?"

D'Andra nodded slowly. "Yes, I am. Night said he'd go with me."

Elaine reached across the table. "I'm glad for you D'Andra; every child deserves to know his parents. I'm hoping for the best."

Elaine finished her Lean Cuisine pizza and continued. "And speaking of Night, I might need to sign up for some one-on-ones. You're looking good, woman!"

"Thank you, Elaine. I feel good too. Both my blood pressure and my cholesterol are down and I definitely have more wind and stamina than I used to."

"Uh-huh. And this stamina is for . . ."

"Whatever," D'Andra said smiling. "But yes, that too," she finished, her body warming as she thought of Night.

"How much have you lost?"

"Twenty-five pounds already. Can you believe it?"

"Looking at you? Yes, I can. When is his gym opening?"

"He's shooting for July fifth."

Elaine noticed the brief frown that crossed D'Andra's face. "Running into a few snafus?"

"Just one really." *And her name is Jazz.* "But he's staying positive and moving forward. He's so excited. And so am I."

For the first time D'Andra went into detail about her plans to take nutrition classes, cut her work at Heavenly Haven to a part-time shift and teach nutrition and health seminars at Night's gym. She also told her about the apartments she'd looked at recently and the low-level, yet continual stress at home.

After her shift was over, D'Andra set off for home and some much needed sleep. Spending time with Night had been great but it had also cut into the previous day's sleep. She'd tried to talk him out of working out tonight but he wouldn't hear of it. She had only one thought on her mind as she walked up the sidewalk . . . bed.

That thought was challenged as soon as she opened the door. Kayla was screaming for Tonia and Antoine to eat their cereal and Mary was hollering at D'Andra through a closed bedroom door.

"Dee! Get those kids ready for school for me!"

D'Andra was so tired she hadn't even noticed that Cassandra's car wasn't parked out front.

She opened her mother's door to find her snuggled under the covers.

"Where's Cassandra?" D'Andra asked in a voice full of agitation.

"She spent the night with Anthony," her mother replied. She didn't bother to take her head out from under the sheets or turn to face D'Andra as she continued. "I think he's getting ready to ask her to marry him."

D'Andra was too tired to argue and didn't have enough energy for anger. "Mama," she said, her voice soft. "I am exhausted. Can you get up and get the kids ready?"

"I'm tired, and my side hurts," she replied.

D'Andra was headed out the door when Mary's voice stopped her. "Oh, D'Andra?"

Mary finally pulled the sheet off her face and grimaced as she shifted to face D'Andra. "She's going to need you to watch them this weekend too. She and Anthony are going to Las Vegas."

D'Andra's heart skipped. She hadn't planned to tell her mother that she was going to Chicago to meet her dad. But maybe, she thought, it was best she knew.

"I can't watch them. Night and I are going out of town."

"That man you work out with? Y'all dating now? I thought you were just friends?"

D'Andra resisted a frustrated sigh. Why did it seem as if her mother lived and breathed Cassandra's life while hers was invisible?

"Mama, I told you a few weeks ago we'd started going out."

"I thought y'all were *working* out. What he look like?"

"He's attractive, Mama. I'm sure you'll meet him soon. At any rate, we're going to Chicago and I won't be here to watch the kids."

"That's where he's from, Chi-town?"

"No."

"Then why are you going there?"

D'Andra took a breath, looked her mother in the eye. "To see my father."

"What?" Mary threw off the covers and struggled to a sitting position. "What the hell are you going to search him out for?"

"I know you don't understand, Mama. But it's something I need to do, for many reasons. You don't want to talk about him, and I have questions that need answers."

"What is there to know? We were together, and then he left. End of story. I never knew my father and you didn't see me traipsing all over the country trying to find him. Why can't you just leave it alone?"

"Why can't you just support my decision?"

Mary's anger propelled her to action. She swung her legs over the side of the bed and stood. That simple act cost her precious breath and she stood for a moment, heaving and holding her side. She then reached for a floral robe, belted it quickly, slipped into a pair of worn, pink fluffy slippers and pushed past D'Andra.

"Go on to Chicago, since I can't tell you nothing. But after you meet him and he's busted your fantasy bubble, don't come back here crying to me."

Mary turned her anger toward her grandchildren. "Y'all get up from that table and get your clothes on. It's time for school!"

D'Andra eyed her mother silently before following the children up the stairs. She couldn't understand why Mary was so angry at her father when she didn't share that same antipathy toward Cassandra's father, Sam. Maybe, she thought as she helped the kids get dressed, it was because Sam helped out financially until Cassandra was eighteen, and was at least remotely in her life. In the end it didn't matter. One, she was too tired to figure it out and two, her mind was made up, she was going to see Orlando Dobbs.

Once the children left for school, D'Andra peeled off her clothes and flopped down on the couch. She didn't even bother to pull out the sofa bed, but covered the cushions with a sheet and herself with a light blanket.

Her heart was heavy as she thought about her family, the mostly acrimonious relationship she had with her mother and sister. *I'm not doing this anymore. Things have got to change.* The phrase repeated itself as she drifted off into sleep. Just before she dozed off, her cell phone rang. She was too tired to answer it but if she had, she might have slept easier. The caller had an answer to her prayers.

22

Night held D'Andra's hand as they sat in Orlando Dobbs' living room, just one week after receiving his wife's phone call. It had been an emotionally draining whirlwind weekend, from the time they arrived on a red-eye Saturday morning until now, Monday, almost noon.

It started with the first meeting on Saturday, after Night and D'Andra had gotten a few hours sleep. They agreed to meet at a Starbucks near the condo where Orlando lived with Sylvia, his wife of almost twenty years. D'Andra guessed the meeting had gone as well as could be expected, but she was unprepared for the bluntness of it.

Night and D'Andra had approached the older Black couple who were already seated and sipping coffee when they arrived.

"Are you Orlando Dobbs?" D'Andra asked the sixtyish-looking man. She tried not to be obvious but couldn't help staring hard at this stranger, trying to find herself in his face.

The man stood, hand outstretched. "I am. And you're Mary's daughter, D'Andra."

"I'm your daughter too," D'Andra replied, openly

staring now. He looked nothing like she remembered, not that her memories were of much. He wasn't a really tall man, around five-nine, but he was big. His stomach hung over the brown leather belt of his navy pants, and his jowls puffed out his face. D'Andra subconsciously placed a hand to her own round face. *Okay, I've got the shape of his face.* His salt-and-pepper short afro framed large, bloodshot eyes. Like D'Andra, it seemed Orlando had slept little in the past few days. Aside from a medium-sized mustache and a mole on the left side of his mouth, his face was clean-shaven.

"I'm Sylvia," the woman who'd remained seated offered. She was not smiling but the words were not said unkindly. She appeared younger than Orlando, with deep brown skin that was smooth and clear. Her hair was short and curly with minimal streaks of gray. Her brightly colored sweater stood in stark contrast to her subdued personality. She motioned to the other side of the table. "Why don't you two have a seat?"

A moment of awkward silence followed after introducing Night and before Orlando spoke. "So how is Mary?"

"She's okay," D'Andra said. She breathed and released, feeling comfort in talking about someone familiar. "I've been trying to get her to lose a little weight, eat healthy, but overall she's doing pretty good. When was the last time you saw me . . . us?"

Orlando cleared his throat and fidgeted before answering. "I think you were around two or so. But . . . just what did Mary tell you about my leaving?"

"Mama hasn't told me hardly anything about you. I asked repeatedly when I was younger, but gave up after I . . . when I was nine years old. And there's so much I want to know. Aside from the obvious questions that any child might ask an absent parent, there are some specific health questions I need answered. A few months ago, I was thirty pounds heavier, suffering from diabetes and high blood pressure. When the doctor asked for a family history of these illnesses, I could only give one side. That's when I became determined to find you."

"Well, I do have high blood pressure; but no diabetes as yet thank the good Lord. That's probably due to Sylvia here. She tries to keep me eating right. If I get fried chicken, it must either be a holiday or my birthday."

D'Andra smiled briefly before abruptly changing the subject. "Why did you leave?"

Orlando squirmed again, clearly uncomfortable. The tension at the table became palpable as all their coffees sat cold and untouched.

Sylvia cleared her throat and broke the silence. "D'Andra, we feel that you should have a DNA test done to prove that you're Orlando's child."

This suggestion, while valid, caught D'Andra totally off guard. It took her a moment to respond. "Of course that's reasonable," she began slowly. "I just never expected to . . . I mean, you lived with my mother until I was about two."

"It's just to be sure, baby," Sylvia said. For the first time since meeting she showed true compassion. "This is a lot for all of us to take in, and if you're Orlando's child, we will welcome you to our family." She looked at Orlando briefly, warmly. "We have three children between us, one I brought in from a previous marriage and two we've had together. If you're his daughter you'll be number four, and the oldest. But we want to be sure before we start reestablishing family ties."

Unbeknownst to D'Andra, Sylvia had used connections with a doctor friend and set up an afternoon appointment for her and Orlando to get swabbed for DNA samples, which would then be delivered to a research lab for analysis. They guaranteed results within forty-eight hours. Now, come Monday, the envelope that held the answer was lying on the coffee table that separated Orlando and Sylvia, who were seated on the blue-and-white pin-striped couch, across from Night and D'Andra, who were perched anxiously on an oversized matching love seat in the Dobbses' living room. The envelope had been delivered less than an hour before Night and D'Andra had arrived.

"Well, do you want to open it?" Sylvia asked Orlando.

"I could," he responded. He smiled tentatively at the couple sitting opposite him and reached for the envelope.

"I'll do it," D'Andra said, grabbing the envelope before Orlando reached it. She was excited. For her the verification of his fatherhood status was merely a formality. She had a feeling she was going to like getting to know the man sitting across from her. He'd been distant until now, but she believed there to be a kind, lighthearted man underneath his guarded exterior. She smiled at Night briefly before tearing open the envelope.

"Here, you read it Night."

"Are you sure?"

D'Andra smiled. "Of course."

Night pulled the paper from the envelope and scanned its content.

"Well?" Sylvia asked.

Night looked briefly at Orlando and then at D'Andra. "Baby, this says he's not your father."

23

D'Andra glared at Mary, who sat nonchalantly on the couch. Her mother had danced around the question ever since D'Andra had returned from Chicago on Monday after getting the results of the DNA test. Now it was Saturday and after five days of "I don't want to talk about it" D'Andra wasn't taking no for an answer.

"How can you sit there and say you don't know?" D'Andra repeated. "If Orlando Dobbs isn't my father, there had to be somebody else, or was it more than one?"

"Who do you think you're talking to? What I do in my bedroom is none of your damn business," Mary retorted defensively. "I knew that fool would lie; he's never owned up to anything in his life."

"It's the DNA test that didn't lie, Mama. For thirty years I've thought a man named Orlando Dobbs was my father. Now I find out he isn't. I also found out the reason he left, at least according to him. He said it was because of another man; and that that man might be my father. Was he talking about Sam or someone else?"

Mary eyed her daughter quietly. For a second, D'Andra thought her mother might cry. Just as quickly, the vulnerability left, replaced by a steely resolve.

"I'm sorry you didn't hear what you wanted to in Chicago," she said without emotion. "But I can't tell you what you want to hear right now. There's a lot of pain surrounding those early years with you and your sister. And I'm just not strong enough to dig around in that pain for the answer you need."

D'Andra wondered about the pain of which her mother spoke, but wondered more about the man whose DNA she shared, the one who now she might never know.

Twenty minutes later, D'Andra was out of the house and on her way to the gym. Shortly after she started her car, her cell phone rang.

"Is this D'Andra Smalls?" a perky sounding voice asked.

"Yes."

"This is Jenny with Palatial Apartments. We called you last week about a one-bedroom that was coming available. You'd listed with Place Finders saying you were looking. Are you still interested?"

"Who is this?"

In all the drama surrounding her trip to Chicago, D'Andra had forgotten all about the message she received the day she and her mother had argued about finding her father. All she remembered from listening to it is that it had said something about "finders." She'd automatically connected it with Peoplesearch.com, the Web site that had helped her locate her father, no, the man she'd thought for nearly three decades was her dad. She was grateful the woman had called her back. A move was exactly the fresh air she needed.

"It's Jenny with—"

"I'm very interested," D'Andra cut off Jenny's reply. "When can you come take a look at the unit?"

"Right now. What's the address?"

Two and a half hours later, D'Andra left Culver City

and headed to Inglewood, and Night's house. She'd decided on the cozy, yet comfortable one-bedroom apartment as soon as she'd stepped into the living room. The layout was open, with a simple bar separating the kitchen from the combined living/dining area. The bathroom was nice-sized and the bedroom had a walk-in closet. It was perfect. She'd filled out the paperwork on the spot and left a check for deposit pending her application's approval. Since it was the third week in March, the manager even offered to let her move in immediately but not charge rent until April first. That offer helped seal the deal. The faster she moved from the chaos, the better. D'Andra's heart still felt heavy, but she was beginning to breathe again.

Night, as always, was a welcomed sight.

"Where are your gym clothes?"

"Hello to you, too," D'Andra responded before kissing him fully on the mouth. She had open access to his lips now and still couldn't get enough. Nor could she believe her luck in finding a man like Night: kind, trustworthy and fine on top of that.

"I wasn't thinking about working out when I came here," she said in response to his question. "Besides, it's Saturday."

"I don't know why not. You know you're my favorite workout partner," Night said. He filled his hands with her buttocks, and squeezed them as if they were ripe fruit.

"Doll . . . you feel so good," he said after placing several kisses across her nose and cheeks. "I love how tight this is getting. But it's still juicy." He squeezed her buttocks again and moaned as he reclaimed her lips.

D'Andra explored his body in kind. She ran her hand over his close-cropped black hair, relishing the feel of its nappiness. She ran her hands along his back and across his hard, tight butt . . . her favorite feature. She felt him harden as she continued to massage his gluteous maximus. *Well, almost my favorite,* she thought as he began a slow grind in the middle of the living room.

"We're going to work out," Night whispered. "And then we're going to *work out.*"

"I told you, I don't have anything to wear."

"Don't worry about that . . . I have everything you need."

Night took her hand and began to lead her toward his bedroom.

"Wait," D'Andra protested. "We need to talk. I've got some things to tell you."

Night's face quickly turned from playful to concerned. "What's the matter? Is this about your real father?"

D'Andra relayed the conversation she'd had with her mother. "I don't know if I'll ever know who he is," she concluded. "And I don't know how I feel about that."

"There's nothing you can do but let it be, at least for now." Night waited for what he felt a respectful time and then said, "Okay, let's get changed."

"Wait just a minute, Mr. Impatient. I have something else to tell you."

"What? You're not pregnant are you?"

"Why would you ask that question? You've always used protection and I'm on the pill."

Jazz. "I'm just teasing you," Night said. But he wasn't. Jazz had used that line on him more than once, and to this day he didn't know whether she'd ever really carried his child.

"I've got a place," D'Andra said. Her eyes shined with excitement. She paced the room as she told Night about it.

He didn't share her enthusiasm. "I wish you would

move in here with me." He'd given the invitation more
than once, after conversations about her less-than-
happy living environment.

"You know how much I care about you. But I'm going
through a lot of different feelings and emotions right
now, making changes in myself, my life. I just need a
little space to sort it all out, and after living with five
other people in a two-bedroom for months, a little soli-
tude."

"I understand, but you know you're going to pay for
this decision, don't you?" He reached for D'Andra's
hand and began leading her toward the bedroom.

"How so?" she asked coyly, her body already tin-
gling in anticipation.

Night reached the bedroom, walked over to his
closet and after a few moments pulled out a pink-and-
white baby doll T-shirt, D'Andra's favorite kind, and a
pair of pink shorts.

"By getting into your workout clothes and meeting
me downstairs. You've put me in a mood, doll. And
I'm going to make you sweat."

Put him in a mood? D'Andra wondered what that
meant. Was it a good mood or a bad mood? She
couldn't tell from his expression. Was he joking? She
sure hoped so. Her stomach was still slightly sore from
the last round of crunches and even though her core,
leg and arm muscles were stronger, she still didn't look
forward to thirty minutes of lifts, squats and stretches.

She dressed quickly in the workout attire Night had
purchased, admiring his taste and attention to detail in
remembering what she liked. When she walked down
the stairs into the home gym, Night was busy doing
pushups on the blue rubber mat. She stopped and quietly noted a body of perfection. How his chiseled arms
bent and straightened, causing his back muscles to
ripple as smoothly as a song. She eyed the slight curve

of his back and the valley at the small of it before it expanded to reveal two dimples above a firm, round behind. His thighs could have been sculpted by an artist, so expertly proportioned was the design. His thighs bulged as his legs helped hold his weight and his calf muscles bulged their participation as well.

"Are you going to stand there ogling me all day, or are you going to join me?" Night asked, without stopping his exercise and without looking up.

"I wasn't looking at you," D'Andra said.

They both laughed at that lie. Night stopped, went to his knees and motioned D'Andra over.

"Let's start with push-ups."

Forty-five sweaty minutes later, they were done. Night had pushed D'Andra physically farther than he'd ever done before: a fast-paced ten minutes on the stationary bike, a ten-minute run on the treadmill followed by kick-boxing, core work including crunches and squats, and exercises to tone her glutes and quads. Both she and Night were sweating and the gym, which Night purposely kept on the warm side, felt a bit similar to a low-heat sauna.

D'Andra sprawled onto the blue mat. "Night, my abs hurt."

Night stood above her with outstretched hands. "Come on, doll."

He guided her gently up the stairs and to the bathroom where he stripped her out of her wet workout clothes. Without saying a word, he turned on the water, hot, and then stripped as well. That's where the loving started.

Soaping her front to back, he used his own body to massage the healing scent of chamomile into D'Andra's skin. He then sat her on the seat Night had installed into his extra wide tub-and-shower unit, took emu, a healing oil for sore joints and muscles, and worked it into D'Andra's tissues. As the water poured over them both, he worked from her toes to her shoulders, around to the back of her neck and back to her thighs and calves, massaging, kneading and releasing tension with every stroke. By the time he finished, D'Andra was as limp as a noodle, and as horny as the brass section of California's Symphony Orchestra.

Night was getting ready to take care of that too. After using a large, fluffy soft towel to dry off D'Andra, he led her into the bedroom.

"Get on the bed," he said, the first words he'd uttered since saying "Come on, doll."

D'Andra hadn't spoken either, partly because she'd initially been too tired to think and partly because she was mesmerized at Night's tender ministrations. She felt cared for, protected, something she hadn't had the chance to feel often. And she was loving every minute of it, her tiredness now replaced by ardent desire.

Night turned D'Andra onto her stomach. For a moment he did nothing, which only heightened D'Andra's anticipation. Then came the feel of cool, soothing lotion and the smell of something delicious— strawberries and white chocolate—as Night began at D'Andra's shoulders and lotioned her body down to her toes. D'Andra loved the way he handled her thick body, as if he were in total control. She'd slimmed down from a size twenty to a size sixteen; and Night treated her extra pounds as if they were cotton candy: licking, nibbling and enjoying the sweetness.

He turned her over and did the same thing on her other side, paying special attention to her breasts and inner thighs. D'Andra moaned softly as beginning at her ankles, Night placed feathery soft kisses along the inner side of her leg before parting them and deeply kissing her passion paradise. She moaned louder now as Night secured her ample hips in his hands and made love to her with his tongue. Just when she felt she would explode he lifted himself up and reached for the protection lying on the nightstand.

"Um, let me," D'Andra breathed. She took the condom out of the package and, with her eyes never leaving Night's, placed it on his massive manhood, using her mouth to unroll it up the length of his shaft. He turned her around and entered her swiftly, forcefully, authoritatively and completely, as if their lovemaking was a matter of utmost importance and urgency. After their initial climaxes they settled into a slow, thoughtful rhythm, memorizing each other's bodies, dancing the timeless, ageless dance of love.

The candles had burned down long ago, the open balcony allowing in a welcomed ocean breeze. The couple lay side by side, settling their breathing after a torrid bout of steamy sex. The man turned onto his side and with a tanned, tapered finger made lazy circles on the woman's bare bottom. She turned and threw her café au lait-colored leg over his.

"That was amazing," he said.

The woman was silent, but simply cuddled closer to the man's slender back.

"Are you going to do it for me?" she finally whispered.

"Do what?"

"You know, make sure that little thing we talked about doesn't happen."

Brad turned over to face Jazz fully. He kissed her again, reveling in the feel of her soft, full lips against his harder, thin ones. Already, he could feel himself once again becoming aroused. He'd wanted Jazz for a long, long time and now here she was, in his bed, and it felt incredible.

"Yes," he answered, as he turned her over on her stomach and knelt over her from behind. "I'll do anything you ask."

24

D'Andra laughed to herself as she hummed along to Chuck Berry's *Rock and Roll Music*. The CD was a gift from Frank, who'd joined her and Night at Jewel's BBQ to review the proof sheet of D'Andra's photo shoot. It turned out to be an evening filled with loud laughter and rich history, as Frank shared stories of his time as a professional photographer in the fifties, sixties and seventies—when along with Chuck Berry, James Brown and other singers, he'd met famous politicians, athletes and actors. The dinner lasted three hours and D'Andra had spent the night in Night's arms.

This Sunday morning started out as beautifully as her Saturday night ended, waking up to Night's incredibly tender lovemaking. He had a client so instead of fixing them breakfast, she drank a protein drink, showered, dressed, and was now speeding down La Cienega Boulevard on her way home.

Her vibrating cell phone indicated an incoming call. D'Andra turned down *Maybellene* and quickly put in her hands-free earplug.

"Hello?"

"Hey Dee, it's Connie."

"Hey girl, what's your prerogative?"

D'Andra automatically used the phrase the Fabulous Four had chimed when calling each other.

"Nothing much. Just got off the phone with Nelly and thought about you. We promised to keep in touch, remember?"

There was a brief pause before D'Andra answered. "I've been busy, plus I'm getting ready to move."

"Where are you moving and what's his name?"

D'Andra laughed. "You know me too well, don't you? I'm moving to this complex in Culver City called Palatial Apartments, and his name is Night."

"Night? What kind of name is that?"

"His real name is JaJuan but everybody, except his mother, calls him Night."

"Well, I'm glad you've got a warm body in your bed, but that's still no reason not to make time for a friend."

The conversation continued for a few more minutes, with Connie filling D'Andra in on mutual associates who'd married, divorced, gotten pregnant or moved. Fortunately no one else they both knew had died. When D'Andra hung up with Connie she noticed she'd missed a call. *Probably from earlier this morning, when I was otherwise occupied with Night,* she thought with a smile.

She checked her messages and was both surprised and delighted to find out she'd been approved for the apartment. It happened so fast D'Andra wondered if they'd really checked her credit report and references. And why was she being called on a weekend? She believed the check she left for deposit and first month's rent may have had something to do with the application being accepted so quickly. She'd barely had time to think about it and now it was happening—she was moving to her own place.

If Night was less than thrilled about it, her family was downright upset.

Arriving home began as it often did, with little hands and feet greeting her at the door.

"Hey, Aunt Dee. Where have you been?" Kayla asked inquisitively.

"You gone all night, Aunt Dee," Antoine added, as if D'Andra didn't know.

"Were you with your boyfriend?" Kayla questioned.

"Can you fix us something to eat?" Tonia interrupted. She couldn't care less about D'Andra's previous whereabouts. It was eleven o'clock and she'd only eaten cereal and a candy bar. When she saw her aunt she saw the beginnings of a home-cooked meal.

"Let me get in the door good, you guys." D'Andra laughed as she noticed Tonia and Antoine vying for position behind her. Kayla's attention was quickly drawn back to the video game she'd been playing while Antoine grabbed his Transformer and followed Tonia and D'Andra into the kitchen.

The twins had just finished helping D'Andra whip up an egg-white omelet when Mary came into the kitchen. She walked to the coffee pot and began preparations for her required three cups a day.

"Where were you all night?"

D'Andra hesitated. "Over at Night's house."

She was not ashamed of sleeping with Night and wondered why she suddenly felt as if she were sixteen and had just been caught sneaking home on a school night. Cassandra often spent nights away from home but if D'Andra arrived with the morning sun on her face, it was because she'd had a date with Heavenly Haven.

Mary sauntered over to the stove and helped herself to a crispy piece of turkey bacon. "This man giving you any money?"

"I haven't asked for any, Mama."

"Humph. Girl, you better learn how to get what

you want from these men. They're not always going to be there."

D'Andra took the English muffins out of the toaster, and began topping them with low-fat margarine and Pure Fruit grape jam.

"Why can't you just be happy for me, Mama? Night's a good guy. Let's just leave it at that."

"Who said I wasn't happy? I'm glad you found somebody to spend time with. But I still can't understand why a Black man would ask to be called Night, actually introduce himself with that name."

Mary took one of the English muffins D'Andra had fixed for the kids and took a large bite.

"Mama, do you want an omelet?" Another day Mary's antics would have bothered her but the smile Night had put on her face would probably last three days straight.

"It does smell good."

D'Andra placed two more English muffins in the toaster and put the kids' plates on the table. "Y'all want orange juice or milk?"

A mixture of answers followed. D'Andra filled the "orders" while pondering how to break the news that their cook was moving out. She decided to wait until they were well into the breakfast, the kids' chatter filling up an otherwise silent room.

"Do you like that omelet, Mama?" she asked.

"Uh-huh. Even though I know the yolks aren't in here. But with the vegetables mixed in, I don't miss them much."

"See, you can eat healthy and have it still taste good."

Mary simply grunted and took another bite. "You are slimming down, I can see that. But when you come off your diet, you better hope those pounds don't creep back on you, and then some. That's what always happens to me and why I don't diet anymore."

"That's just it; what I'm doing is not a diet, but a lifestyle change. Yes, I've been using some diet foods, but my long-term goal is to make eating healthy and exercising a way of life."

Cassandra came into the kitchen still dressed in pajamas even though it was close to noon. "Something smells good."

"You just get up, Mommy?" Antoine asked.

"Mommy ain't up yet," Cassandra replied with a yawn. "But the smell of this food got me out of bed."

Cassandra took a plate out of the cabinets and put the remainder of the omelet and two strips of bacon on her plate. "Where's the bread?"

"There are some muffins in the refrigerator," D'Andra answered.

Cassandra sighed. "Why didn't you fix enough for everybody?"

"I fixed enough for everyone who was in here when I started cooking. And you're welcome for the food."

The sound of Cassandra's slippers sliding across the tiled kitchen floor was the only reply. The next sound was that of the upstairs bedroom door closing.

The short but somewhat snippy exchange with her sister reminded D'Andra of what she wouldn't miss. Unfortunately moments like those outweighed the lighter, good times. It gave her the push to break the news to Mary. Hoping for the best she got up from the table and began gathering the dishes.

"I've been looking for a place," she said casually as she stacked the dishes in the dishwasher.

"A place for who?" Mary asked.

"Me, Mama."

"Why do you want to move? What's wrong with here?"

D'Andra started the dishwasher then turned and leaned against it as she continued.

"Mama, I've been sleeping on the couch for months. And while I love the kids, they are really cutting into my being able to get good sleep. But more than that, I'm just feeling the need for my own space. I found this cute little place over in—"

"And just what am I supposed to do when you take half the rent with you? Did you stop and think of anybody but yourself? You know my disability payments stopped and I still have to help Cassandra with these kids. Did you stop and think about that?"

This conversation was going exactly how D'Andra thought it might, but hoped it wouldn't. She joined her mother at the table.

"I did think about that, Mama. But that on-the-job injury happened more than a year ago. It's more than healed now. It might do you good to get back out there, back in the workforce, to be productive. Plus, Cassandra gets child support; enough to cover my part of the rent and more. Cassandra could find a job if she really wanted one."

Mary put down her coffee cup and crossed her arms. "This is about your father isn't it? This is about your being mad that I want to let the past stay in the past."

"I've been thinking of moving out for a while now," D'Andra countered, not feeling it necessary to admit that the who's-my-daddy fiasco did play a part in her desire to move quickly. "And since I'm dating," she added, "I need more privacy."

"How come we've never seen this man you're dating?" Cassandra asked as she entered the kitchen and walked over to the refrigerator. She wore a pastel, multicolored halter top paired with light yellow jeans that fit her curvy figure like a glove and complemented her golden brown hair and bronze skin. She didn't wait for the answer.

"Can you watch the kids for a couple hours, Dee? I've got an errand to run."

"D'Andra's moving out." Mary intoned the words like a funeral dirge.

"Why? Where are you going? Are you moving in with the man you met?"

D'Andra couldn't gauge whether Cassandra's incredulity was because she was moving or because Cassandra thought her overweight sister might land a provider before she did.

"I found an apartment in Culver City," D'Andra replied. "I didn't expect it to go through so soon but since it did, I'm going to move out right away. So, no, I can't watch the kids. I've got to pack my stuff and don't worry; I'm not taking any of my furniture, just my clothes and personal items. Oh, and the computer."

"Well, Dee, the kids can help you. Since this is the last time I'll be able to ask you, please help me out."

"You going out with Anthony?" Mary asked with obvious pride. She had her eyes set on having this professional ball player for a son-in-law and often fantasized about the house she'd live in with them and the kids, or the condo he'd buy her.

"No, I have to drive to Santa Monica and meet a prospective employer."

"On a Sunday?"

The truth was, Cassandra didn't know how much longer she'd be in Anthony's life. She'd heard it through the grapevine that he'd been cheating on her for months with at least two other women. Her rapper boyfriend Hollah had hollah'd at someone else, a Latina and Black drop-dead gorgeous model he'd met on his debut rap video. Cassandra hadn't been without a boyfriend since she was fifteen, and was already wondering about the availability of the man she was getting ready to meet.

Cassandra shrugged. "He's a businessman looking for a personal assistant. He asked if I could see him today and I said yes. So can you watch them? Mama, will you help? I'll leave some money for pizza and movies; they'll practically watch themselves."

"Oh, all right. Go on, girl. And remember you said a couple of hours."

"Thanks DeeDee!" Cassandra placed a half-empty glass of orange juice on the table and ran out the door.

"I don't want you to move," Mary said. "I'm not ready to go back to work and I can't take care of San's kids. Why don't you wait a couple months, until she and Anthony get together? Then we'll probably move anyway, into a bigger house."

"Because I've already paid a deposit and the first month's rent. And I want to move."

"Well when you run into trouble and can't pay your rent, don't think you're going to be able to come back here. If you move out, it's for good!"

With that, Mary heaved herself from the kitchen table, went to her room and closed the door.

So much for you helping to watch the kids, D'Andra thought as she walked into the living room where Kayla and Tonia were watching cartoons.

"Where's Antoine?"

"Outside."

"Y'all get your shoes on, you're coming with me."

Two hours later, D'Andra returned home with a supply of cardboard packing boxes and other packing supplies. She worked steadily for two more hours and was surprised that even though she wasn't taking any big items, she still had a great deal to pack: books, DVDs, CDs, toiletries, and all the other odds and ends that one accumulates over time. She planned to pack her clothes tomorrow. They would be the last thing she picked up.

Sitting down to finally eat a salad and take a break, D'Andra had just reached for the remote when her phone rang.

"I am so pissed," Night said as soon as she said hello.

"What's the matter?"

"Brad! He just called me with some lame excuse about a delay on closing escrow and the deal going through. I told him if there were any problems to let me know before now. I planned to have the contractors start working next week!"

D'Andra had never heard Night this angry. Her first instinct was to comfort him, her second to keep him from losing his dream.

"I'm sorry, Night. But stay positive; everything will work out."

The sound of her soothing voice brought immediate solace. Night took a deep breath and tried to calm down.

"I'm watching my nieces and nephew right now, but why don't you come over? You can tell me all about what Brad said while you help me pack."

"Pack? Where are you going?"

"I'm moving, remember?"

"Of course, I just didn't think it would happen so soon."

"So . . . are you going to come by?"

"What's your address?"

"You told me to dress casual; I hope I'm okay." Cassandra settled into the large black leather chair in a well-appointed corner of the plush hotel lobby.

"You're a very attractive woman," the businessman replied. "I hope you don't mind my saying so."

Cassandra smiled coyly, happy she was having an effect on this handsome, brown-eyed blonde. She'd taken his full measure in an instant: about six feet tall, athletic, strong legs, expensive clothing and no wedding ring. Memories of Anthony were already starting to fade from her head.

After ordering tea from a roving waitress, her potential employer got down to business. He spoke of his company and described in detail the type of work he'd require from an assistant.

"Do you think you can handle this type of position? I admit, it can get demanding at times."

Cassandra shifted in her seat, deftly exposing cleavage as she leaned forward. "Listen, I've got three kids. There's no job that gets more demanding than that."

The man could not hide his surprise, nor the quick once over he gave Cassandra's small, tight frame.

Cassandra's laugh was throaty and real. "You can't believe I'm a mother? Well I am. And I take very good care of . . . my babies." She reached for her tea glass and teased the straw with her tongue. Halfway through the businessman's explanation she decided she would put her cards on the table and leave no doubt just what types of duties she was willing to perform.

The businessman hardened as he watched Cassandra's tongue dart around the straw. He struggled to keep focus.

"So what if your work runs into the evening? Is your, uh, husband okay with handling the children until you get home?"

"I'm very single," Cassandra replied with the perfect mix of purr and professionalism. "But don't worry; I have a reliable sitter and a network of helpers. My work will be my very first priority."

"When can you start?"

"Would a week from tomorrow be okay? I want to

take the time to make sure everything is in place with my family, so I can give you my undivided attention."

In reality she knew it would probably take her that long to convince her cousin Jackie—who swore she wasn't taking one more kid into her daycare center— to take not one more, but three.

"I was hoping you could start sooner, but I like your confidence and your drive. I think you'd be perfect for what I need."

They talked several moments more, Cassandra getting the pertinent information she needed: address, work hours and of course salary and benefits. After that they stood. The interview was over.

"I'm looking forward to working with you, Cassandra."

Cassandra shook the businessman's outstretched hand. "Brad, I can't wait to get started."

25

By Monday afternoon, D'Andra had checked several items off her to do list. She'd picked up her apartment keys and made two trips to her new home: one with an SUV full of boxes and the second with her car full of clothes. Night made her promise to leave him the heavier boxes but she already felt guilty about taking a personal day. She wanted to get done as much as possible. Now she was once again in her car, headed to the store for cleaning supplies and a few groceries before returning to her new home in time for the one piece of furniture she was determined to get delivered ASAP . . . a king-sized bed.

As she navigated the mid-day traffic, she ruminated on the events of the past twenty-four hours. Night had been an invaluable help when he came over, and the children took to him right away, especially Antoine. After Night showed the little tyke a couple kick-boxing moves, Night was his hero. Cassandra had come home all excited about a new job, something D'Andra believed was the direct result of her prayers. While she'd refused to feel guilty about moving, and had even gone so far as to pay half the rent for the upcoming month, she only wished the best for her family and didn't want them to suffer in any way. So when Cassandra came home with a job announcement it was like passing go and collecting two hundred dollars. Cassandra's news had made D'Andra that much more excited about her new abode.

Her sister's reaction to Night had been interesting. D'Andra was sure Cassandra was unaware—at least she hoped she was—of how her body language and demeanor had changed as soon as Night came out of the bathroom, where he'd been when she first walked through the door.

"*You're* Night?" she'd asked, when D'Andra introduced him. She looked at him as if he were a chocolate bar with nuts.

"That's right. Nice to meet you."

"D'Andra said you were a personal trainer but, wow. You're really . . . in great shape."

Cassandra tossed her shoulder-length curls away from her face. "Maybe I need to start working out. Are you taking any new customers?"

Night walked over and put his arms around D'Andra, hugging her to him tightly. "No, I've got my hands f ull right now," he said, planting a kiss on the top of D'Andra's head for emphasis. "But I have a friend who works at Bally's. He's looking for clientele. If you'd like I can refer you."

D'Andra could not have loved Night more than she did in that moment. The sister who'd never been considered a catch, the one dubbed least likely to get a man, much less keep one, had an obvious prize by her side. D'Andra was sure her sister was happy for her, even if she didn't say it. Shortly after that conversation, Cassandra had scooped up her kids and within five minutes was back out the door.

Mary was a different story. D'Andra had knocked on

her door as soon as Night arrived and told her mother there was someone she wanted her to meet.

"Who?" Mary asked, after a long pause.

"My friend Night."

"I'll be out there in a minute; I'm asleep."

She never came out of her room.

D'Andra's thoughts were interrupted as her cell phone rang again. She tried to read the caller ID but traffic was thick and she decided to just answer it.

"Hello."

"D'Andra?"

"Yes?"

"This is Orlando, Orlando Dobbs."

For an inexplicable reason, D'Andra's heartbeat quickened. Even with the DNA results, there was a small part of her that wanted him to be her father, if for no other reason than to know who that man was.

"Hey, how are you doing?"

"We're fine, fine. But me and Sylvia have been thinking about you and wondering how you're doing. It was a brave thing for you to come all this way and then to get disappointed like that . . . it's a lot."

"I'm okay, good actually."

"Did you talk to Mary when you got back home?"

"Yes, but she still won't tell me anything. She even accused you of lying to me until I told her about the test results." D'Andra thought about her mother's odd behavior the day before when she refused to come out of her room and meet Night. "I think she's angry with me for contacting you."

There was a brief silence on the other end. "Don't judge your mother too harshly," Orlando said when he spoke once again. "Your mama went through some things back in the day, some things that are hard to talk about."

"Like what?"

Another pause. "It's not my place for me to share your mother's business. In time, she may feel strong enough to tell you herself. But know this. Your mother loves you. I can tell you that from the few years I was with her."

"Maybe I can ask you another question. Do you know who my father is?"

Another pause. "I know the people who Mary hung around with when you were conceived. For the first couple years, I thought you were my child. But then a few things happened and I began to question it. Your mama wouldn't talk to me either and eventually . . . if you don't have communication in a relationship you don't have anything."

"Well . . . I appreciate you calling. Tell Sylvia I said hello."

D'Andra heard Orlando relaying her message. "She says hello back and wishes you the best."

D'Andra tried to fill in the empty spaces left by Orlando's conversation as she shopped for groceries. What could have happened to her mother that she didn't want to talk about? she wondered. Was Orlando involved? Was her real father? Had her father done something illegally? Was he in jail? There were more questions than answers as she loaded up her food items and headed back to her apartment. At this point she saw little else she could do to find out about her father. The man she'd thought was him wouldn't give her any hints, and the only person with all the answers wasn't talking.

D'Andra decided to try a different route back to her new home. She headed north on Sepulveda Boulevard and turned on a street she thought would take her around to the back of her building and to the gate to the underground parking. Instead she found herself on a quaint side street with a mixture of shops. Upon quick glance she spotted a bookstore, a plant and fish shop and an Indian food restaurant on the corner. That's when she realized that it was lunchtime and she hadn't eaten yet. Not wanting to wait and prepare something herself, she decided to pick up lunch from the restaurant and take it home.

She quickly found a place to park and went inside. The atmosphere was colorful and cozy and the smell of deliciously spicy food greeted her as soon as she opened the door. The menu was filled with mouth-watering fare and as hungry as she was she had trouble making up her mind. She decided on a flat bread called Punjabi, lentil soup, vegetable curry and chicken masala. At the last minute she decided to double the order, in case Night was hungry when he came over later.

As the cashier helped bag up her order, the bell over the front door clanged. A customer came in and stood next to D'Andra, looking at the menu.

"Have you eaten here before?" D'Andra asked as she turned.

"Yes, the food's . . . oh . . . you."

"Hello, Jazz."

The cashier placed D'Andra's large bag on the counter. "I see you've lost a pound or two, all Night's doing I'm sure. But you're still eating like a fat person."

D'Andra resisted the petty comeback that included the mention of her soon-to-be dining companion. "Fat girls do love food," she said instead.

She picked up the bag and turned once more to Jazz. "Take care."

She was almost to the door when Jazz asked in a pseudo silky voice. "How's Night?"

"Fine," D'Andra said, not turning around.

"What's he going to do now that his dream to be the next Billy Blanks has hit a wall?"

That comment stopped D'Andra. She stopped and turned. "What are you talking about?"

Jazz seemed unsure, but only for a moment. "It's a small town," she said once she'd regained her poise. "I hear things. And Brad Gilman is a dear friend of mine."

With those words she turned back to the menu, a pointed sign that the conversation was over. D'Andra opened her mouth to speak and then thought better of it. Her time and energy would be put to better use talking to Night instead.

She saw his GMC Acadia as soon as she turned the corner.

"Hey, baby. Go to the front and I'll let you in as soon as I park. Hope you're hungry!" she added as she sped away to the back and the garage gate.

The apartment building door hadn't completely closed before D'Andra spilled her news. "I think I know what happened with your gym space, why it hit a snag."

"You do?" Night easily kept up with a fast-moving D'Andra as she headed back to her car.

"Jazz."

Night stopped. "Jazz?"

"I just saw her at the restaurant where I got the food that's in the car."

"What did she say?" Night reached into the back of D'Andra's SUV and easily carried two bags of groceries, a bag of cleaning products and a box containing a four-piece dish set.

D'Andra took the bag of food from the front seat and locked her car. She recapped the brief conversation as she and Night headed toward the elevator.

"How would she know that your deal fell through if she wasn't involved?"

"She and Brad are good friends. That's how I met him."

"Do you think he would purposely do something to prevent your deal from closing; I mean, can he do that?"

"Anything can happen," Night answered.

They entered the apartment. Night put the groceries on one counter while D'Andra unpacked food containers on the opposite counter by the stove.

"I hope you're hungry."

"I wasn't until I smelled that food." He peered over her shoulder into one of the containers. "Is this from Mayura's?"

"You've eaten there?"

"Yes," Night said, and then answered the unasked question. "With Jazz."

D'Andra quelled her feelings of jealousy and sudden inadequacy and quipped, "Trust me when I tell you the food will taste better eaten with me."

She fixed their plates and handed one to Night. "Have a seat," she said dryly.

They sat with their backs against the dining room wall and ate in silence before D'Andra continued.

"You thinking about Jazz, wondering how she blocked your getting the gym?"

"Knowing Jazz, I know how. But it's all good though. I know a few people in L.A. as well. This is far from over. I've already got another possibility, but the price is twice as high."

Night told D'Andra about his meeting with Frank's associate, and the space opening up in another prime location not far from Ladera Heights, the location of his first space. D'Andra thought of Jazz and realized her attempted punch at hurting Night hadn't landed as hard as she'd hoped. Night was just as excited, if not more, about the possibilities of opening up in the space he'd just seen. The bottom line is her baby had his smile back. That was all D'Andra wanted.

* * *

Jazz sat in a corner booth of Mayura's restaurant. What little appetite she'd had left when she ran into D'Andra. She pushed aside her partially eaten samosas, a crispy vegetable-filled crust that any other time would have been scarfed down in minutes, and idly sipped ginger beer. *Why isn't Brad answering?* she wondered. She picked up her phone and dialed him again.

Brad rolled over, exhausted yet thoroughly satiated. He'd just experienced, without a doubt, the best sex he'd ever had. And having so recently been with Jazz, he didn't think that was possible.

"Damn, you are incredible, absolutely incredible."

Cassandra accepted the compliment without responding. Rather she took Brad's hand and placed it in her wetness. She'd employed every trick in her erotica playbook and knew the trap was set to catch her latest prey. Now it was time to begin the subtle shift in power. Cassandra knew only one way to play the male/female game—on top.

She kissed Brad quickly, rolled out of the bed and headed to the shower. She was well aware of the picture she painted as she walked naked across the room. She stopped and turned just before going into the bathroom. Brad was staring at her, as she'd imagined.

"What?" she asked coyly, as if she didn't know.

"You haven't even started working for me yet and I already don't know what I'd do without you."

"Well if you play your cards right, Mr. Brad Gilman, you'll never have to find that out."

26

The next three weeks passed by in a blissful blur for D'Andra. March had melded seamlessly into April as she settled into her new apartment, found a Bally's in her area, continued her day and nighttime workouts with Night, at least the nights when she wasn't working, and registered for an online course on nutrition. She felt bad about canceling her plans to attend college, but she'd determined her life was too chaotic for a full load of courses. The online course made her feel that she was staying somewhat on track with her goals.

On top of that, she felt physically better than ever. She'd lost another five pounds and almost screamed two days ago when she put on a size sixteen dress at Lane Bryant and had room to spare. Thanks to peace, quiet and a king-sized bed she felt more rested than she had in months, even with the extracurricular activities of the Night kind. But undoubtedly the most significant event that happened was the conversation she finally had with Chanelle.

It all started when D'Andra called Connie. They discussed getting together during the summer, among other things. Near the end of their conversation, Chanelle's name came up.

"You guys still haven't talked, I take it."

"No."

Silence, and then, "She was your friend for twenty years, D'Andra. I'm not asking you to believe what she tells you. But don't you think you at least owe her the courtesy of hearing her out, of maybe a ten, fifteen minute conversation before you close the door for the rest of your life?"

Until now, the answer had been no. But she knew what could happen when one assumed, without all the facts. For the first time, she seriously thought about taking her friend's advice.

"So Connie, if you walked in and saw Will screwing another woman, you honestly believe you'd give her an opportunity to tell her side of the story?"

"I would if it were you, D'Andra. I'd want to know how my best friend, who'd been with me since we were ten, could betray me like that. I'd definitely have the conversation. Now, I may kick your ass after hearing the explanation, but I'd want to know what you had to say for yourself."

The conversation ended, and after another thirty minutes of intense thinking, D'Andra phoned Chanelle. They agreed to meet, and were soon sitting at an outdoor café in Leimert Park, a Black business enclave in south Los Angeles.

"I'd had too much to drink that night," Chanelle began shortly after they'd gotten their coffees and were seated. "Me and my date got into an argument, and he left without me. You'd already gone by then, and when I saw Charles, I asked him to drive me home.

"On the way, he asked if I was hungry. I knew I needed to put something in my stomach to soak up all the alcohol, and said yes. We stopped, got some KFC, and then Charles wanted something to drink and stopped at a liquor store."

Chanelle paused and looked at D'Andra, who returned her unflinching gaze.

"When we got to my house," she continued, "Charles said he had to use the bathroom. After he finished, he asked if I wanted a wine cooler. That's the biggest mistake I made that night . . . saying yes. He asked me for a bottle opener. I gave it to him and then went to wash my hands.

"D'Andra," Chanelle said, her eyes beginning to water. "He had to have put something in it, because I only drank one cooler and the next thing I knew I was waking up with my panties down by my ankles and that muthafucka's cum on my thighs."

D'Andra slowly digested this information. Chanelle's explanation shed a whole new light on what D'Andra thought she'd seen that night. D'Andra had noticed Chanelle's drinking, and her date was partying too. After leaving the club, D'Andra became concerned and called to make sure Chanelle was okay.

She tried the cell and home phone several times and when there was still no answer at two am, decided to drive over to Chanelle's and check on her. She remembered being startled to see Charles's car, and instead of knocking, looking into the living room window. When she didn't see anyone, she'd used the extra key they had to each other's homes and went inside. She tiptoed to the bedroom, and saw her worst fear realized.

"That's why you didn't answer when I hollered at you," D'Andra said. "Because you were passed out. I thought it was because you didn't give a damn.

"I never for one minute thought what was happening was against your will. But as long as we'd been friends, I should have known better. I'm sorry, Nelly."

"You came and checked on your girl," Chanelle answered. "To make sure I was all right. There was no way you could have known what was really happening. If I had seen what you saw, I probably would have jumped to the very same conclusion."

"He should be in jail for what he did."

"I tried to press charges. The courts wouldn't prosecute. Said that even with DNA proving we'd had sex, it would just be my word against his. But what goes around comes around. Charles is going to get what's coming to him. Watch and see."

Another interesting development had occurred. There was a new patient on D'Andra's wing of the rehabilitation center—Night's mother, Val. Bringing her thoughts back to the present, D'Andra smiled as she walked down the hall toward her newest patient's room.

It was just after twelve-thirty in the morning. D'Andra tiptoed into the room. She didn't want to wake Val if she was sleeping; just wanted to do a quick check before she began her regularly scheduled round of patients. She placed a finger under her nose to feel her breathing and noted the tone of her skin. Her breath was full and even; her color rich and healthy. All looks fine here, D'Andra thought.

"You leaving without saying hello?" Val asked.

D'Andra turned around. "I didn't mean to wake you, Miss Val. How are you doing? Are we treating you okay?"

"Everybody here is so nice. I'm being treated like a queen. But then, I think you have something to do with that."

"You mean that death threat I put out on anybody who mistreated you?"

They both chuckled.

"Are you sleeping okay? Would you like some medication to help you rest?"

"No, baby, I'm sleeping fine. Just a light-sleeper is

all, have been ever since I gave birth to Night all those years ago."

D'Andra took Val's blood pressure and temperature, and then adjusted her pillows.

"Get a good night's sleep," she admonished. "We want you fresh and ready to go when Bryan comes to work that leg in the morning."

"You mean that pretty boy with those deep blue eyes?"

"May I remind you that you're a married woman," D'Andra teased.

"There's nothing wrong with admiring the product, as long as I don't sample the merchandise."

A little after seven, D'Andra was ready to clock out. Elaine met her in the hallway.

"Have you heard the word, Girlfriend? Your honey is creating quite the buzz."

"Yes, I heard," D'Andra responded dryly. "Even Miss Daisy talked about the nice-looking *colored* man she saw in the hall."

"I'm told that for some mysterious reason Miss Val's vitals get taken much more often when Night's in the room."

"Don't tell me, Rita and the new girl, Allison."

"Watch Allison, that girl is hot to trot. She's the type to slip him her phone number."

"That's why I thank God I'm with a man I can trust. Are we still working out together this weekend?"

"Foot loose and fancy free for one of the rare times in life? You bet!"

Elaine's husband, Max, had joined friends in Big Bear for fishing, poker, too much drinking and male bonding. The children were in San Diego, with Max's mom. Night would be busy Saturday checking out more potential locations for his gym. So the two work colleagues made plans for a rare weekend get together:

a workout at Bally followed by a non-diet dinner and a movie, comedy preferred.

Her thoughts back to the present, D'Andra showered and got ready for bed. She'd just gone into the kitchen for a glass of water when her phone rang. She frowned slightly. It wasn't even eight in the morning and she could count on one hand who had her number. As she went into the living room to pick up the receiver, she fought against the rising blood pressure that came with thinking an emergency had occurred.

"Dee, it's Cassandra."

"Hey, Cassandra. What's wrong?" Belatedly she realized there was no anxiety on the other line. *This is a surprise.* Of the people on one hand she'd figured were calling, her younger sister was not one.

"Sorry to bother you but I wanted to catch you before you went to bed. I need a favor."

"What's that?"

"Can you watch the kids this weekend?"

"Sorry, Cassandra, but I have plans."

"Come on, Dee. I really need you to watch them. I've got an invitation to fly to Palm Springs for the weekend."

"You'll have to take a raincheck," D'Andra replied, yawning. "It's too late for me to change my plans. I miss the little rugrats though and will be happy to watch them another weekend, when we have time to plan ahead."

"Thanks, sister. Maybe next weekend?"

Thanks, sister? First of all, D'Andra thought, Cassandra was not a morning person. Secondly, she usually stomped and pouted for at least five minutes before giving up on a babysitting request and, thirdly, she never *ever* called D'Andra "sister." Something was going on.

"What's the reason for this sunny mood? Did Anthony or Hollah propose?"

"Anthony and Hollah are history. I've got a new man now."

"Girl, I can't keep up with you."

"For the first time in our dating history, I'm trying to keep up with you. I took one look at that chocolate candy you pulled in and knew I had to step up my game!"

"There's a first time for everything. It sounds like you're happy, San."

"Happy is relative; I'm going for satisfied and paid. I just may have found my bank account."

D'Andra didn't respond to this comment. In this area, Cassandra had taken a page directly out of Mary Smalls' playbook.

"Call me later," she said instead. "I'm about to fall asleep talking on the phone."

D'Andra made one more call, canceling her Tuesday workout with Night. After threatening to work her double on Thursday, he wished her sweet dreams. There was a smile on D'Andra's face as she drifted off into dreamland. For the first time in a long time she and Cassandra had had a civil, even friendly conversation. It felt good, and D'Andra hoped it was the start of good things to come.

D'Andra awoke to the sounds of a dog barking near her open window. She looked at the clock and was surprised she'd slept solidly for almost nine hours straight. After a lazy stretch, she rolled over and reached for the cell phone she'd placed on silent before going to sleep.

The first message was from Night, optimistic about another building he'd looked at in Culver City. He teased her about coming over and waking her up for some noonday nooky and said he'd call her later. There was a message from the moderator of the online nutrition course wanting to know if D'Andra would be interested in meeting with those participants who lived in Los Angeles and setting up a regular, monthly pow-wow to share information, experience and needed support. The third message was Cassandra, again. But this time the sunshine in her voice was gone, replaced by sheer panic.

"Dee, what's wrong with your phones? I've been calling and calling. Call me as soon as you get this message. And get down here to Martin Luther King Hospital. It's Mama, Dee, it's Mama. She's had a heart attack. I don't think she's gonna make it."

27

D'Andra threw down the phone and jumped out of bed at the same time. Five minutes later she was in her car, driving erratically and breaking speed limits to get to MLK Hospital and her mother. In the middle of this NASCAR-style speed racing she managed to speed dial Night, Elaine and Chanelle on her cell phone. She made a regularly twenty to twenty-five minute trip in half the time.

She parked in the closest spot to the emergency ward doors, not caring that it was a handicapped space. She raced into the building and looked around frantically. Kayla spotted her first.

"Aunt Dee!"

D'Andra ran over to where Cassandra, Jackie, the kids, and a couple of Mary's friends stood huddled together. They were listening attentively to a tired-looking doctor in a wrinkled white coat.

"How is she?" D'Andra gasped out, trying to catch her breath at the same time.

The doctor turned to her. "You must be the other daughter. I'm Dr. Wein—"

"I know who you are." Dr. Weinstein was the same doctor who'd spoken to D'Andra when she was in emergency five months ago. "How is my mother? Is she alive?"

"You've got to calm down, Ms. Smalls," the doctor said in a firm yet gentle voice. "The doctors are still working to stabilize her, but we believe she's going to pull through."

D'Andra visibly relaxed, or almost collapsed is a better description.

"As soon as she's completely stable, we'll have to run a series of tests to see exactly what's going on in the old ticker," he said, trying to ease a very tense situation. "I don't want to say anything further until there is specific, concrete information available."

The doctor looked down at a sudden and somewhat forceful fist on his leg.

"You better fix my grandma!" Antoine's face was serious, his stance one of the kick-boxing positions Night had taught him.

Dr. Weinstein, a grandfather himself, knelt down to Antoine's eye level. "I tell you what, little man. The other doctors and I are going to do everything we can to make sure you get your grandmother back as good as new. Do you know what you can do to help me?"

Antoine shook his head no.

"You can send a whole bunch of love to your grandma by thinking good thoughts about her. This situation is scary isn't it?"

Antoine nodded yes.

"Well, whenever you begin to feel that little shiver of fear, just send a whole bunch of I-love-you thoughts to your grandmother. You'll be helping all of us doctors help your grandma get well. Deal?"

"Deal." Antoine then shook Dr. Weinstein's outstretched hand.

The small group of Mary supporters was silent as they watched the doctor's retreating back go through the double doors down the hall. Antoine hadn't been the only one listening to Dr. Weinstein's instruction. Everybody in the huddle, in that moment, was sending Mary Smalls a "whole bunch of love."

D'Andra wiped away tears even as she felt arms come around her.

"Baby doll, I'm here." Night turned D'Andra into his chest and hugged her tightly.

D'Andra fought against breaking down completely. "Night," she whispered. She held on to him for dear life, as if she were a sailboat flailing in a storm and he was the life anchor.

"I got here as soon as I could. How's your mother?"

"She's alive, thank God. The doctor said he thinks she'll make it." D'Andra remembered Dr. Weinstein's words. "She'll make it," she said with more confidence.

Night hugged her again.

"Wait," D'Andra pulled back from Night. "What about your other clients, your meeting . . ."

"D'Andra, nothing is more important than you and my being here to make sure you're all right. Surely you know that by now."

D'Andra nodded her head against his strong chest. "I love you," she whispered.

Night wondered if he'd heard what he thought he heard. He squeezed her to him a little tighter. For now it was enough to believe that he had.

Within the hour, several more people joined the vigil for Mary taking place in the emergency room waiting area. Elaine came in bearing gifts: donuts, fruit and an assortment of coloring books and crayons for Cassandra's children. D'Andra marveled at her maternal thoughtfulness even as she realized that care and compassion came as natural as breathing to her dear friend Elaine. Chanelle arrived about fifteen minutes after Elaine. When D'Andra looked up and saw Frank coming through the doors she almost lost it again, and ran into his arms.

"Thanks for coming, Frank!" she cried.

"You know I wasn't going to leave a Berry fan hanging. How's your mother, doll?"

"We think she's going to . . . she's going to be okay."

"What about you? How are you doing?"

D'Andra smiled into the kind, worn face of this gentle man. "Better now."

The cast of characters in Mary's drama expanded then decreased over the next three hours. Everyone stood to their feet when Dr. Weinstein came into the room. That he was walking over with a smile on his face relieved everyone.

He walked over to Antoine and once again held out his hand. "You did a very, very good job," he told the wide-eyed five-year-old. "Your grandmother is doing well, she's resting comfortably, and I am positive she felt your love."

Antoine looked solemnly at the doctor for a moment before throwing his little brown-skinned arms around a ruddy neck. Everyone watching held back tears.

Dr. Weinstein then addressed the larger group, telling them that they would be keeping Mary a while, that a series of tests had to be run and that everyone should go home and try and get some rest.

"When can we see her?" D'Andra asked.

"She's pretty groggy right now. If we could limit these first visits to the daughters and maybe one or two more people, and only for a few minutes, that would be best."

Within minutes D'Andra, Cassandra and Jackie were standing around a sleeping Mary Smalls. D'Andra held her mother's hand tightly while Cassandra kept smoothing Mary's hair. Without thinking, D'Andra found and took a fast-beating pulse. Jackie whispered

The Lord's Prayer under her breath. Mary's eyes fluttered open.

Her voice was barely above a whisper. "What . . . what are y'all doing? Why . . . are . . . you . . . standing . . ."

"Shh, Mama. Don't try to talk. You had a heart attack and are in the hospital. Everything's going to be okay."

"I . . . what?"

"Just take it easy, Mama," Cassandra said. "Try and get some rest."

"Auntie, what are you doing? Trying to scare the hell out of me? Well, just for the record, it's working. I think I'll go to church next Sunday, and I haven't been since I don't know when!"

Jackie's outburst brought the slightest of smiles to Mary's lips.

"Good," she whispered. *I need to go too, if I make it out of here*, Mary thought. Her eyes lit up when she saw Cassandra, and her smile widened when she turned and looked at D'Andra. She looked at her eldest daughter a long moment. "I love you," she mouthed. Then her eyes fluttered closed.

After a few moments, a nurse came into the room. "Sorry folks, but we need Mary to get her rest now. She'll more than likely sleep for at least four to six hours. So if I were you, I'd go get something to eat, and some rest, and then come back tomorrow. Everyone, including your mother, will be feeling better."

D'Andra was touched by the nurse's bedside manner. "Oh, you're good, you're real good," she said with a smile. And then she whispered in the middle-aged blonde's ear. "And that's spoken from one nurse to another."

The nurse winked at her and then her demeanor changed from personal to professional as she began checking her patient. D'Andra blew a kiss to her mother and the familial trio quietly left the room.

Night looked up as D'Andra reentered the waiting room. He quickly finished his call, flipped shut his phone and met D'Andra in the middle of the room. His facial expression was a question mark.

"She was only awake for a few minutes, but there's color in her cheeks and her breathing was fairly normal. The doctor said there was nothing we could do right now and the nurse admonished us to try and get some rest."

"Where's your car? I'll follow you home."

"That's so sweet of you baby, but really, I'll be okay. I know yours has been an incredibly long day already. Elaine and Chanelle are here and said they'd stay with me as long as I needed."

"But I want to be here for you too."

"You already are, and I appreciate it more than you know. But you've been working so hard, and these long hours will take their toll if you don't get some rest. I'll call you later, promise."

Night hesitated, visibly torn about leaving D'Andra at such a vulnerable time.

Elaine walked up and put a hand on his arm. "We'll take really good care of her," she said softly. "And we'll make sure she calls and keeps you updated on everything going on."

"She's lucky to have a friend like you," Night replied to Elaine. "You too," he said to Chanelle.

"We're the lucky ones," Elaine and Chanelle said in unison.

Their joint laughter lightened the mood of the room and while Mary's friends decided to stay a while longer, everyone else headed to the parking lot. Night walked D'Andra to her car.

He opened her door and made sure she was buckled in before giving her a gentle, probing kiss full of all the love and compassion his heart felt at that moment. The poignancy of his touch moved D'Andra to tears.

She cupped his face. "What did I do to deserve you?" she asked.

"Be born," he said simply. "Make sure you keep checking in with me so I know you're okay."

A short time later, D'Andra, Elaine and Chanelle sat at a 24-hour diner.

"Try and eat something," Elaine coaxed D'Andra. "You'll need your strength later.

D'Andra managed a few small spoonfuls of the aromatic vegetable soup she had ordered. Meanwhile both Chanelle and Elaine had finished their meals and sat silently watching their friend.

"You know," D'Andra began, fiddling with the spoon in her soup. "My mother said 'I love you' to me today. I can't remember the last time that happened."

"Being close to death always puts things in perspective," Elaine offered. "Maybe out of this horrific incident can come a new, more agreeable relationship between you and your mom."

"You know Miss Mary loves you," Chanelle said. "Some people just have a hard time saying it. My mother's the same way. That just makes the words even more special when I hear them."

D'Andra nodded. "I know that Mama loves me. But it sure felt good to hear the words, even whispered."

While Chanelle and Elaine ordered dessert, D'Andra called the hospital for an update on Mary's condition and then checked in with Night.

"I'm checking in," she said with a smile.

"Thank you, doll. Any change with your mother?"

"No, I just called the hospital and they said she's resting comfortably. They'll run tests later tonight, or tomorrow, depending on how she's feeling. Now, why aren't you asleep already?"

"I was waiting for your call."

His thoughtfulness nearly moved her to tears. "I love you Night."

Night was sure he'd heard the words this time, and his heart swelled at the sound. He answered without hesitating. "I love you, too."

D'Andra had just hung up from Night when her phone rang again. She didn't recognize the number but answered anyway.

"Baby, it's Miss Val," said the voice on the other end of the line. "Night told me about your mother. I hope you don't mind that he gave me your number and I'm calling so late."

"Not at all, Miss Val. It's so sweet of you to call."

"I know how upsetting something like this can be, especially when it's your mother. I've been there, and wanted you to know I was thinking about you, and praying for you, your mother and the rest of your family."

"That means more to me than you know. I'll carry the thoughts of your prayers with me. Now, how's that leg?"

"You know, baby, it's the strangest thing. But every time that cute little therapist gets to touching it I feel better."

Val's light humor instantly lifted D'Andra's spirits. "You're a mess, Miss Val. But isn't Bryan off today?"

"Yes, child, but I'm talking about the other one, Matthew."

D'Andra had heard about the part-time therapist the hospital had hired, but she'd never met him. She shared this information with Night's mother. "I'm sure you'll tell me all about him when I see you."

"Uh-huh. I even sent Carter out for some magazines just so I could, you know, have some private time with my new friend."

D'Andra's laugh was genuine. "I can see I might have to come in early and make sure you behave."

"Don't worry, I have another new friend who's taking care of that."

"Who?"

"Her name is Frieda. She heard me humming a hymn when she was doing her hall walking exercise. Came in and introduced herself. She come calling me Grace the next time she came in, and I told her that if she wanted to keep coming into my room, to get my name right."

D'Andra howled at this news. "Well, you're a better woman than I am. She calls me Grace too, and I just call her Miss Daisy."

"You know where that name came from, right? Now I don't know how true this is but my mother, who was born in Mississippi, said her mother told her the old masters would often go through several housekeeper maids in as many years and instead of bothering to remember their real names would simply call all of them Grace."

D'Andra was appalled; she'd had no idea.

"So I wanted to make sure—who do you call her— Miss Daisy and me got off on the right foot. That she understood I wasn't born yesterday and that she'd have to get up mighty early if she wanted to pull an insult like that over on me. Anyway, you take care, baby. I'll see you soon."

Val's phone call totally changed D'Andra's demeanor and lifted her spirits. For the first time she truly believed that her mother would live. The realness of this belief revitalized D'Andra.

"Waiter?" she called out as the young man passed their table. "Can you heat up my soup?"

* * *

Jazz sat and gazed at the doors to Bally Fitness, wondering for the umpteenth time why she was there, why Night wouldn't return her calls and why she couldn't get him out of her thoughts. At first she placed her fixation on the fact that he'd been by far the best lover she'd ever had. Then she wondered if it had to do with knowing she'd been replaced by a woman twice her size. Finally she gave up trying to figure out why. She just knew she'd do anything to win Night back.

She straightened out her carefully chosen outfit as she walked toward the gym to demand a conversation with Night. An earlier phone call to the gym had confirmed he was teaching his Wednesday night kickboxing class, a fact further evidenced by seeing his car in the parking lot.

Appreciative male eyes and envious female ones turned toward her as she walked into the gym. Her form-fitting white mini-skirt showed off a tight, round derriere and firm, scar-free legs, further elongated by three-inch strappy white sandals. The matching white midriff she wore emphasized a flat stomach and played up her surgically enhanced orbs. She walked up to the glass of the room where Night's class was being conducted and tossed back her long, straight black hair while lifting her chin in greeting when he noticed her. Then she sat on a workout bench directly in front of the glass, crossed her legs and waited patiently. She looked as though she'd been torn from a fashion magazine, with the poise and grace of a princess.

"Why didn't you take the class?" Marc asked as he sat down on a bench next to hers.

"Hey, Marc."

"You're looking beautiful, as usual."

Jazz simply smiled.

"So you just came down to stare at your ex?"

Jazz's smile disappeared. "Is why I'm here any of your business?"

"Whoa, what's with the attitude? I just asked a question. You're not a member here; it's not like I had to let you in."

"You're right, Marc. I apologize for being snippy. I'm here to see Night for personal reasons." Jazz flashed a come-hither smile. "Is that a better answer?"

"Much."

"What time is this class over?"

Marc looked at his watch. "In about ten minutes."

Jazz turned her full attention back to Night, drinking in his amazing physique as he kicked his leg to the side and straight up. His posture was perfect, his hands balled into fists and positioned at waist level. His body glistened with sweat, its darkness further enhanced by the stark white drawstring pants he wore. Jazz's body hummed as she remembered the feeling of that mass of muscle covering her. She wanted to feel it again.

Night toweled off and patiently answered questions from his class of mostly female boxers once his class ended. He knew that Jazz was waiting on him and therefore was in no hurry to leave the room. At the same time, he knew D'Andra was also waiting on him, which spurred him into action. He gathered his personal items and placed them in a black leather gym bag. The rich scent of a luxury perfume alerted him that Jazz was in the room before he turned around.

"I forgot how beautiful your body is," Jazz said.

"What's up, Jazz?"

"Once again, you're not returning my calls."

"I've been busy. Besides, since we're no longer business partners I don't know what it is that we have to talk about."

"What about responding because we were lovers for almost four years? And friends as well, or so I thought."

Night headed out of the room. Jazz followed beside him. Those observing noted they looked the perfect couple, made a striking pair.

"I thought we were friends, too," Night said. He acknowledged people here and there in the gym with a wave or a nod. "But that was before I found out you played a part in sabotaging my building in the Ladera Heights mall."

"I what?" Jazz asked incredulously.

"Oh, please. Don't even try it. I know what good *friends* you and Brad are. Do you want me to believe you had nothing to do with the sudden complications that cropped up regarding getting the sale finalized?"

Jazz stood in between Night and his door after he got into his car. "Night, I admit I know about the problems you're having, but I swear I had nothing to do with them. Please don't be mad at Brad for revealing confidential information but he's how I know what happened. I coaxed the information out of him, swore to end our friendship if he didn't tell me."

Night's smile was predatory. "I just bet you did. I can just about imagine your *coaxing.*"

Jazz stifled her anger. Now was not the time to lose her cool. She sidled up to Night and placed a soft hand on his hard arm. "I wasn't responsible for your deal falling through," she said softly. "But I'll do whatever I can to be responsible for getting the sale back on track. If that's what you want."

Night sighed as he looked squarely at Jazz. There was no denying her sex appeal.

Jazz, believing in the effect she thought she was having, leaned into Night, her breast rubbing against Night's firm biceps.

"What I want right now," he said after a moment. "Is to leave the parking lot. Someone very special is waiting for me. And I'm late."

Jazz could no longer hold her ire. His blatant dismissal of her was too much. "Fine," she said, her chest heaving with each angry breath. "But understand this Night Simmons. You *will* come back to me. We are perfect for each other and you know it. And after you get through playing at the fat farm . . . you'll be back."

Night could feel the tension ebbing away from his neck and shoulder muscles as he turned onto the street of D'Andra's apartment. She buzzed him into the building and he entered her place with the sounds of the Temptations' *My Girl*. He immediately put down the bottle of wine and bouquet of flowers he was holding, grabbed D'Andra around the waist and began twirling her around the room as he sang:

I don't need no money, fortune or fame. I have all the riches baby doll, one man can claim . . .

D'Andra melted into Night's arms, swaying and moving as if she were Ginger Rogers and he Fred Astaire. They danced until the song ended, and then shared a passionate kiss, their tongues moving and swirling as their bodies had done seconds before.

"What have you brought me?" D'Andra squealed as she broke their embrace. "Look at the flowers, Night. They're beautiful. And how did you know how much I love crystal? The vase is perfect."

She took the bowl of iris, larkspur and white roses, with similarly colored beads resting in the vase bottom, and placed them in the center of her living room's coffee table. The colors blended perfectly with her purple, ice blue, silver and black color scheme.

"How's your mother doing?"

"I just talked to Chanelle. She and Jackie just left and said she was still pretty much in and out of sleep. I plan to be there first thing in the morning."

"Now aren't you glad you took a personal day?"

"Yes, JaJuan Night Simmons. This is one order that I'm glad I followed."

"So . . . we're in for the night?"

D'Andra smiled. "Uh-huh."

Night wriggled his eyebrows.

"Is sex always on your mind?"

"Only when I'm around you." Night remembered his reaction to Jazz earlier and knew this statement to be true.

"So are you hungry?" D'Andra asked as she looked at the label on the bottle of wine. "Something to go with this Bordeaux?"

"Yes, I'm ready to eat," Night replied. He walked over and did his favorite thing: cupping D'Andra's ample yet increasingly firm bottom and pressing her to his manhood. "And everything I need to go with that bottle is right here."

While Night took a shower, D'Andra rifled through her cabinets and came up with the fixings for a simple pasta dish. The single glass of wine that each of them had with dinner was the perfect complement. She scooped up the last piece of pasta, swirled it in the remaining tomato sauce and relished the bite. When she opened her eyes, it was to see near black irises boring into her hazel ones.

She licked her lips in anticipation, all too aware of what that look signaled. Night was going to ravish her. It was exactly what she needed.

He came around the table and took her hand. Instead of the bedroom, he walked into the living room where the Temptations had been replaced by Smokey Robinson and the Miracles talking about seconding an emotion.

"I didn't know you liked old school," he said as he lifted D'Andra's top over her head.

"My mother is the fanatic," D'Andra replied. "I put these CDs on because the sounds remind me of her."

"Your mother has excellent taste," he said, nibbling her neck, licking the sides of her mouth. "You taste good too."

D'Andra returned the fervor of Night's kiss, noting that his mouth tasted like the fine wine they'd just consumed. She stepped away from him to loosen the string on the black, baggy drawstring pants he now wore. They dropped to the floor. He wore no underwear.

"Oh my," she said, as she wrapped her fingers around the large engorged head that sprang up its greeting. "It looks like you have something for me."

Night didn't answer but instead placed his fingers in the sides of D'Andra's elasticized pants and pulled them down. He followed the pants down to the floor, placing his mouth directly in front of D'Andra's throbbing womanhood. He began licking her through the sheer, pink panties she wore, placing his hands on her butt and pulling her even closer. D'Andra gasped even as Night commanded her to spread her legs.

She did as she was instructed and barely managed to remain upright as Night assaulted her senseless. He pulled her panties to the side for a more intimate exploration of her feminine treasure, his tongue probing, licking, his teeth nipping, teasing.

D'Andra's legs turned to butter. "Night, please, I can't . . ." She melted to the floor.

"Just where I want you," Night said. He reached behind D'Andra and unlatched her bra. D'Andra's vagina felt his absence immediately, and she instantly yearned for what threatened to be her undoing just seconds before. But her thoughts were quickly shifted as Night lifted a full, heavy breast and placed her hard, extended nipple into his mouth. He suckled her as if she were an aphrodisiac, his hands gently

kneading and exploring the rest of her body as he
gave first one nipple and then the other pleasure.

Just when D'Andra thought she could take no
more he lifted his head, stood up and reached for
her. D'Andra didn't question, simply raised herself
from the floor to greet him. Night walked toward her
recently purchased pewter-and-tan-colored dining
room set. On the way, he stopped and reached into
his small traveling case for protection, and then proceeded to lead them to the dining area. He sat down
in one of the straight-back yet comfortable wood-
finished chairs.

He silently handed her the condom and whispered.
"Put it on me."

D'Andra smiled as she knelt down in front of Night's
masterpiece. She took his massive shaft into her hand
and stroked it lovingly. But instead of putting on the
condom, she placed as much of him as she could in
her mouth, her tongue swirling around the tip, her fingers tickling his heavy balls. Night's groan was long and
audible.

"Baby doll, doll . . ."

Emboldened by this power, D'Andra took him in
as far as his gargantuan size allowed. She sucked him
hard, his power rod lengthening even more. She in-
creased the rhythm of her hand strokes along his
shaft, as her head bobbed up and down and her
tongue swirled to catch the love juices he emitted.
Night placed his hand on the back of D'Andra's head,
pushing himself farther into her soft, moist oral cavity.

Now it was Night's turn to call for surrender. "Baby,
please, I'm getting ready to . . ."

D'Andra lifted her head and in one smooth movement protected them both. Then she straddled him
and eased ever so slowly down on his pulsing piece
of flesh. They both moaned this time, grinding into

each other, their tongues matching the lower parts of their bodies, Night's hands massaging D'Andra's aching breasts as his mouth alternated between them and her mouth. He tried to take in the whole of her even as he arched up to reach the very core of her soul with his love sword. It was as if he were trying to draw her very essence into himself.

Their dance started off slowly and then quickened in pace as their ardor heightened. After several moments of D'Andra riding Night as if she were a jockey in the Kentucky Derby, Night lifted D'Andra and himself from the chair and while remaining connected to her, placed her up against the wall, held her leg in the crook of his arm and pounded into her relentlessly. D'Andra had never been a screamer but she soon realized the teeming sound coming into her ears was her own voice. Tears poured down her face as Night continued to unite their flesh, pulling out to the tip and then ramming deep, all the time whispering questions in her ear. "Is this good for you baby? Is this what you want? Where's my love button, doll? Is it here?" He shifted to another angle and rammed deeper into her. "Is it here?"

D'Andra continued to moan, groan, scream and cry but Night wasn't finished. He led her over to the couch, placed her on all fours and entered her from behind. He grabbed her cheeks and spread them wide, allowing himself access to all parts of her treasure. D'Andra's breasts swayed back and forth as she matched his rhythm, pushing her butt even higher in the air for his easy access.

"Yes, Night. Yes! Yes!"

"Give me more, doll. I want it all. I want everything you've got. Now give it to me!"

He lifted her to the couch in an angle that allowed him to enter even more fully. D'Andra's cries had dropped to a hoarse whimper. She continued to have one orgasm after another. Night's hips moved at a frenzied pace as he neared his own release. When he finally exploded, propelling them both toward the heavens, D'Andra's name was the one shouted from his lips.

28

The next morning, D'Andra left her Culver City condo and arrived at the hospital a little before ten o'clock. Several vases of flowers and a couple of green plants were placed on various surfaces throughout Mary's semi-private room. The partially draped window let in shards of sunlight that danced across the pale green linoleum floor. For the moment Mary was alone, the patient in the bed beside her having been wheeled out for tests. D'Andra entered tentatively, quietly, not wanting to wake her mom if she were sleeping.

She stood at the foot of her mother's bed watching her breathe. For the first time she fully took in the stress lines etched around her mother's mouth, which stood out in juxtaposition to the excess fat hanging from her jaw and melting into her neck. Her mother's stomach rose several inches higher than her head and the thin sheet could hardly hide the massive hips and thighs that lay beneath it. D'Andra swallowed her emotions and cleared her throat.

"Mama?" she almost whispered.

Mary's eyes fluttered open. "I wasn't asleep."

D'Andra walked around to her mother's side and

gingerly sat on the edge of the bed. She brushed her
hand across her mother's forehead, then placed her
fingertips on her mother's wrist and took a quick pulse.

"Where is everybody?"

"You just missed them. They're down in the cafeteria getting a bite to eat; Jackie and Karen, Boss, San
and some new friend of hers, White man."

"Aunt Karen's here?" It had been a long time since
D'Andra had seen Jackie's mother. It touched her
that she'd flown in from Vegas, where she lived.

"How are you doing, Mama?"

"Always the nurse, huh, D'Andra?"

"Yes, I guess so."

"I never told you but I'm proud you're a nurse."

Mary was right. She'd never told her. The profess-
ing of this truth threatened to open the floodgate of
tears that swam so near to the surface for D'Andra
these days.

"Thank you for telling me, Mama. It means so
much for me to hear you say that."

"There's so much I haven't told you. But now . . . I
think I should."

D'Andra accurately guessed the reason behind
Mary's change of mind about opening up with her
daughter. She'd found out earlier, through a phone call
with Dr. Weinstein, that Mary would have to have
open heart surgery, a triple bypass. While Dr. Weinstein
tried to assure D'Andra the surgery was fairly routine,
D'Andra was well aware of its severity. How routine
could it be to cut into and open up one's heart?

But she could tell her mother was still very weak.
The voice that usually boomed now spoke just above
a whisper. Maybe now was not the time. That's what
she told her mom.

"Maybe later, when you're stronger," she offered.

Mary shook her head. "What if later never comes?"

When D'Andra started to protest she held up a weak hand. "They want to perform the operation as soon as possible and I'm believing that I'll come through it with flying colors. But I'll feel better going into that room if I've left nothing behind that remains unsaid. This conversation is long overdue."

D'Andra waited as her mother tried to find a more comfortable position. She helped by shifting pillows and bringing the bed up to a more upright position. Now that the moment had arrived, D'Andra wondered just how much she really wanted to hear of what her mother planned to tell her. She'd just recently begun to reconcile herself to the fact that like thousands of other children she might never know her father and was in the process of trying to become okay with that idea.

"You and Cassandra were always so different," Mary began again. "Not only in looks, but in personality too. You were and are the more serious and more compassionate one. Cassandra is more how I used to be—wild and rambunctious, giving in to the pleasures of the moment.

"She got something else from me that I wish she hadn't. But it's my fault because its how I raised both of you—to believe that all a man is good for is money.

"Around the time I got pregnant with you, I was seeing several different men, intimately. I'm not proud of this D'Andra, but at the time it's what I did. I never had to work more than a part-time job because one would pay my rent, another my utilities, another my car payment, and so on and so forth. There's not many pictures of me from those days but baby, I was the stuff. It wasn't hard for me to get a man, just hard to keep one.

"But there was this one man that came on the scene that I fell hard for. He was nice-looking, hard-working, no nonsense, a man's man if you know what I mean. He knew I was seeing other men and in the beginning he went along with it. But things quickly got serious and he told me that if I wanted to be with him, he'd have to be the only one. I told him if he was the only one we'd have to get married and he'd have to take care of me in the same way I was being taken care of by all the other men. He told me what he couldn't give me in material things, he'd make up for in the way he loved me. And I believed him.

"Orlando was one of the men I was seeing and as much as I loved your father, I had a thing for Orlando as well. He was wild, like me, and provided the excitement I felt I was getting ready to give up by staying with this other man. I was ready to, mind you, because I was getting tired of the revolving door and wasn't getting any younger. But it was still excitement that I knew I'd miss.

"Orlando was driving a truck then and he came into town the same day your father went out of town. He was going to some seminar for the sales job he had. I invited Orlando over for one more wild time before I gave up all the other men for your daddy. I told Orlando it was going to be the last time and we really whooped it up, drinking and smoking and carrying on. Then we went to bed. A little while later your father walked in on us in the middle of, well, you know. The seminar had been cancelled at the last minute and his boss had given his employees the day off. I'll never forget it. He had a dozen red roses in one hand and a box of my favorite donuts in the other. He dropped them both as soon as he opened the door. I thought a fight was getting ready to break out but that didn't happen. Instead, he just looked at both of us a long moment, and then turned and walked out the door. He never came back."

A single tear rolled down Mary's round cheek as she relived the agony of losing the only man she'd truly loved and the promiscuous past she'd long since left behind. D'Andra's pain mirrored her mother's. Yet having caught Charles directly in the act, she had a feeling of what her father must have been feeling as well.

"So how is it that Orlando thought he was my father?"

Mary took a sip of water and cleared her throat. She grimaced slightly and D'Andra caught it.

"Are you okay? Where are you hurting?"

"I'm fine."

"Are you sure? Maybe I should get the doctor."

"I'm fine, D'Andra. I want to get this out." She closed her eyes for a brief moment and then stared out the window as she continued. "Orlando knew how I felt about your father and felt bad that he'd been the one responsible for our break-up. Of course, the fault rested solely with me but Orlando chose to share the blame because he was there. He also knew your father; they'd been casual associates. They both rode motorcycles at the time and would see each other at the club or at some of the biker events. So even though I stopped seeing most of the other guys, I kept seeing Orlando. Eventually he moved in and shortly after that, I found out I was pregnant.

"At first he didn't question that you were his. You favor me much more than your father, but there are definite attributes of his that you inherited. One of them is your strong, compassionate personality and another is your hard work ethic. But as you got older, Orlando did start questioning whether or not you were his child. By then I'd gone back to my old habits and had started seeing Cassandra's father on the side.

"I'm not proud of this," she repeated, as if her daughter needed convincing. "Cassandra's father swept me off my feet with his good looks and smooth talk and even though he was married, I couldn't resist the charm. When I got pregnant with San . . . that's when Orlando left me. I only saw him occasionally after that and after he left town, moved to Chicago, I never saw him again."

D'Andra's heart pounded as she pondered the question she must ask, and ask she did. "What happened to my father?"

"He moved away for a while as well. I heard he'd moved to the east coast, I even think he spent time overseas. Then he came back here and found the type of woman he was trying to make me, one who acted like she had some sense. And when he found her, he married her.

"I wish I could say that's all to the story but there's one more part. When your father came back, I was determined to get him back. I went to him and told him I had a child by him. He wouldn't listen for a second, didn't want to know your name, see a picture, refused to even speak to me. I didn't know it at the time but he'd gotten married. It didn't matter. I still pursued him relentlessly. This was before tests and DNA and all of that stuff. He simply refused to believe he could be the father of my child and that was that. I can't say I totally blamed him. Given my history he had every right to be skeptical.

"One day I ran into his wife at the store. One look and I could see she was pregnant. Things got ugly, real ugly. I ended up assaulting her physically, we ended up falling down on the sidewalk. The jut of the curb hit her in the abdomen. She later lost the baby.

"She didn't press charges but looking back, she should have. It was a horrible thing I'd done and while I don't know for sure what her doctors told her . . . in my heart I know I caused her to lose that child.

And what's worse, at the time, I was glad I did. Then the reality of what I'd done began to sink in. I caused a type of pain no mother should have to go through. To this day, I feel guilty. I don't think your dad and her ever had a child together."

D'Andra sat stunned. So this was the shame Orlando spoke about, why he'd asked her not to judge her mother too harshly.

"Orlando knew?"

Mary shrugged. "He may have heard about it. Like I said, he and your father knew some of the same people from the motorcycle club. It may be one of the reasons he washed his hands of me. At one point, I tried to get Orlando back, sent him messages through mutual friends we knew. But he had met someone in Chicago and let it be known that in no uncertain terms he was not interested. I fell into a deep depression for a while after that. For almost two weeks, I barely got out of bed."

Although Mary spent a lot of time in the bedroom now, D'Andra couldn't remember her doing so when she was a child. In fact, all through high school, she remembered her mother always on the go.

"So how did all this happen and I not remember?" D'Andra asked. "Your staying in bed, being depressed, I don't recall any of this."

A faint smile appeared on Mary's face. "You can thank your Aunt Karen. Remember when you and San went to stay with her in Vegas that time, for about a month?"

D'Andra remembered it well. She'd turned nine years old that summer; Cassandra was six and Jackie was seven. It was hot as Hades but Aunt Karen brought an inflatable pool, some beach balls and snorkeling sets. They'd played in the pool all day, almost every day, and would come out with hair spongy as wool and skin shriveled as raisins. That month was one of D'Andra's favorite childhood memories.

"Karen knew everything that had happened. She called me the day I found out Orlando got married. I was crying like a fool, talking crazy. She was concerned for me and even more for y'all; she knew it wasn't healthy for you girls to see your mama all out of sorts. And I was a mess. So she and Ann worked together to get y'all down there. She bought the bus tickets and everything."

D'Andra nodded, remembering when Dominque's mother had taken them to the bus station. Dominque had cried because she couldn't ride the bus too, even though at that time, they barely knew each other. It wasn't until two years later that they became best friends. Then, D'Andra remembered something else.

"Mama, did you ever talk about this with Sam?"

Mary looked surprised. "Cassandra's daddy? Yeah, why?"

"Remember that day you found me asleep in the closet? It was shortly after we returned from Vegas."

Mary creased her brow, trying to remember. She finally shook her head no. "Y'all were always doing silly stuff. I probably didn't pay it any attention."

"Well, it was because I overheard a conversation, and you called someone a b-i-t-c-h. I think you might have been talking about this woman, but I thought you were talking about me. That's why I hid."

Mary's eyes teared up once again. "D'Andra, I would never, ever do that!" Her voice softened. "But I must admit, there was a time I hated you. I'm so sorry, but I hated you because I *wanted* to be a part of your father's life and you *are* a part of him. I'm so sorry!"

Mary cried openly now. D'Andra walked over, sat on the bed, and quietly rubbed her mother's shoulders as the tears flowed.

"Shh, Mama, don't do this to yourself. Don't get any more upset than you are already." D'Andra wrapped her hands around her mother's arms and rocked her gently. Finally the crying stopped, but the tears still flowed.

The admission and deliverance of indescribable pain brought a pallor over the room and with it silence. It was almost a full five minutes before either of them spoke again.

"What's my father's name?" D'Andra asked finally, her voice barely above a whisper, her eyes brimming with unshed tears.

Mary looked her daughter in the face and pronounced a name she'd rarely spoken aloud in decades. But it was time. Her daughter deserved to know.

"Johnson," Mary said, feeling the weight lift from her conscience even as she uttered the name. "Your biological father's name is Carter Johnson."

29

D'Andra sat stunned. She was sure she'd heard incorrectly. Had her mother just uttered the name Carter Johnson? The same name as Night's stepfather? There was no way, absolutely no way she could have heard right. Her mother's voice was weak, she'd almost been whispering. D'Andra relaxed the tension that had immediately built up in her shoulders. She took a deep breath, determined to hear better this time.

"Who'd you say, Mama?"

"Carter Johnson," Mary repeated in a slightly stronger voice. "The woman . . . his wife's name is Valerie," she added, furthering the proof that D'Andra had heard correctly the first time.

"I'm so ashamed to tell you this but your father's right here, D'Andra, in Los Angeles. He's been here this whole time, practically the whole time you've been begging to get to know him."

Mary placed her head in her hands and sobbed quietly into them. D'Andra sat and watched her, dazed, partly wanting to reach out, partly wanting to run out. There were so many emotions running through her, she couldn't tell which one was more prevalent at any given moment: love for her mother finally telling the truth, hate for it having taken so long, shock at the fact that her father was alive, and living in L.A., sadness for all the time together they'd missed; numbness at how she could possibly break this news to Night and his mother. Her biological father had raised her lover as his son.

D'Andra rose from the bed and walked to the window. A couple chatted animatedly as they walked to the parking lot, hospital employees walked with heads down and purposeful strides, others talked on their cell phones. A plane flew overhead and a bicyclist navigated between the sidewalk and the grass. Outside, life went on as normal. But here in this room, D'Andra's world had been turned upside down.

"Talk to me, D'Andra. I know that after all these years of your asking me to do it and me acting a fool and refusing I have no right to ask. But talk to me. What are you feeling, baby? I know you probably hate me now, but do you think there might come a time when you forgive me?"

"It's a little more complicated than you realize," D'Andra answered, still looking out the window.

"I . . . I don't understand. Granted, I don't have Carter's number but I know some people who are still in contact with him. I can make sure you have his information . . . to contact him. I know that's what you want."

"You don't have to look him up, Mama. I know where he lives." She turned around to find Mary's surprised eyes fixed on her.

"You mean to tell me you already know Carter Johnson?"

D'Andra's laugh was without humor. "Yes, in fact I met him in this very hospital a little over a month ago. He was here visiting his wife, Val."

Mary's frown deepened, not making the immediate

connection. "But what were you doing here? Were you doing some type of work or something?"

"No, Mama. I was here specifically to see her. Carter Johnson is my boyfriend's stepfather, Mama, and Val is Night's mother."

"Oh, my God." The full ramifications of Mary's secrecy slowing began creeping through her initial veil of disbelief. She looked at her daughter, now standing dry-eyed and resolute. "D'Andra, I'm so sorry. I'm so, so sorry. Oh, God," she repeated. "What have I done?"

Cassandra and Jackie entered the room laughing but immediately sobered.

"What's the matter?" Cassandra asked. "Dee, why is Mama crying?"

"It's a long story," D'Andra answered. "About my father."

That night, despite the strong desire to take another personal day, D'Andra went to work. But the closer she got to the hospital, the slower she drove. She dreaded walking into the lobby and onto her ward. Night's mother, Val Johnson, was there waiting for her visit. Waiting for her to pop in around twelve-thirty, the way she usually did, soon after beginning her eleven to seven shift. D'Andra didn't see how she could avoid Night's mother, but she also didn't see how she could face her. Or Night, who was probably already wondering what was going on. He'd called her three times and left two messages. It was the first time since her initial encounter with Jazz that she hadn't returned his calls.

Elaine noticed something wrong immediately and as soon as they'd gotten their assignments from the chief nurse, she pulled D'Andra into a supply room and closed the door.

"I know Black people don't pale, but you look like you've seen a ghost!"

"I have," D'Andra responded. "The ghost of my mother's past."

Elaine could sense D'Andra was fighting back tears, trying to keep herself together. She placed a gentle arm around her friend's shoulders.

"Sometimes it helps to talk about it."

D'Andra shook her head. "I don't know where I'd start. I'm still trying to sort it out myself. You know the saying that truth is stranger than fiction?"

Elaine nodded.

"I'm living that strange truth right now."

Elaine didn't understand, but instead of asking probing questions remained silent.

"It's about my father," D'Andra said a few seconds later.

"Oh, honey," Elaine said, hugging her friend more fully. Now D'Andra's tight-lipped, pained expression made sense. She stepped back, placed her hands on D'Andra's shoulders and looked her in the eye. "So . . . you now know the name of your father?"

"Yes," D'Andra answered. "And that's all I can say right now."

The two left the supply room after that and before long were absorbed in their work routine: taking vitals, passing meds, making reports. Her first patient was Frieda, who wide-awake at eleven-thirty, wanted to chat. That in itself wasn't unusual to D'Andra. She often slept during the day, lay awake at night, and talked one's ear off. No, the point that made its way through D'Andra's muddled emotions was that Mrs. Frieda Lee Miller did not call her Grace.

"Well there you are, D'Andra," she'd said smoothly, as if she'd said her name that way every day.

D'Andra offered a half-hearted greeting and then focused on her work.

"Did you know I have a new friend?"

"No."

"Well I do, her name's Val. She's a smart lady, that one there." Mrs. Miller's voice dropped down to a conspiratorial whisper. "And I'll tell you something else. She's colored."

Rather than respond, D'Andra motioned for Mrs. Miller to lift her tongue so her temperature could be taken.

"Do you know we know some of the same hymns? She grew up Baptist just like I did, except I was in Georgia and she was in Mississippi. Everyone knows Georgians are the true Baptists."

In her depressed state, D'Andra became agitated. But when she looked up, Mrs. Miller had a twinkle in her eye.

"Yep, that Val Johnson is a mighty fine woman and she's raised a strapping son." She looked at D'Andra a moment before continuing. "Well my word, I don't know why I didn't put two and two together before. He's perfect for you, D'Andra. Val's son." Mrs. Miller squealed with delight, as if she'd just discovered the cure for cancer or the secret to youth.

"He's kind and considerate and loves his mother. He came to visit her the other day when I was in her room. Brought her some candy and I made such a fuss over it that the next day he brought me some too. Now that's a kindly gentleman if ever there was one."

D'Andra never said a word. She felt if she so much as opened her mouth, a flood of tears would come out.

But Mrs. Miller had never had any problem with one-sided conversation. She touched D'Andra's arm lightly. "If you want, I can put in a good word for you. I think he respects this old woman," Mrs. Miller said, pointing a bony, purple-veined finger towards her chest. "He'll listen to me."

D'Andra shook her head and said, "No, Mrs. Miller. Don't do that." And then she fled the room.

By sheer will, D'Andra finished her rounds. She took her break, but instead of going to the cafeteria, she walked outside to the smoker's area. Here, in the quiet of the early morning, D'Andra finally gave into her tears.

She'd been crying for several minutes when she felt a soothing hand on her shoulders and a warm body sit down next to her.

"I saw you come out here," Elaine said gently. "Thought you might like some lavender tea . . . and some Kleenex."

D'Andra looked up and smiled through her tears. She took a tissue from the box Elaine offered, wiped her eyes and blew her nose. Then she took the cup of tea laced with just the right amount of honey and sipped slowly. After a few more moments, Elaine spoke again.

"I also brought you the biggest chocolate chip cookie I could find. I know it's not medically proven, but I personally think chocolate cures just about any ailment one could have, including a shattered heart."

"Thanks, friend," D'Andra said, before going into another round of sobbing. Elaine held her gingerly, patiently, until the moment of anguish subsided. As she did so, she tried in vain to figure out what finding out about her father had to do with D'Andra avoiding their new favorite patient, Val Johnson.

"Val asked about you earlier," Elaine said after D'Andra had once again blown her nose and was now absently munching on the cookie. "She's used to you stopping in as soon as you get to work and wondered why she hadn't seen you. Night called as well, first his mother and then the front desk. Still don't want to talk about what's going on?"

In that moment, D'Andra knew that sharing the burden of the truth she'd learned might help to lighten it from her heart. She felt she could barely breathe, and knew from personal experience that situations often looked different in another person's eyes. She knew Elaine's would be a fair, non-judgmental perspective. She was the only one D'Andra could even imagine sharing this with: she didn't want to talk to Cassandra about it and the thought of discussing it with Chanelle or Connie felt equally uncomfortable. But after looking at her watch, she knew that now was not the time.

"I do want to talk about it," she said rising. "Maybe that will help me gain perspective. But there's no time now, and I know you have to rush home right after work, so Max can leave for work."

"I can spare a few minutes," Elaine said readily. "Plus I can call my next door neighbor's teen. I don't think she has to be at school until nine. I'll tell her I'll drive her to school if she watches the kids. Then we can talk."

The rest of D'Andra's shift went by in a blur and before she knew it, it was a quarter to seven. She seriously considered not going to Val's room, but that act felt cowardly even with her hurting. She decided to just pop her head in, say hello, and then use having to clock out as an excuse to not stay long. After five more minutes she gathered her courage, walked down the hall and peered around the door into Val's room.

Val was awake, alert and watching television. She turned her head almost before D'Andra's face was barely visible. "There's my angel! Girl, you had me worried about my favorite nurse in all the world. Now come on in here and tell me how your mama's doing."

D'Andra willed herself calm and dared her eyes to

shed a tear. "I just stopped by to say hi," she said quickly, before the dam burst again. "Sorry but I was really busy tonight. I'll see you later, Miss Val."

"But baby, I've got something for you, something I made."

Whatever she had would have to wait. D'Andra fairly ran down the hall, to the clock out center and then to her car, forgetting all about sharing her burden with Elaine.

30

She wouldn't be able to run away from Night as easy. Seeing his GMC as she purposely passed instead of turned down her street, she circled the block and entered the alley to her garage from behind the building. Cautiously she walked to the elevator, being careful not to be seen through the large paned windows.

Once inside her apartment, she peeled off her clothes and headed straight for the shower. She ran the water as hot as she could stand it and then stepped into the stall. More tears flowed as she tried to wash away the events of the past twenty-four hours and the questions that entered her mind and refused to leave. Why had she kept asking about her father? Why had she insisted on knowing his name? Why had her mother had a heart attack now, just when things between her and Night were perfect. D'Andra was convinced that if her mother hadn't gotten sick, this ugly truth would probably have never gotten out. Some people said that what you don't know can't hurt you, D'Andra thought snidely. *No, but it can kill you*. Of that, D'Andra had no doubt. Because a part of her spirit died at the mere thought of a life without Night in it.

D'Andra stayed in the shower until the water

cooled and then stepped out and toweled herself dry. After quickly spreading cocoa butter lotion over her skin, she walked naked to her bedroom, ready to crawl into bed, pull the covers over her head, and hide herself from her own reality. But it was not to be. She almost jumped fifty feet when she walked into her bedroom and found that she was not alone.

"Night! How . . . how did you get in here?"

"You gave me a key, remember?"

Belatedly, D'Andra remembered giving Night her extra key the morning the furniture store had called to say they were delivering her living room furniture. D'Andra had had a doctor's appointment on the other side of town and couldn't be there to let the men in. She'd never even thought to ask for the key back. Now, she wished she had.

"Why are you avoiding me?"

"I wasn't. I mean I'm not. I was busy last night and left my phone on silent and—"

"Didn't you see me when you passed by the street and circled around to the back of the apartment? Isn't that why you were trying to hug the wall like a shadow when you walked to the elevator, hoping that I wouldn't see you? What's going on, D'Andra?"

D'Andra felt as naked emotionally as she was physically. Suddenly she became aware of her nudity and reached into her closet for a bathrobe. All the while she was trying to concoct some kind of believable story. But D'Andra had always been horrible at making up stories. In the end, she was simply too drained emotionally and physically to lie. She knew this truth would be the end of her fairy tale romance. Mary's confession had already cut out part of her heart. She figured she may as well give Night the information needed to finish the job.

She walked across the room, as far away from him as

she could get, and took a seat on the floor. With her head down, she recounted the story as she had heard it. Her voice faltered a couple times and at times she wondered if she could actually utter the words about her mother's complicity in Night's mother's miscarriage. But she did.

Night sat still and quiet as D'Andra talked, his expression going from concern, to confusion to something unreadable. At one point, D'Andra wondered if Night truly understood what she was saying, how her story affected them. When she finished, she repeated the most important part.

"Your stepfather, Carter Johnson, is my biological dad."

Night continued to sit quietly for several minutes, his chin resting on his closed fist, his brow creased in concentration. D'Andra stared at him silently and watched his love for her ooze out of the room.

"Do you hate my mother now?" D'Andra asked, eerily similar to the question Mary had asked regarding D'Andra's feelings for her.

It seemed another eternity before Night spoke. He didn't look at her. "I don't know what I'm feeling right now, to be honest with you. Never in a million years could I have imagined this story."

"Your mother never said anything about it?"

"I knew she'd lost a child, the little girl who would have been my sister." Night cut a quick glance in D'Andra's direction. "But I never knew why."

D'Andra dared to approach the bed. She sat down next to Night and lay a shaky hand on his thigh. The gesture she'd done on countless occasions now seemed foreign, invasive. Night was stiff as a board.

"If your mother was with so many men, how is she so sure Carter's your father?"

"She seems very sure, but I guess there's always the

possibility that he's not." For the first time in her life D'Andra found herself hoping someone was *not* her father. "We should do a paternity test," she continued. "If your stepfather, if Carter is willing."

Night rose from the bed. "I need to go see my mother."

"Are you going to tell her what I've shared?"

"Of course," Night said, a little too forcibly.

"Do you think she'll tell my, my father?"

Night looked at D'Andra then, really looked at her for the first time since he entered the apartment. Now he saw the paleness underneath her flushed cheeks, took in the bloodshot eyes, swollen from crying. He imagined the lone, lost girl who for years had searched for the other part of who she was and the mixed emotions she must be experiencing now that she'd found him. He knew the story she'd relayed to him wasn't her fault, but he couldn't help that his feelings toward her had shifted.

"I'm sorry for what you're going through," he offered. "I can't imagine how you feel."

"And I can't imagine how you feel," she replied.

"I'll call you later," he said as he walked out of the bedroom toward the front door.

He hugged her briefly. Not the deep, all encompassing, breath-taking hugs he usually gave upon their parting, but a see-you-later-bye hug, an it's-been-good-knowing-you hug. There was no kiss. And then he was gone.

D'Andra stared at the closed door for long moments after he'd gone. She was all out of tears but stood, breathing deeply, trying to catch breath that suddenly seemed in short supply. She felt herself getting light-headed and quickly sat on the sofa. She knew her pressure was rising, and she practiced the breathing exercises she'd learned to restore some semblance of calm.

When she was able, she got up from the couch, walked into her bedroom, closed the blinds, turned off her phones, slipped off her robe and slid under the covers. She pulled the downy comforter over her head, pulled herself into a fetal position. All her life she'd wanted to know who her father was. Now she knew. But would the knowledge she gained be worth what it had cost her?

31

Night's heart was heavy as he walked toward his mother's room. He replayed the story D'Andra shared over and over in his head, as he drove from her apartment to the hospital. At once he was angry, hurt, confused and sad. He'd *thought* that Jazz was the love of his life but he *knew* D'Andra was. But how could his love survive what she'd told him? Her mother had caused his mother to lose a child, his sister? How did a love, no matter how great, get beyond that?"

He took a deep breath, squared his shoulders, put a smile on his face and entered Val's room.

"Hey, Mom," he said, placing a kiss on her forehead. "You look good today."

"I wish I could say the same about you, son. If I didn't know better I'd say you just lost your best friend."

"Who, me?" He said this even though he wasn't surprised at his mother's perceptiveness. She'd been reading his mind since the day he was born; in fact nothing much anybody did got past her.

"Does this have something to do with why D'Andra ran away from me this morning? Barely poked her head in the doorway as if I had the plague."

Night dropped the façade and slouched into the

chair next to his mother's bed. "There's no fooling you, Mom," he said with more than a hint of admiration mixed with sadness. "You're not going to believe what I have to tell you."

Val listened intently, not revealing the shock that Night had been expecting or that she was feeling. That sweet, thoughtful girl who'd stopped by to see her every night since she'd come to Heavenly Haven was Mary Smalls' daughter. How could an angel be born from such a devil?

"Can you believe it, Mom? Can you believe the woman I love might be the daughter of someone who could have done something so awful?"

"It's hard to believe, son," Val admitted. "Lord, I haven't thought about that whole incident for a long, long time. I've often thought about the daughter I carried, but not about the ugly incidents surrounding her leaving.

"I forgave Mary Smalls a long time ago," she continued. "But I guess forgiving isn't forgetting."

Her eyes narrowed as she looked far back into a distant past. She didn't like what she saw, or the feelings that stirred from those memories. She shook her head to rid herself of the picture that had sprung up as clear as day: Mary and Val scuffling in front of the grocery store. She remembered her bag busted: all of the items tumbled to the pavement, a bottle of vinegar dropped and shattered and oranges rolled everywhere.

And then it was Val who went rolling, after she and Mary had fallen off the curb and onto the ground. Val landed hard on her five months pregnant stomach; the pain was immediate and intense. She remembered grabbing her stomach and looking up into Mary's face with a look of shear panic.

"Call the ambulance. I think you hurt my baby!"

Mary said absolutely nothing; simply turned and

walked away. A couple who'd witnessed the incident stepped in to help. They drove her to the hospital and the husband called Carter. They hoped against hope that no damage had been done but she ultimately lost the baby. Val shared none of this with her already miserable son. She saw no need to add to his hurt; one look at him and she saw the pain he felt written all over his face.

"What are you going to do, son?" she asked softly.

Night shrugged. "Don't know." He looked at his mother a long moment. "What are you going to do? And how are we going to tell Carter?"

"Tell Carter what?"

Both Night and Val looked up as Carter walked into the room. He was carrying Val's favorite cinnamon rolls, a container of orange juice and the morning paper. He placed the items on a table and walked over to kiss his wife on the forehead, much like Night had done.

"Tell me what?" he repeated.

"Sit down," Val sighed.

Carter looked from Night's anguished face to Val's drawn expression. His heartbeat quickened as he braced for bad news. "Tell me, Val. I can hear just fine standing."

Val's expression softened as she drank in the vision of the strong, good-hearted man she'd met and fell in love with twenty-one years ago. Even in discomfort, he formed a formidable and distinguished picture.

"Give me one of those cinnamon rolls and have a seat, Carter Johnson," she said with a comfort level that only comes with true intimacy. "And trust me when I tell you . . . you're going to want to be sitting down for this."

* * *

D'Andra awoke in the late afternoon. Her head ached and she felt a wave of anxiety, as if she'd had a very bad dream. And then it hit her. The nightmare had occurred during her waking hours and it was in sleeping she'd escaped.

D'Andra fell back against her pillows, wishing she never had to leave the cocoon of her bedroom, that somehow if she stayed isolated long enough she would come out and find that in her absence the world as she'd known it had righted itself.

But she didn't have time for wishful thinking. She'd agreed to take a co-worker's Saturday shift and there was much to do beforehand. She had errands to run, wanted to visit her mother, hoped Elaine could come to work a little early so they could talk and, more than anything, she wanted to be with Night. With that thought, she reached for her cell phone sitting in its charger on the nightstand. She tried to keep down the hopes that there'd be a message from him, but she couldn't help it. She wished fervently that Night had called her and told his doll that everything between them was okay.

He hadn't. She had no messages. And while showering, fixing a bite to eat and preparing to leave her apartment she tried to tell herself it didn't matter, that he was just getting over the shock of her unexpected news, but she couldn't quell the deep sense of foreboding that in gaining a father, she'd lost his son.

The more D'Andra thought about Night leaving her, the more real the possibility became. By the time she prepared to leave the house, their break-up was as good as final in her mind. She determined that she would take the alone time to keep working on herself and her health and that instead of taking the online class, she'd go back to school and get a degree in nutrition, as she had first planned.

That's it, D'Andra thought. I don't need a man in

my life to be fulfilled. If Night makes a decision to leave, I'm not going to go begging for him to stay. If he's going to blame me for what my mother did, then maybe he isn't the man I thought he was after all.

Her home phone rang just as she was preparing to lock the front door. Hoping it was Night she dashed back into the living room and caught the call on the third ring.

"Hello?"

"Dee, Nelly."

"Oh, hi girl."

"Well don't act so happy to hear from me."

"It's not that. I thought you were Night calling."

"I'm so happy for you, that you found a good man, one who isn't bullshit like Charles was."

D'Andra remained silent. She'd promised herself that she wouldn't shed another tear.

"Dee, you there?"

"Look, I need to go."

"Dee, what's wrong? What's going on with you and Night?"

"Did I say anything was going on?"

"This is your girl you're talking to, you didn't have to. Now, do you want to talk about it?"

"Not really."

"Well, will you tell me if y'all are still together at least?"

"I hope so," D'Andra responded softly.

"Look, I don't know what happened or who did what or whatever, but take it from a friend who's been single for far too long. From all you've told me and the little I've seen your man is one in a million. Men like him don't come along everyday. And honestly watching you two interact at the hospital—I've never seen you this happy. So I don't care whatever it is that has y'all trippin', it isn't worth throwing away a good relationship over.

"When you saw Charles in my room that night, you ran away without asking for an explanation, giving your opinion, or entertaining discussion. I understand your reaction. But don't do that this time. Anything keeping is worth fighting for. Don't run, D'Andra."

She's right, D'Andra thought as she navigated rush hour traffic on the way to MLK Hospital. *I need to know exactly what Night is thinking.* She dialed his number and got voice mail.

"No problem," she said aloud as she waited for his outgoing message to end. "I'll just leave my message at the sound of the beep."

Carter sat with arms crossed, unconsciously shielding himself from a past he'd hoped was dead and buried. Of course, he and Valerie had talked long ago about Mary Smalls and her brief obsession with all things Carter. He'd assured Val that although at one point Mary meant something to him, that was long ago. Val was the only one for him and that was the end of it. What Val didn't know was that after she lost the baby, Carter paid a visit to Mary and literally threatened her life. He told her that he wasn't a violent man, and he believed in God and hell, but if she ever came near his wife again, or tried to contact him again, it would be the last thing she did on this earth. It wasn't his proudest moment, but he had no regrets. That's why the harassment stopped, and that's when he and Val went on with what, until today, had been a relatively peaceful, predictable life, just the way he wanted.

"I wonder why Mary would tell her daughter this story," Carter pondered, almost to himself. He looked up at Night. "And then why would she come and tell you?"

She wouldn't, she couldn't, Carter thought. Surely Mary wouldn't try something like this after all these years.

This is the hard part. "She was avoiding me and I forced her to tell me why. But in the end that isn't the only reason," he looked at Val, "and Mom, I didn't have a chance to tell you this before Carter came in but the main reason she felt she had to tell me was because—"

"She thinks I'm her daddy," Carter finished.

This time, Valerie was the one surprised. "I thought you said you didn't have children, Carter."

Carter set his jaw with the determination of a man who would not be moved. "I don't."

32

It wasn't often Jazz felt like a fish out of water. And she refused to admit that's the way she felt now. But if she *had* admitted she was out of her element, it would have been true. Jazz was used to being in control and to getting what she wanted. But in the last few months, with first Night and now Brad choosing a life without her, things had changed. And in her life *she* did the leaving, thank you very much. It had been almost two weeks and Brad still had not returned her call. Soon it would be May. The deal should totally be off by now. If not, Brad Gilman would need to step up his game. She was getting ready to make that fact very, very clear.

"Where's Brad?" she demanded, bursting through the door. She was brought up short when instead of seeing Nancy, a mousy middle-aged woman who doted on Jazz's exquisiteness, she encountered an equally beautiful, fashionably dressed woman with attitude sitting behind the receptionist desk.

"Who are you?" she demanded, a little less forcefully.

"Who's asking?" Cassandra replied, with enough force for the both of them.

"Never mind," Jazz gave Cassandra a dismissive gesture before walking toward the hall and Brad's office.

Cassandra cut her off. "Look, bitch, you don't just walk up in here like you own the place. I asked for you to introduce yourself. And if you can't do that then you can find the door and make your exit."

For all of the secretarial school professional polish she brought to the position, she had not left her street skills at home. The unexpected combination of beauty and brawn was a total surprise to Jazz. It made her feel like, well, a fish out of water.

"Brad!" Jazz yelled around the unmoving Cassandra.

"He's not here," Cassandra said calmly, crossing her arms and leaning her weight on one leg. "And from the looks of it that might be a good thing because we need to have a conversation."

Jazz's look of incredulity could have been next to the word in the dictionary. "*We* don't have to have anything but *you* need a course in office etiquette."

"You won't be the one who gives it to me."

"I'm outta here."

Jazz turned towards the door and then quickly spun around. She hid the hurt she felt behind haughty sarcasm; hurt at being replaced in Brad's life by a lowlife tramp.

"Wait! I get it. You're the new flavor of the month, and your newfound yet limited success has you feeling pretty sure of yourself. You get a weave, a fake designer outfit from the swap meet and a bus ticket out of the ghetto, and you think you've arrived. Well I have news for you. Brad and I have been friends for years. I was here before you came and I'll be here long after you leave."

"That may be the case," Cassandra countered as cool as a cucumber. "But if you stay here for any longer than five seconds, I'm calling security."

* * *

"Who's Jazz?" Cassandra asked a freeway traveling Brad just seconds after Jazz had huffed, puffed and left the office.

"Why, is she there?"

"No, but she was. And I must tell you Brad, I didn't handle the situation very professionally."

"What happened?"

Cassandra told him.

"That's all?"

"It's enough. Who is she?"

"An ex-friend. We were good friends for a while but then we added sex to the equation and then I met you. I didn't think the two of you would work well together so I stopped calling her. From what you're telling me of what went down in the last five minutes, I'd say I was right."

"Ooh, baby. Are you saying you put her down because of me?" Cassandra said in a sultry, sexy voice. "I'm going to have to give you a special reward for that as soon as you get home."

Brad smiled with satisfaction as he hung up from Cassandra. He was whipped and knew it; the woman had come in out of nowhere and totally snatched him from the game. He always said he wouldn't date a woman with one child, let alone three. But something about this street-smart yet vulnerable woman had brought out his caveman side. He didn't look it but he was almost fifty years old. Being around Cassandra and hearing her talk of her children had for the first time in his life made him think about leaving a lineage. He'd already asked Cassandra to move in with him, and offered to hire a housekeeper and nanny. So far, she'd said no. She spent every evening with him before going home to be with her kids, giving him the kind of love and mind-blowing sex he'd barely believed was possible.

Less than a month and he was already wondering what kind of diamond she liked.

Brad pulled into the parking lot of a large electronics store. He decided to leave the top of his Porsche down since he'd only be a few minutes. After entering the store and looking up at the directive signs, he headed down aisle three.

"Brad Gilman," a voice behind him said.

Brad closed his eyes briefly before turning around. Then he fixed his face with a smile. "What's going on, Night?"

"Everything's cool."

There was an awkward moment as each man paused to collect his thoughts.

"You know man, I'm really sorry about what happened with your real estate deal. I feel real bad about it."

"Why?" Night responded. His tone held no anger. "You're the reason it fell out of escrow."

Brad didn't have to say anything; his guilt-ridden face said it all.

"I understand man. At one time, I was under Jazz's spell. And I have no doubt in my mind something she told you is the reason I don't have the keys to 10281 Centinela Boulevard. And I'm equally sure that whatever she told you is not the truth. But it's cool. I'm looking at some other spots. Nothing is going to keep me from my dream."

"What can I say man? I screwed up."

"Yes, you did."

"Tell you what. Why don't I make a few phone calls, see if we can get the deal going again? I know that a couple other people were interested in it but I don't think any paperwork has gone through yet."

"Brad, you don't owe me anything."

"I owe you an apology. Let me make it by helping you get your building back."

33

The dinner conversation was quieter than usual. Carter had brought Val her favorite rib dinner from Jewel's BBQ, complete with baked beans and potato salad, but somehow the meal felt incomplete—stilted by words left unsaid.

Val was first to try and bridge the gap. "Maybe you should consider it, Carter."

"Consider what?" But he knew what; it was the same conversation they'd had all weekend.

"That D'Andra could be your child. At this point in our lives, especially with her grown and all, it wouldn't be the worst thing that could happen. She's a beautiful girl. I considered her like a daughter from the first time she came into this room. She's warm, sincere, a lot like you when I think about it. Now look, I'd have to do a reassessment with these new eyes of knowledge, but she definitely has some of your temperament."

"That woman has wanted to get me back ever since I left her."

Val placed her finished plate on the table beside her. She wiped her hands and took a long sip of tea before she spoke again.

"Maybe it's time you put what Mary did behind

you," Val said. "And at least be open to helping heal somebody who's done you no harm."

Carter was reminded all over again why he loved Valerie Marie Johnson. "How would you feel about that if it's true, that D'Andra's my child?"

Valerie smiled, her answer both instant and sincere. "I'd say it would be poetic justice if after all these years the daughter Mary had becomes the daughter I've always wanted. Now will you take the paternity test?"

Night couldn't believe the emotional rollercoaster he was on. While still reeling from the news that D'Andra may be his stepsister, he was now excited about perhaps getting his dream spot after all. He sauntered into his mother's hospital room with her favorite butter pecan ice cream.

"Between you and Carter, I'm going to gain twenty pounds by the time I leave here."

"Oh, I'm sorry. I can always take it home with me." Night began putting the container back in the bag.

"Boy, you are cruisin' for a bruisin'. Did you bring me a spoon?"

Night placed the ice cream beside him and reached for the paper bowls and plastic spoons he'd brought.

Val watched silently as her son pulled everything they needed from a plastic bag. *He's so thoughtful,* she thought. *He and D'Andra would be good for each other.*

"Have you talked to D'Andra?" she asked.

"No."

"Why not?"

"What do I say to her Mom? Her mother made you lose a baby. Carter may be D'Andra's father. She'd be my stepsister."

"She could be your wife."

Night's hand stopped in the mid-scoop. "Where is this coming from?"

"It's coming from knowing how happy you've been since meeting D'Andra. And seeing with my own eyes what a beautiful woman she is, inside and out. I just don't want you to stop talking to her because of some misplaced sense of loyalty or obligation to Carter or me. Son, like I told you, I forgave Mary for what she did a long time ago. Surely you can forgive a woman who hasn't done nothing at all."

Val told Night about Carter's decision to have the paternity test. "I've come to love D'Andra and hope she is Carter's child. That way, if you decide to act stubborn, like you don't have the sense God gave you or I taught you, she'll still be family to me . . . one way or another."

Night ate his ice cream in silence, digesting what his mother said. She was right. Night figured he couldn't continue seeing D'Andra because it would hurt Carter and his mother to do so. Her words had given him permission to put his heart back in his chest.

"I'll be right back," he said and left his mother's room.

Once in the hall he pulled out his cell phone. Voice mail picked up on the other end. Night thought about leaving a message but decided against it. The things he wanted to tell D'Andra needed to be said face to face.

D'Andra battled mixed emotions as she left MLK Hospital. She'd convinced herself that there was no bitterness at her mother's indirect participation in her losing the man she loved. D'Andra knew she'd lost him. How could it be any other way? Her mother had done a horrible thing to his mother. If D'Andra knew nothing else, she knew how Night loved one Val Johnson.

Once on the highway, she put in her hands-free and

pulled out her cell phone. She'd meant to call Elaine before getting to the hospital but had been lost in thought of what might have been with Night. She hoped it wasn't too late to ask her friend to come to work a little early. After rushing off without talking to Elaine, D'Andra had spent the entire weekend battling with her pain. She was desperately in need of a compassionate, non-judgmental listening ear.

"Where did you disappear to on Friday?" Elaine asked in place of hello.

"Sorry, Elaine. I was more upset than I realized."

"I worried about you all weekend but was stuck in no man's land on a camping trip we promised the kids. The Sequoia National Park is beautiful, but phone reception sucks! I'm glad you called, but I still might ring your neck for putting me in a panic by running off."

D'Andra knew Elaine was trying to lighten the moment, but couldn't force a laugh. "Look, can you come to work early, so we can talk?

"Absolutely."

After making their plans and hanging up, D'Andra realized she had a missed call. She punched the received calls button. *Night!* But there was no message. Not a good sign, she thought. But that he'd returned her message inspired a sliver of hope. He'd listened to her message. And he'd called.

"Thanks for coming early."

"No problem. Max was boring me anyway, going on and on about his latest fixation: trout fishing."

"Where on earth did he get that idea?"

"The sports channel. Yes, it's considered a sport. Now he wants to buy a boat and sail the trout-filled waters."

The conversation faded as they walked past

colleagues in the cafeteria and took a more secluded table near the back.

"Okay, out with it. What on earth is going on?"

D'Andra took a deep breath and dove into the story. She left out what her mother had done to Val, and focused on the fact that Night's stepfather was her biological one. D'Andra told the story by rote, as if what she shared had happened to someone else. Her condensed version took less than five minutes.

"So why are you so sure Night will break up with you over this? What your mother did is not your fault and neither is the fact that Carter might be your father."

"Yes, but the reality is it messes up their peaceful life and brings back painful memories to a mother he loves dearly. I can only imagine her reaction when he broke the news. Or how she'll treat me now that she knows.

"I do want to talk to Night, though, tell him how I feel. I don't think it will change his mind but at least I can walk away knowing that I laid my heart on the line and that nothing is left unsaid."

"Looks like you'll get your chance," Elaine replied.

"Why do you say that?"

"Because Night just walked in the cafeteria and he's headed in our direction."

D'Andra whipped her head around before she could remember to play it cool. Her eyes locked with Night and suddenly they were the only two in the room. He moved like a panther, sleek and confident. Her heart flip-flopped. How could she have thought even for a moment about not fighting to keep this man?

"D'Andra," he said as soon as he approached the table. "Can we talk?"

34

There was no conversation as Night and D'Andra navigated the short walk from the cafeteria to the outside patio. A few other employees were out there; one busy texting on his BlackBerry, another engrossed in a novel and a couple others smoking in the smokers' area.

D'Andra and Night walked past the small crowd to a bench several yards away. D'Andra sat on the edge of the bench; Night straddled the bench to face her.

"I'm sorry," he began.

D'Andra's heart dropped but she kept her head lifted. If she didn't come away from this meeting with her heart, at least she'd have her pride.

"For what?" she dared ask.

"For not trusting my heart."

The answer wasn't what D'Andra had expected. She looked him squarely in the eye for the first time that evening.

"I don't understand."

"When you told me what you'd found out the other morning, I was in shock. That's just for starters. I was confused, angry, hurt; and those emotions were distributed among several people I love and one person

I don't know, your mother. I should have focused on you; how you must feel to know that the man who raised me may be your biological father, how you must feel about your mom, and what she did to a woman you've grown to care a lot about.

"But I didn't. I admit, my first and foremost thought was about my own mom and how yours had hurt her. My heart told me to call you, talk it out, work through this together. But my head said I couldn't see you after what your mother had done. It may not have been a rational thought but it felt like I'd be taking sides against my mother if I chose to stay with you. Plus I didn't know if Mom knew about Carter's past relationship with your mother, nor did I know how she would take the news that he might be your father.

"So you told your step . . . Carter? What did he say?"

"At first he said he was positive you weren't his daughter. But later, after Mom talked to him, he agreed to a paternity test."

His response didn't sound too welcoming but given the circumstances, D'Andra couldn't say she blamed him. She hoped that maybe time and getting to know one another could heal some of the wounds.

D'Andra hesitated with the next question. "And what about Miss Val? What did she say?"

Night smiled. D'Andra's heart flip-flopped.

"She said what only somebody like my mother would. That she's always wanted a daughter and that she hopes it's you."

The tears D'Andra had sworn not to shed came instantly. So did her arm around Night's neck. The position was awkward but she kissed him anyway. It was a light kiss, tender.

But not enough for Night. He turned her until she was cushioned in the crook of his arm and proceeded to ravish her mouth relentlessly. They'd only been apart three days, but that was a longer time than Night wanted to spend without her. His tongue circled and plunged; it took years of martial arts discipline to keep his hands from roaming D'Andra's shapely, thick body.

D'Andra gave as good as she got. She was at work but she didn't care who saw her. She hadn't dared dream this moment was possible. But instead of running away she'd put her heart on the line with the message she left on his cell phone. And just like that she was back in his arms.

Reluctantly Night and D'Andra broke the kiss. She knew it was nearing the time for her to clock in.

"There's so much I want to say to you," she said. "Like I said on my message—"

"What message?"

"The message I left on your cell phone. I thought that's why you came by. You didn't get it?"

Night pulled out his cell phone and checked for messages. There were none. D'Andra hugged him tightly and whispered in his ear. "That makes your coming here that much more special."

"Come home to me when you're off," he whispered back. "I've got something even more special for you."

D'Andra went warm from her navel down to her womanly core; her nipples instantly hardened. Every part of her body remembered Night's specials. Seven o'clock in the morning couldn't come fast enough.

Night strolled to his car and popped the lock. For a moment he just sat there, trying to wrap his mind around all that had happened, and was happening. He'd be the first to admit how crazy it was that the woman he loved might end up being his sister by marriage. But life was just going to have to work out the details. Now that he'd reunited with D'Andra, he would never let her go.

Just as he started his engine and headed toward the parking lot entrance, a tone on his cell phone signaled he had a voice mail.

I didn't hear it ring, he thought, but he touched his Bluetooth to hear the message nonetheless.

It was D'Andra. Somehow the voice mail had just been delivered. However in the idiosyncrasies witnessed in the past several hours . . . it was right on time:

> *"Night, it's D'Andra. I have so much to say and then again for what I'm feeling there are no words at all. When you left the other day, my heart stopped. And suddenly any joy in finding my father paled in comparison to the thought of losing you. I understand that you're upset. I'm upset too. I wish I could change the past. I can't. But I'm hoping to affect the future with this message. I love you JaJuan Night Simmons, more than I've ever loved anyone. Please return my phone call. Please don't let us end this way. I love you."*

35

Night woke up and wondered if he'd slept with a smile on his face. He wouldn't have doubted it; life had never been better for him than it was right now.

It had started at seven-thirty this morning when D'Andra rang his doorbell. He'd greeted her naked, leaving no doubt about his *special*. The lovemaking had been quiet, tender, as if each body wanted to speak words of love that weren't in his vocabulary. They'd slept several hours and then woke up again with love on their minds. The coupling was more urgent this time: frenzied, powerful, nasty, raw. They worked up a crazy appetite and after a luxurious shower Night made D'Andra a healthy dinner of poached salmon in dill sauce, mashed cauliflower and salad. Their plan was for him to be at her house when she got off the following morning, but Night looked forward to the day when their households combined and when he thought of the plans he had for their future, his smile widened. Could the day get any better?

Obviously so. His phone rang with good news on the other end of the line.

"Night, my man!"

"Brad, what do you have for me?"

"Good news! Not only is the space still available, but after your deal fell through—"

Night cleared his throat.

"Okay, after I pulled your paperwork, the owners lowered the price by ten grand. They want to expand their property portfolio in Arizona and New Mexico; they're using the profits from this sale to buy a small strip mall just outside Santa Fe. So they want to sell quickly."

"Well, you know what to do then. Make it happen."

While Night was talking to Brad, D'Andra was talking to Cassandra. She and her sister, along with Jackie and about half a dozen other friends of Mary, were at the hospital, praying and pacing while a team of specialists performed open heart surgery. The procedure had been scheduled for two days later but after Mary complained of pain in her chest and x-rays showed a potential clot forming, the medical team decided not to wait a moment longer.

It had already been two hours and D'Andra and Cassandra had broken away from the group to catch a little private time in the cafeteria. The one good thing that came from Mary's heart attack was that it had brought the sisters closer.

"You scared?" Cassandra asked.

D'Andra nodded.

"You tried to help her, Dee. Telling her about nutritious foods and wanting her to exercise with you. And look at you! Girl, I don't know when I last saw you this size. How much have you lost?"

"Around thirty-five pounds, I think." Her usual joy at this disclosure could not be heard in her answer today.

"That's great, D'Andra. Hey, while we're talking, we need to figure out what to do with mama once she gets out of here. Brad said we could move to a place with a guesthouse so that maybe Mama could live back there. At least while she's recuperating from surgery."

"Uh-huh," D'Andra said half-heartedly. And after a moment, "Who did you say?"

"Brad. It's been a while since we talked, huh? Brad is the name of my boss who's also my man. He's whom I've been spending time with. I can't believe I might actually snag this big fish."

"What's his last name?"

"Dee, you don't know him."

"I might."

"Trust me, you don't. But you will. He's coming here later, after he finishes with his last client."

"So he sounds rich. But do you love him?"

"What's love got to do with it? This man has mad cash, girl. He loves me, accepts my kids, even suggested I get their fathers more involved in their lives. Made me feel bad I haven't made more of an effort to do that. Oops, sorry Dee. I know how talking about daddies gets to you."

D'Andra came close to sharing the news that she may have found her father but instead decided to wait until the paternity test was over. They were going to a diagnostic center for the testing and would have the results back five days later. D'Andra wanted to go a faster route, and even suggested DNA kits that could be ordered online. But Carter didn't want to take any chances that a mistake could be made. He'd made the appointment with one of the top paternity testing companies in Los Angeles. D'Andra steered her thoughts and the conversation back to Cassandra's new man.

"Money is good, San, but love is better."

"Oh, so you're an expert now that you're dating? What's it been, four months? Wait until the glow wears off, until you have your first big argument or he

has his first affair. That's when it becomes not about
the man, but about his money."

Fortunately or unfortunately, D'Andra's cell phone
saved her from having to respond. The name on her
caller ID instantly made her feel better.

"I'm pulling into the parking lot. Where are you?"
Night asked.

"In the cafeteria, but I'll meet you in the waiting
room."

Night found a parking space not too far from the
hospital entrance D'Andra had suggested was closest
to where she'd meet him. He was just about to cross
the pedestrian walk to go inside when a horn honked.
The car was close. He turned around and sauntered
over to the driver's side of the car.

"This is the last place I'd expect to see you," Night
teased. "I didn't think you came south of Wilshire
Boulevard."

"I'm not going to apologize for being more Santa
Monica than L.A., but I'm here to be with a friend
who's mother is having heart surgery."

Night frowned. "So am I. What's your friend's name?"

"Cassandra. Cassandra Smalls."

Night started to laugh, a reaction that confused
Brad. But the mirthful sound was so contagious that
soon he found himself laughing as well.

"I wish you'd let me in on the joke," he said.

"You're not going to believe this, but Cassandra is
D'Andra's sister. And D'Andra is the woman I'm going
to marry."

36

D'Andra smiled as she watched her mother move around the kitchen, gathering preparations for her blueberry banana smoothie. The transformation in Mary Smalls following her open heart surgery was nothing short of a miracle. In just a few short months, she had totally changed her diet from fried and greasy to baked and well-seasoned with herbs and extra virgin olive oil, and actually looked forward to thirty-minute walks with her new best friend, a gentle, black English cocker spaniel named Girl.

It probably also helped that these walks took place in Mary's new upscale neighborhood in Calabasas. Brad, Cassandra and her children had moved into their five-bedroom, four-and-a-half bath, Tudor-style home the previous month and after remodeling the large, one-bedroom guesthouse, had invited Mary to move there. She joined a rambunctious yet well-oiled family unit that also included a nanny and full-time housekeeper.

"You sure you don't want one?" Mary asked. "I'm a professional smoothie maker now you know."

D'Andra laughed. "Of course you are. I taught you everything you know! But I really should be going.

Night is running around like crazy preparing for tonight and I still have some errands to run as well. I just picked up the disco ball and strobe lights for our seventies-and-eighties-themed party and had to stop by since I was so close. I was also hoping that a personal visit may help you change your mind and join us tonight."

"Maybe some other time." Mary sat at the table opposite D'Andra and took a long sip of her drink. "I'm sure that, you know, everybody is going to be there."

D'Andra knew the *everybody* Mary was talking about. "Yes, Mama, Carter and Val will be there and they made it very clear they'd be totally fine with you being there as well. We're all trying to turn the page on a new chapter in our lives and let the past stay in the past."

"I know but I . . . maybe another time."

The truth was Mary hadn't quite forgiven herself. All these years later, she still felt immensely guilty for what she'd done to Carter, and the pain she'd caused his family.

"Another time should be next Saturday. That's when the first J.E.W.E.L.S. class starts."

Mary smiled. "The one for big girls?"

"That's right." D'Andra walked around the table and hugged her mother. "I've got to run, Mama. I'll call you later."

Several hours later, D'Andra pulled into the Ladera Heights Shopping Center and drove toward the brightly lit corner property. It was Labor Day weekend, and the weather was divine. At first, Night had been disappointed in having to push back the opening from July. But it had given them time to work out the kinks and plan the type of bash worthy of a dream fulfilled.

D'Andra smiled as she looked up at the fluorescent marquee, more reminiscent of a nightclub than a gym. It was exactly the look Night wanted, one that would underscore his gym's uniqueness: the late hour party atmosphere, subdued lighting, themed weekday work-out classes from "Seventies Sweating" to "In Shape In Eight"—a full-body workout regimen combining aerobics, step, pilates and dance and designed to shed major pounds and inches in eight short weeks.

The gym was bustling with activity when D'Andra stepped inside. The caterer from Jewel's BBQ was laying out a mouth-watering feast, the DJ was setting up in the corner and various workers were performing last minute cleaning details: wiping down the shiny chrome of the exercise equipment, vacuuming rugs and making sure the glass and mirrors were spotless.

"Hey, Marc. How's it going?"

"D'Andra, there you are. Night's looking for you." Marc was busy punching member information into the computer, and organizing a pile of paperwork spread across the lacquered wood reception area.

"I see you're busy, but it looks like you've got everything under control. Night is lucky to have you managing the place."

"Are you kidding? I'm the lucky one. I mean, Bally's is all right and all but there ain't another gym in southern Cal like this one. Once the word gets out, it's going to be off the chain, just watch." Marc grinned sheepishly, showing off an attractive dimple on the right side of his face. "Of course, it didn't hurt that Night offered to bring me on as a partner."

"I'm sure it didn't," D'Andra replied, laughing. She spotted Night in the hall leading to several classrooms. He was talking to a group of personal trainers. "Hey, is Lindsay coming tonight?"

"With all the fine honeys that are going to be here? That woman will be holding the chain to the ball around my foot."

"And with your reputation for flirting with women, that's probably a good thing."

Night finished talking to his employees just as D'Andra walked up. "Hey doll." He gave her a brief kiss on the mouth.

"Everything looks great, baby. Excited?"

"In shock is a better description. This has been a dream for so long, I can't believe I'm here, actually walking around in the reality." He grabbed her hand and started down the hall. "Come do a final walk through with me. Doors will open in about an hour."

They started at the far end of the hall, in the largest room. Here·the various cardio classes would be held: various levels of aerobics and step, kick-boxing, African and Latin dance workouts, the senior stomp for those sixty and older and the daily era-themed routines. On one wall was a variety of workout poses Frank had taken of Night, Marc and the personal trainers and on the opposite far wall were D'Andra's before and after shots and under them the J.E.W.E.L.S. slogan: *Join Exercise With Enthusiasm and Look Sensational!* Chairs had been placed along the wall for the revelers who would surely make their way to what tonight would be a dance space, grooving to the music that would be piped through the entire building. Down the hall was a smaller room for yoga, pilates, callanetics and meditation, and a slightly bigger room for classes on nutrition, fitness, health and others that would be added as D'Andra developed the educational curriculum. Across from that room were two doors: one room would be used for massage and aromatherapy, the other a general office for all of the gym personnel.

The hall opened up to the large rectangular shape of the gym's main floor, which housed every type of exercise equipment imaginable. Cool gray carpeting offset off-white walls with bold red-and-black stripes running the perimeter of the room. On the other side of the gym were the restrooms, dressing rooms, co-ed Jacuzzi, co-ed sauna and Night's large, glass-front office where he could look out over his fitness domain. For the party, chair groupings of two and four had been strategically placed throughout the room and at the front of the gym where later P.T.'s would give their private lessons.

"It's perfect," D'Andra gushed when their final inspection was finished. "Is it what you imagined?"

"Better," Night said without hesitation. "Especially because of the person who's standing beside me sharing this moment."

He pulled her into the personnel office and closed the door. "Did I tell you that you look stunning this evening?"

"Yes, but I could stand to hear it again."

"You have become the dollhouse I envisioned," he whispered, as he nibbled and licked her earlobe before continuing down her jaw to her neck. He kissed her eyes and cheeks before circling her mouth with his tongue and plunging inside it. He rubbed his hands over the silky fabric covering D'Andra's tight derriere, pressing her cushiony 38 DD's into his hard chest. In losing the weight, she'd also lost a couple inches, but there was still more than enough of her voluptuous mounds for him to handle.

"You keep that up and we won't be ready when the guests arrive," D'Andra said, a bit breathlessly. "And just in case I haven't told you: tonight you will no doubt be the most handsome man in the room. You are my Night in shining armor. I love you."

They shared one more searing kiss and then Night's phone rang. They exited the room as he answered it and entered a controlled chaos. Several of the VIP guests had arrived and were enjoying the pre-party:

Carter and Val, Robert and a new lady friend, Mildred,
Elaine and Max, Chanelle and her date, Cassandra
and Brad, Jackie and Thomas and a smattering of
news media. Several of Night's high-profile friends
were also circling through the gym, drinks in hand
and dates by their side, appreciating Night's vision and
handiwork. There were pro athletes (noticeably not
including Cassandra's baseball-playing ex, Anthony),
actors, singers and hip-hop artists (noticeably including Cassandra's now chart-topping ex, Hollah, and his
video-vixen wife), and a couple politicians. Everyone
was dressed, as the invitation had requested, in workout attire though many of the outfits were designer
and not meant to see sweat. A few hardcore revelers
were actually using the equipment, which made Night
smile. His hope was that every machine would be in
continuous use once the doors to the members and
then the general public opened. Frank was in his element, taking pictures everywhere.

Night looked outside and was surprised to see a
long line. Clusters of people dotted the sidewalk and
the parking lot. Those passing by would definitely
think of a night club and feel the excitement. It was
just what Night wanted. Taking one last look around
he went to make sure Marc had everything he needed
and then went over to unlock the doors.

It didn't take long for the party to start in earnest.
The line Night saw must have stretched around the
building because all the chairs were taken and there was
barely room to stand within an hour after he opened
the doors. Extra security quickly had to be added to
monitor the door: only letting people come in as others
left. It was crazy and beautiful: some people dancing,
others exercising, still others doing line dances in front
of the gym.

D'Andra was in the group exercise room with

Chanelle and Elaine and about seventy-five others getting sweaty to the sounds of the eighties: New Edition's *Cool It Now*, Earth, Wind and Fire's *Let's Groove Tonight* and Levert's *Casanova* kept the floor crowded.

By the time the Force M.D.'s slowed things down with *Tender Love*, D'Andra was ready to take a breather. She navigated her way through the crowd and had just turned the corner onto the main floor of the gym when she heard a scream. Her startled expression turned to chagrin and then laughter as she turned to see Connie running toward her.

"D'Andra! Is this you, girl?" Connie hugged her tightly before stepping back for a full appraisal. "I can't believe it."

D'Andra obliged with a full pivot and turn. "In the flesh." She looked past Connie to the handsome, stocky mocha man standing just behind her. "Hi, Will," she said to Connie's husband.

"I am so proud of you Dee. Is this the body referred to on the marquee?"

D'Andra laughed. "One of them, for sure."

"I can't get over it. How much weight have you lost?"

"Around fifty pounds. I've gone from a size twenty to between a twelve and fourteen, depending on the outfit."

"You've never looked better."

"I've never felt better. And I'm so glad you guys are in town for this. Come on, let me show you around."

On the way to showing Connie around, she bumped into Carter, Val, Robert and Mildred who said their good-byes.

"You've really helped Night do a grand job," Carter said sincerely. "I'm proud of you."

D'Andra would have to ponder the thought that she'd heard something for the first time in her life: a compliment from her father. Since the paternity test, their relationship had been cordial, neither pushing to make it something it wasn't. It was too late for father-hood, so they navigated the journey to knowing each other as friends. Like Night, D'Andra called him Carter.

Other people came and went as the night went on. D'Andra often caught glimpses of Night, who seemed to be everywhere at once. Someone was constantly pulling on him, and his energy was boundless. He looked sexy as hell in his trademark white drawstring pants paired with a cropped, white sleeveless T-shirt. Her mouth watered as his muscles bulged and she re-membered the promise he'd made just before she left for Calabasas, a special after-hours workout he'd de-signed just for her.

As if sensing her watching him, Night looked her way and motioned her over. He introduced her to one of his financial backers and once finished, con-tinued around the room with her hand in his.

"I need to keep you close to me, Doll," he said. "Too many brothahs looking at that tight, juicy butt of yours."

Night had picked out D'Andra's outfit, the same one she wore in the after picture on the gym wall. The fitted pink stretch pants had a silky feel but were ac-tually a smooth polyester blend for durability. Her v-neck cotton top, in a lighter shade of pink, showed off her breasts to perfection, the cleavage deep and inviting. A tear-drop diamond necklace on a thin silver chain had been on a breakfast-in-bed tray that morning, and it was the perfect complement to her pink-and-silver tennis shoes. The entire outfit was chosen to show off her thick, hourglass figure, and from the looks of male admirers, both covert and overt, Night had succeeded in his goal.

Jazz stood in a corner of the room, watching. She'd purposely dressed out of character in a baggy T-shirt and leggings, her hair pulled into a ponytail and a baseball cap pulled low over her eyes. The crowded gym made staying incognito easy yet from where she stood she could see everyone in the main room, the only place she'd ventured since coming inside fifteen minutes before.

Eyeing the happy people surrounding her, Jazz tried to figure out why she'd even come. It was obvious the two men so prominent in her life a year before had both moved on. She'd heard that Brad, who she thought would be a Santa Monica fixture forever, had relocated to the valley. She'd seen him tonight, squiring around his ghetto girl receptionist as if she were a queen. And Night—well tonight was proof of what he'd done. Jazz admitted to being taken aback and grudgingly impressed when she saw the new and improved D'Andra at his side.

Night had gone and done it. He succeeded in achieving his dream without her. She'd thought she was invaluable, that he'd never be anything without her. But now, as she watched celebrities mix with people from the neighborhood and beyond, everyone congratulating and cheering him on, she realized he could do everything without her.

"Jazz? I thought that was you." Marc came from behind her, Lindsay by his side.

"How are you doing, Jazz?" his wife said. "We almost didn't recognize you."

"That was the point," Jazz said sarcastically.

"Too hard for you to resist, huh?" Marc asked, ignoring her caustic remark. "It can't feel too good to see what Night has been able to accomplish, even after you tried to thwart his plans."

"Yes, I wanted to see for myself the calm before the storm. Everything's wonderful now. That's not unusual for a business that's just opened. Talk to me in six months, when I'm finished with my smear campaign. Then let's see if you're still gloating."

Marc stepped to within inches of Jazz's face. "Give it up, Jazz," he said quietly but with veiled anger in his tone. "You're a beautiful woman. Why don't you move on, meet somebody new, get on with your life? It will be the best thing for all of us, but for you most of all.

"Now, tonight is a special night. I'm asking you nicely to leave the premises, but I'll only ask once. After that you'll be forcibly removed. Any questions?"

Jazz cut daggers at Marc, her fists clenching and unclenching in anger. She wanted to slap his smug face but knew such an action would draw the very type of attention she wanted to avoid.

"I was just leaving anyway you arrogant asshole. There's no place for me in this room of losers."

Marc and Lindsay shook their heads as they watched Jazz walk along the outer wall and out the door.

"Do you think she'll really do it?" Lindsay asked. "Does she have something on Night that could potentially ruin his reputation?"

"All Jazz has is hot air and attitude," Marc answered. "Come on, let's see if you can keep up with me on the dance floor."

As Marc passed Night, they chatted a few minutes. Marc assured him everything he'd requested had been handled. Satisfied, Night talked to a few more people before searching out D'Andra, who was relaxing with Chanelle and Connie in the classroom.

"Excuse me ladies, but I need to borrow this pink confection for a moment. It's time to get our midnight workout on, baby."

"Let's take the night off," D'Andra countered, not moving. "Connie's only going to be here one more day and we still haven't caught up. Plus, the last time I was out there all the machines were taken anyway."

"That's no problem," Night answered. He walked over, took D'Andra's hand and gently pulled her out of the chair. "I've got a connection with the owner and he's reserved two treadmills side by side with our names on them. I figured we could do an easy ten minutes, like we did the first day I met you."

"Aw, you're such a sweetheart," D'Andra answered as she remembered that day around eight months ago, when she almost passed out after only a few minutes of slow walking. "I'll gladly join you, especially if we can put the pace where it was when I started this journey."

"A piece of cake for you now, huh babe?" Night kissed D'Andra on the cheek.

A few onlookers applauded as Night and D'Andra took their places on the treadmill, but after a couple minutes everybody was back to doing their own thing. D'Andra and Night chatted easily, but after a couple minutes settled into enjoying the walk and watching any one of three channels playing on the dozen flat screen TVs placed throughout the room.

They had almost finished their ten minutes when the flat screens suddenly went out, the crisp color pictures replaced by gray snow.

D'Andra looked at Night. "Oh no, baby. What happened?"

Night's brow creased as he looked and saw that every single television showed the same snowy picture. He stopped his treadmill and got off. "Let me go investigate," he said. "But you," he continued in an authoritative tone, "don't you stop until you've given me the full ten."

D'Andra rolled her eyes as she placed her hands back on the treadmill bar. *He's so bossy*, she thought, and that's why she loved him. It was his drive, determination and dedication to her getting in shape that inspired her to meet the expectations. And now, here she was, living the life she'd envisioned as she looked into the fluorescent lights of MLK Hospital's emergency room ceiling. She had her health, her mother was well and she'd found her father. Her relationship with Cassandra was better than at any time in their lives and she was in love with the man of her dreams. And in just three short weeks, she would go from full to part-time at Heavenly Haven. The rest of the time she would work as a trainer and nutritional consultant at Night's gym. She couldn't think of anything that would make her happier than she was right now.

D'Andra looked at the television screens and noticed that Night had switched them from cable to the built-in camera system he'd installed so that at various times people could see themselves working out on television. Good move, she thought. People would enjoy this bit of electronic wizardry while Night worked to fix the problem with their satellite dish.

She looked down at the timer on her treadmill: one minute to go. When she looked up at the screens, there were weird, psychedelic colors flashing. Soon everyone, like her, was staring at the screens. And then they went black.

Oh no, D'Andra thought as she stepped off the treadmill. She was about to turn around when she saw her name begin flashing on the screens: D'Andra, D'Andra, all over again. And then this message:

D'Andra, get back on the treadmill and give me ten more minutes.

Oh cute, real cute, D'Andra thought. Night always loved his toys and was obviously playing with the computer hook-up also connected to the flat screen TVs. It didn't matter. She hadn't even broken a sweat during the first ten minutes and since the celebration was winding down and most of her personal friends gone, she didn't mind following his command . . . this time.

She set the timer for ten more minutes and began walking at a little faster pace. Night soon joined her on the other treadmill.

She looked at the screen, still flashing crazy colors. "What are you doing? You're just going to leave the screen like that?"

"Marc is working on it," Night responded. "I told him I had to get back to my number one client." He winked at D'Andra.

They both continued walking and then the flat screens went blank again, just like the first time.

"Damn," Night said, but kept walking.

"You think Marc might need you back there?" D'Andra asked.

"In a minute."

They both turned back to the now black screens. The psychedelic colors began flashing on the screens again, and then the word: D'Andra, D'Andra . . .

"Oh, oh . . . somebody forgot to press delete," she said, laughing.

Night smiled and kept walking.

"D'Andra, D'Andra," the blinking message said. "I love you, I love you," it continued. "Will you marry me?" The blinking stopped and those words stayed etched on the screen, all twelve screens around the room. Suddenly the blaring music dimmed, replaced by the familiar guitar beginning to the Temptations classic, "My Girl."

Somebody on the far side of the room started clapping. Soon others joined in. D'Andra, who'd stopped her treadmill, stood staring at the words, wondering if what she thought she was reading was actually on the screens. She looked at Night, who by now was grinning broadly. He stopped his treadmill, climbed down from it and got on his knees next to D'Andra's.

"You are the dollhouse I dreamed of," he said. "And together, we can turn my house into a beautiful home. I love you, D'Andra. Will you marry me?"

"Yes!" D'Andra literally fell into Night's arms. He staggered back before regaining his balance, lifting her from the ground and twirling her around.

"Yes! Yes! Yes!" she repeated with joy.

When they stopped and enjoyed a tongue-driven kiss in front of everyone, the cheers broke out in earnest.

"Take off your clothes," Night demanded. He and D'Andra were alone in the now empty gym. They were back in the sauna room, but the heat wasn't on.

D'Andra's hands trembled as she reached for the edges of her shirt, to pull it over her head. She kept her eyes locked with Night's as she undid her bra, freeing her melon orbs. Night licked his lips. Her nipples hardened immediately, as they always did under his intense gaze.

"Now the pants," he demanded. He leaned back against the sauna's back bench and spread his legs to give his lengthening member room to grow. His fingers itched to massage the heavy breasts gently swaying in front of him. He knew their softness, could hear the moans his touch would cause. But he stayed seated.

D'Andra stepped out of her pants and began to pull down her lacy pink thong.

"No, leave that on. Now come and lay down on this cover."

D'Andra did as she was told, fully aware that Night was drinking in the sight of her backside as she passed him. He confirmed her thought by squeezing her cheek gently as she passed by. She lay faceup on the cover, with one foot planted on the floor and her other leg folded at the knee. Even though it was narrow, the bench was more comfortable than she thought, especially with the comforter Night had thoughtfully brought along. This seduction was obviously preplanned and had, along with the engagement, been well thought out.

"Close your eyes."

D'Andra complied and soon after she did, she felt the slightest hint of Night's tongue on the ball of her foot. She gasped. Night continued a leisurely journey up her ankles to the calves of her leg, first one and then the other. He slowed down when he reached her sensitive spot, a place on the backside of the bend in her knee. D'Andra's moans began low in her throat. Night continued his tongue bath to her inner thighs, and then on to her navel, stomach and then buried his head between her two golden mounds before pushing them together and lavishing attention on her dark brown nipples. D'Andra moaned louder this time.

After a couple deep kisses, Night retraced the steps of his previous journey, stopping at the breasts, the stomach. Then he straddled the bench and put his hand underneath D'Andra's knee. He lifted her legs and spread them wide, giving him open access to her golden paradise. He took full advantage of this freedom, his tongue parting her folds and licking her with relish. He took his job seriously, making sure that every crevice of her body received his full attention. By now, D'Andra was beside herself, her former moans becoming soft screams. Night took her to the edge and then over, and her scream became louder as she reached a seismic orgasm.

"We're just beginning," Night said. "Stand up."

D'Andra could barely hear. She was still trying to

get back into her body, having sworn her spirit had left it and raced to the heavens in the moment before. She swore she saw Venus and maybe Mars. She knew she saw stars and just as she began to regain her bearings, she remembered the dream she'd had so long ago, of her and Night in the sauna, which with the exception of the heat not being on, was a moment just like this.

"Stand up," Night repeated.

D'Andra did so and was led to a rectangular cushion on the side of the room. That wasn't there before, she thought as she watched Night spread the comforter over it and motion her forward. They knelt down on the soft, downy material together and proceeded to give each other pleasure before falling asleep. They woke up as the first rays of daylight streaked across the night sky.

"Come on, baby doll. The morning crew will be here in an hour. I don't have a problem with it, but I'm sure this is not how you want them to find us."

D'Andra stretched, yawned, and sleepily found and put on her clothes. Night straightened the area, sprayed air freshener and turned on the rocks, generating steam for his first customers and making sure that no signs of the lovers' rendezvous remained for the morning crew to discover.

"Leave your car here, ride home with me," Night said as he steered D'Andra past her Suburban to his Acadia.

"You sure are bossy," she said with a yawn.

"Just like you like it," he responded.

D'Andra looked back toward the gym as Night drove out of the parking lot. The fluorescent sign looked especially good, framed as it was in the cover of darkness. She thought of Connie's comment about her newly slim body and smiled. Because of her friend's words the sign would forever have new meaning to D'Andra, and as they drove toward Inglewood D'Andra was busy thinking of the surprise she would give to Night: a supply of T-shirts, mugs and other items to sell at his shop, emblazoned with the logo and the gym's name: *Body by Night*.

Want more?
Turn the page for Zuri Day's
LIES LOVERS TELL

Available now wherever books are sold.

1

Maya fumed, the steady tapping of her foot an outward sign of her annoyance. The man standing five feet in front of her was taking forever at the ATM. On another, less harried day she might have welcomed the sight. He was tall, she guessed about six-two, broad-shouldered, with long, thick legs encased in jeans that emphasized nicely rounded, tight buns. She'd wondered what his face looked like until his transaction had taken longer than the sixty seconds she thought appropriate, considering the hurry she was in. As if Monday mornings weren't busy enough, her assistant had phoned to inform her that Mr. Brennan was waiting on her in his office. Zeke rarely came into the office before 10:00 a.m. on Mondays; she couldn't imagine the urgent matter that had changed his normally predictable schedule.

The stranger at the ATM looked at a receipt he'd retrieved from the machine, and began another transaction. Maya looked at her watch and sighed audibly, hoping the man would get the message. *Will you hurry up? Jeez!* She no longer cared about his attractive backside; he was making her late.

"Excuse me, but could you hurry? There's a line,"

Maya said in a firm, authoritative voice. The fact that she was the only one in line was beside the point.

The stranger stopped punching in information, looked up from the ATM screen, and slowly turned around. Maya breathed in quickly, and almost forgot to breathe out. The man was platinum fine, at least what she could see of him. He wore a Dodgers baseball cap and sunglasses, so she couldn't really see his face. What she could see was mouthwatering: a strong, firm chin with perfectly groomed day-old stubble, a strong aristocratic-looking nose that tapered over the most delectable lips she'd ever seen in her life. A small cleft in his chin gave him a roguish air.

The stranger's mouth turned up in a slightly amused grin. Maya realized she was staring at the man's lips and tried to regain her composure. She slowly exhaled, set her shoulders back, tilted her head slightly, and continued in her best authoritative tone. "Are you finished?"

The smile deepened in the stranger's face. "Are you?"

His teeth were straight and white and lit up Maya's heart like a fluorescent lightbulb. She looked briefly at his chest, slightly exposed by two open buttons, revealing a light layer of curly black hair. Maya blinked her eyes, tried to get her mind to work. She couldn't figure out what was wrong with her, what about this man had her so flustered. She figured it must be the phone call making her nervous, the phone call that said her boss was upstairs, waiting.

That thought shook Maya from inactivity. "Look, I'm in a hurry. Are you done?"

Maya watched the smile fade from the stranger's face and she could tell his eyes were intense, even hidden as they were behind dark glasses. He shrugged, turned to the machine, canceled his transaction, retrieved his card, and stepped away from the machine.

"It's all yours," he said, unsmiling.

Maya hurriedly conducted a transfer and retrieved two hundred dollars from the ATM, all the while aware that she was being watched. She tried to forget about the stranger as she stuffed the bills into her purse, retrieved her card, and headed toward the elevator. She'd glimpsed the stranger step back up to the ATM after she walked away and couldn't help but consider what he'd done chivalrous. She also found herself wondering what was hidden behind the ball cap and dark shades.

There was little time to ponder that though; duty called. She phoned her brother to tell him she had transferred money into his account, and that it was the last time she was going to rescue him from his irresponsible actions. He was her beloved twin brother and all the family she had left in the world. The night before her mother died, Maya had promised to watch after him. All of eight minutes older than Stretch, she'd always been the sensible one, he the rebel. But she couldn't continue to clean up the messes he made. It was time for somebody to man up.

As soon as the elevator doors opened onto the penthouse floor of Brennan & Associates, thirty-three stories above the hustle and bustle of downtown Los Angeles, Maya was all corporate business. She bypassed the luxurious break room and her roomy corner office, not even stopping to put down her purse or briefcase. She'd been summoned by Zeke Brennan. And when Zeke called, people came running—quickly.

"Good morning, Zeke," Maya said. She'd called him "Mr. Brennan" the first three years of her employment. But last year, when she was promoted from first assistant to executive assistant, working directly with Mr. Brennan on a daily basis, he had told her it was okay to call him Zeke. She only did so when they were

alone, however. Whenever clients or other staff was
around, he was still "Mr. Brennan."

"Maya," Zeke replied simply, shuffling through
papers on his desk.

"You're here early," Maya said. She sat down in a
chair opposite him, set down her purse, and opened
her briefcase to retrieve a pen and notepad. Sensing
Zeke was in no mood for chitchat, she remained quiet,
waiting. She casually scanned the immaculate office:
an exquisite blend of African mahogany and stainless
steel. The floor-to-ceiling windows covered the east
wall, giving Zeke an uninterrupted view of not only
downtown, but miles beyond, into Orange County.
Unlike the rest of the carpeted offices, the CEO
office's floors were a rain-forest-brown marble, im-
ported from India. Matching, maroon suede area rugs
under his massive desk and the large conference table
on the office's opposite side warmed both the floor
and the room, as did the freshly cut bouquet of bird-
of-paradise, yellow callas, reddish orange amaryllis,
and vibrant blue mokaras, set in Tiffany crystal, and
adorning the middle of the stately table for ten. Maya
had been a key player in the office's redesign; and the
weekly delivery of freshly cut exotic flowers created especially for the executive office was her idea. She
noted that the cleaning team had done an exceptional
job, as she demanded. There was not a speck of dust,
or a paper out of place. She was pleased.

Zeke opened a folder and took out another docu-
ment. He handed it to Maya. "Ever heard of this company?"

Maya's attention immediately returned to business.
She took the paper from him, scanning it quickly. It
provided scant details of an investment company, S.W.I.,
International, from London, England. Their holdings
were listed at an impressive twenty billion, with proper-

ties on all seven continents. Several personnel were listed, one of them highlighted, a Mr. Sam Walters.

Maya shook her head, handing the paper back to Zeke. "No, I haven't. But it seems as if I should have, they're impressive."

"I thought the same thing," Zeke said, rising from his chair and walking over to look out the window. "How did a company of this size and with this reach elude my radar? Unless . . ." Zeke turned to Maya and continued. "Unless this is a new company being developed under an old, established investment company, created to keep the competition in the dark about who's actually buying what."

Maya knew this was a definite possibility. Investors weren't known for shouting their transactions from proverbial rooftops. Research was one of Maya's fortes, and what had led to a bachelor's degree with honors. And she loved a challenge. "You want me to find out more about them?" she asked, already making a list of various resources she could tap for information.

"Actually, I want you to find out more about *him,*" Zeke said, this time handing Maya a photo with a name highlighted at the bottom. "Sam Walters."

"Me?" Maya knew Zeke employed men and women from various occupations, geographical areas, communications and background check companies, etc., to research competitors and others' histories. What could she possibly do that a professional background check company couldn't?

Zeke smiled for the first time that morning. He sat down in the chair next to Maya instead of behind his desk. "I know what you're thinking, and you're right. I've done the background checks, reviewed the buzz on this guy, and he comes up legit, a land developer who made billions redeveloping for the rich in Africa. Sold his company and is now looking to expand his land ownership portfolio, primarily in the large metropolises of the United States."

"So what do you think I can find out that your people couldn't?" The guy sounded legit to Maya too, so much so that if not for her professionalism, she'd ask if he was married.

"I don't know," Zeke responded. "It's just a feeling I have, a gut instinct, that all's not how it looks with Mr. Walters. He comes out of nowhere, no one knows about him over here . . ."

"Did you ask Mr. Trump?" Zeke and Donald Trump were golfing buddies, and had also participated in several joint real estate ventures.

"He doesn't know him either. Knows about the parent company, though, the one we think is serving as an umbrella for S.W.I."

"So how can I help?"

Zeke leaned forward, choosing his words carefully. "I need someone to get on the inside of this company, to get close to Sam Walters, someone who has the smarts to obtain confidential information and the savvy to pull off the duality this job will require. In short, I want to find out if this Sam Walters is really who he says he is."

Maya frowned. "I don't understand. Do you think this man isn't the *real* Sam Walters, or do you think there is no Sam Walters at all?"

"I'm not sure what I think," Zeke answered. "But what I know is that my gut instincts have guided me accurately for over forty years, and something . . ." he paused to look at Sam's photo, "is wrong with this picture."

Maya studied the photo again. "So you want me to try and get a job at"—she looked again at the paper—"S.W.I. Company?"

"Not exactly."

Maya was still confused. Was Zeke asking her to try and date this Mr. Walters? That had actually been the first thing that came to mind when Zeke mentioned "getting close."

"Ahem, how do you suggest I get close to Mr. Walters?" Maya was usually very comfortable talking with Zeke, even when discussing multimillion- and billion-dollar business deals. Now, however, was not one of those times.

"Well, I'm certainly not going to ask you to sleep with him," Zeke said, once again reading her thoughts.

"Was I that obvious?" Maya asked, relaxing.

"No, I'm that smart," Zeke countered lightly, before turning serious. "I do want you to become a part of his household, though, and I've got it all prepared, all worked out."

"How do you propose I do that?" Maya asked, confused once more.

Zeke hesitated and then answered, "As his maid."

GREAT BOOKS, GREAT SAVINGS!

When You Visit Our Website:
www.kensingtonbooks.com
You Can Save Money Off The Retail Price
Of Any Book You Purchase!

- **All Your Favorite Kensington Authors**
- **New Releases & Timeless Classics**
- **Overnight Shipping Available**
- **eBooks Available For Many Titles**
- **All Major Credit Cards Accepted**

Visit Us Today To Start Saving!
www.kensingtonbooks.com

All Orders Are Subject To Availability.
Shipping and Handling Charges Apply.
Offers and Prices Subject To Change Without Notice.

More of the Hottest
African-American Fiction from
Dafina Books